Penguin Books
The Man who Held th
Sent Parliament Pack

Peter Van Greenaway gave up work in 1960
in order to devote himself to writing. Since
then he has written *The Crucified City* (1962)
and *The Evening Fool* (1964). His latest
book, *The Judas Gospel*, is shortly to be
published. He lives in Ramsgate.

Peter Van Greenaway

The Man who Held
the Queen to Ransom
and Sent Parliament Packing

Penguin Books

Penguin Books Ltd, Harmondsworth,
Middlesex, England
Penguin Books Australia Ltd, Ringwood,
Victoria, Australia

First published by Weidenfeld & Nicolson 1968
Published in Penguin Books 1972

Copyright © Peter Van Greenaway, 1968

Made and printed in Great Britain by
Hazell Watson & Viney Ltd,
Aylesbury, Bucks
Set in Linotype Times

With the appearance of the wise man the State expires.

Emerson: *Politics*

1

From the deposition of Sergeant Edward Shaw, a volunteer:

Certainly I knew what it was all about. We all did. We're not all
square-bashing clots y'know. Politics? Well why not? We can read
as well as a mufti man *and* keep our eyes skinned – that's what
we're trained for. So? So we liked the look of what we saw and
volunteered. I know the Colonel says he objected now – but he
didn't at the time. How could he? If the DM said okay he'd got no
choice had he? No I didn't know Captain Wyatt very well – who
did? Heard him talk though – that was enough for me. Yes I know
all about her but she isn't dead is she? – when I've got something
to cry about I'll let you know.

From the deposition of Sergeant George Turnbull, volunteer:

There were about fifty of us, a mixed bag – came from all over
the place. I was at Colchester myself. Don't think I was the only
one because I wasn't. So many wanted to do a spell in London
we had to draw lots. I was one of the lucky ones or unlucky ones
... politics? Nuts! The Captain was doing all right – he needed
volunteers – Sunday in Colchester raining cats and dogs – course
we volunteered. Anyway he had the right idea ... me personally –
in detail? We'll be here all night then ...

From the deposition of Hardwicke, former adviser to Wyatt
on foreign affairs:

I was approached by Captain Wyatt several months before the
coup. It was about the time I stood as an Independent at the last
General Election. I had six members in an audience I remember –
he was one of them. No, he wasn't in uniform. I felt despondent
naturally. He came up to speak to me when the others left – made
an extraordinary impression on me; perhaps because he appeared
to be so well informed about my political convictions. I learned

7

he had read a series of my articles contributed to an obscure political quarterly – yes they're the ones ... dissatisfaction? Possibly, at the very least I felt our foregin policy left much to be desired which in turn reflected on the quality of our representation ... I'm sorry, but you did ask. A question of personal aggrandizement? I don't think that was true of anyone who worked for Wyatt.

From the deposition of Colin Treece, a one-time fellow-officer and friend of Wyatt. Subsequently joined an engineering firm in the North. One of the few area leaders so far arrested:

He was an incredible man, don't make any mistake about that ... I know what everybody's saying about him now but there's nothing new in slinging mud when the tables turn. Very well, you make your comparisons and I'll stick to mine; whatever he was then so am I by reflection and I'll be glad to take my share – I was right behind him from the start. I'm ready to go his way too if I have to.

From the examination at the preliminary hearings of Malcolm Maudsley, Second Secretary at the Treasury:

Of course I continued to work under him, so did thousands; this is a good moment to protest against completely arbitrary victimization. Very well you choose to make a distinction between active and passive collaboration. Some perhaps cooperated more wholeheartedly than others; but what could any of us do in the circumstances? One must eat, whoever governs. If the machinery breaks down – no one eats. I really don't see why I should be singled out ...

Abstract of evidence given by Major-General Hurst, also from the preliminary hearings:

Yes I obeyed orders – illegal? Maybe, but I didn't have much choice did I? My frame of mind? Is a soldier supposed to have one in peace time? Oh very well, my feeling was that if no one else objected very strongly, if at all, why should I play St George? I'd have found myself out in front without a shred of support anyway. Of course I could have resigned. What good would that have done? There's always someone ready to step into one's shoes even if they don't fit. My opinion of Wyatt? If that's a booby trap I refuse to touch it. Yes I know he was this that and the other, what the devil d'you want me to say – Wyatt was good for the country? Was that my what – my opinion? I've told you I'm a soldier . . .

Extracts from the notes of Chief Inspector Drew, taken at the preliminary interrogation of Sergeant Jennings, Wyatt's personal aide:

. . . since Korea . . . yes I knew him like the back of my hand so don't tell me he was Adolf the Second because I know better . . . politics? I'll tell you something, sonny – when I started I didn't know a Member of Parliament from a Military Policeman – when I finished I knew there wasn't any difference as far as a few million voters was concerned . . . think so? Go on try me . . . who was Prime Minister in '31? You must be joking – never mind the kid's stuff – I'm telling you he taught me the lot – suppose I asked you what was Keynes's definition of the division of Labour in '32 . . . alright I'll tell *you* — 'one lot ardent to do things because they're economically sound; the other lot just as ready to do things admitted to be economically unsound'. That's the last Labour Government in a nutshell, friend. Wyatt showed me the score – and if he said there was something better that was good enough for me. Knew what he intended to do? You lot are gorgonzola green alright. Knew! I was in on the ground floor planning, co-ordinating the groups – even the arms deal . . . and I'll tell you another thing – we'll be back . . .

Sergeant Jennings strode across the barrack square with more haste than triple striped propriety demanded. Captain Wyatt watched him for a moment, smiled, took one pace to his desk and sat down to wait for the burly NCO's breathless arrival. Time to gaze round at the shabby utilitarian office smelling aseptically of a Unitarian chapel. He would leave it with no regrets . . . Then Jennings entered, sketching a semaphorical salute, marring its regulation perfection with a broad grin.

'Compliments of the Colonel . . .' he barked.

'*Pianissimo,* Jennings, for heaven's sake, we're not on the parade ground now.'

'Yessir,' he dropped into a conversational register. 'About the transport, sir.'

'Request granted.'

Jennings showed surprise. 'How d'you know sir?'

'For one thing you looked so pleased with yourself.'

'Oh.' Jennings changed down to disappointment.

'For another I took the precaution to ring him just now.'

'Oh.' The sergeant was plainly hurt.

'It's all right, Jennings, I wanted to assure myself of his reaction. "I told your man you can take what you damned well like, Wyatt, but have it all back for general inspection by 08.00 hours on Thursday – and good luck."'

The sergeant's face was a noncomposmental study. 'Good luck?'

'Looking incredulous will get you nowhere.'

'I look it because I feel it. I've seen you do a lot of things I thought impossible; but getting transport and men out of Colonel Blacker *and* a blessing thrown in for starters –' he checked rapidly as an idea almost visibly impaled him. ''Ere! don't tell me the Colonel's in on this.'

Wyatt's smiled broadened: 'Very well, I won't, if you prefer.'

'What I mean is, is he?'

The smile faded. 'Jennings, I've kept you and the rest posted about everything except this. The Colonel knows what we intend doing – because I told him. I can't go into his reasons for helping now. All I can say is, he's the only man I trust outside our organization.'

'Then why isn't he in it?'

'He's not for us because he doesn't think we can do it. He's not against us because he believes it's all to the good if we can. There'll be a lot of people like him to begin with ... meantime let's thank God he does no more than wish us luck.'

'He doesn't know details?' Jennings persisted.

Wyatt regarded the sergeant mock despairingly.

'No, Jennings,' he said. 'He doesn't.'

Further extract from Chief Inspector Drew's notes, taken at the second interrogation of Sergeant Jennings:

I didn't say he was cold-blooded – you're bloody well twisting my words! I said he was cool. Well that's what you expect in an officer isn't it? Examples? I could give you a dozen. The day we took over. Is that good enough for you?

Big Ben chimed the half and Jennings glanced at his watch for no very good reason. Otherwise he showed little sign of nerves.

'Fifteen minutes to go, sir.' No movement. The words fighting through a barricade of set teeth. He sat in the driving seat of a large green Hillman; Wyatt in the rear made no reply, continued to gaze out at the grey Gothic pontificating Victorian virtues. They sat in silence for a minute or two, the Captain deep in thought, Jennings listening intently to the crackle of the two-way radio.

'Tally sticks,' Wyatt said.

'What's that, sir?'

'The old Palace of Westminster was burned down in 1834 by a surfeit of tally sticks.'

'I didn't know.'

'When Parliament discussed a new site, William the Fourth offered them Buckingham Palace.'

'I don't blame him.'

'The Duke of Wellington was against the idea.'

'He would be – Conservative bastard.'

'He was right strategically speaking. Houses of Parliament should never be situated, in his view, so they could be entirely surrounded by the mob.'

Jennings chuckled, but made no comment.

'I think I'll take a stroll.' Wyatt sounded calm and relaxed.

'Right, sir.'

'Keep an ear open.'

'Will do, sir.'

Wyatt left the car and a more relaxed Jennings to follow a five-minute schedule previously and meticulously worked out to the second. He wandered casually across the square, noting the disposition of police constables on duty, nodded affably to a sergeant at the New Palace Yard entrance and bought an *Evening Standard* at the stand nearby. Then a stroll as far as Richard the First and back again; no signs of recognition as he passed familiar faces in the short queue waiting to see 'Democracy in action'.

Two men were intent on photographing the ornate St Stephen's entrance adjoining Westminster Hall. Not far away in a street leading from Smith Square an army lorry would be waiting ...

Almost in spite of himself he paused to study the coal-black statue standing alone, apart from the rest. The outsider, the russet-coated captain, 'the great practical mystic' stood where he belonged, isolated, a man to be reckoned with.

Wyatt caught himself mouthing a Latin valediction, *'Bonus intra melior extra'*, smiled and knew in part why he'd taken five minutes off. He returned to the car while Cromwell, gripping Bible and sword forever, frowned eternally on the passing world, all triviality and nothing of God.

The captain quickened his step at sight of Jennings painstakingly striving to keep agitation from his expression. Jennings was hardly succeeding.

'Well?'

'Bad news, sir. Objective One's behind schedule.'

With detached interest Wyatt watched colour return to the sergeant's features. 'How long?'

'Fifteen minutes.'

'Inform the scouts – alert all vehicles. Plans A and B now operational at sixteen hundred hours.'

'Do we have time?'

'Only if you hurry.'

'Right, sir.'

Wyatt tossed the evening paper – late lunch edition – on to the front seat.

'You might like to look through that while we're waiting.'

Private Jackson showed no concern, no emotion of any kind as junior prosecuting counsel rose with a benign Friar Tuck smile suggesting anything but the fact that the soldier was on trial for treason. He stared ahead with parade ground fixity.

'Now, Jackson, you admit that you were in charge of a heavy lorry on the 23rd. So far as I can gather you drove the empty vehicle out of your camp at approximately nine o'clock in the morning and arrived in London at twelve. The defence wishes us to believe that you then made a number of scheduled stops at various points to pick up a complement of uniformed men; that you then drove to the vicinity of Smith Square, waited till the moment for action arrived and then participated in the events described – all this! in ignorance of what it was all about?'

'I never said I didn't know what it was about. I was asked if I obeyed orders. I did.'

'Illegal orders.'

'It wasn't for me to say one way or the other.'

'You wish us to believe then that you knew nothing of Wyatt's subversive activities until zero hour on the 23rd?'

'You know damned well I did!'

The Judge intervened to warn the accused against the use of intemperate language. Counsel continued:

'What I may be presumed to know is beside the point. My concern is to make it abundantly clear that you acted voluntarily and of your own accord in a situation leaving you complete freedom of choice. In those circumstances it is derisive to talk of obeying orders. Now, will you tell the court how you became involved in the events of the 23rd?'

Jackson seemed not to have heard. He was staring into the depths of the great vaulted roof, lost in a prospect of carved angels . . . or he may have been too uninterested to care. Counsel repeated his question.

'Involved? Well it was through the discussion groups mainly.'

'Discussion groups – in the army?'

'It's common practice. The officers often give talks to the men – keeps 'em occupied.'

'The officers or the men?'

'Both if you like.'

'And the subjects discussed?'

'Regimental history – they were more like lectures really. Strategy Ancient and Modern, that kind of thing.'

'And politics?'

'Naturally.'

'Naturally. A subject admirably taken care of by Wyatt no doubt?'

'By Captain Wyatt – yes.'

'The subversive nature of his political beliefs, such as they were, required a degree of caution on his part?'

'He didn't make a secret of 'em if that's what you mean.'

'Was that not risky?'

'Maybe, but that was his affair. The Captain knew what he was doing.'

'So Wyatt took Politics as his subject and aired his views for the benefit of all and sundry?'

'The Captain chose Current Affairs – you can't help discussing politics then can you? I mean it covers a multitude.'

Counsel tittered in the wake of the court to show he too was human without particularly meaning it. The man was showing signs of intelligence incompatible with his rank and former profession.

'Now Jackson,' he continued, 'about these "discussions" . . .'

It was a cushy number. They'd gather together one or two afternoons a week in a NAAFI recreation room. Most times it was a perfunctory sort of performance; blackboard stuff – How we Broke Through at Alamein, Jungle War in Burma; typical Service bull. Most of the men got through it with the best grace possible, industriously making notes on their pads; more often than not their jottings looked suspiciously like naked women.

Wyatt they listened to, even looked forward to his sessions. He'd enter briskly followed by Jennings who stood smartly at attention and remained statuesque throughout the period. The Captain would pace the length of the room as he spoke, watching no one in particular, aware of every single one of them, yet always apart somehow. They were forced to watch him as he moved restlessly about the room as though weaving a pattern of invisible footsteps. And all the time – words, words and ideas, outrageous, novel, revolutionary; they had to listen as they watched, and therefore they were forced to think.

'I thought it might be profitable if today we consider the

role played by class distinction in a society that claims largely to have discarded such a notion while practising it privately, pleasurably, and with a sense of shameful satisfaction, as a small boy practises masturbation.'

One or two of the newer recruits coloured visibly, but already Wyatt had one hundred per cent attention.

'Now,' he continued, 'I'm going to stick my neck out and say that class distinction was never more prevalent than it is today. Anybody care to contradict me?'

Several of the men grinned and glanced at Corporal Dunwood, the Kinplingesque barrack-room lawyer, veteran of Normandy, Korea and a dozen assorted punch-ups in and around the barracks. He was Wyatt's oldest sparring partner – the best punch bag in the gym. The Corporal pushed a formidable jaw forward and the others sat back happily. He was full of confidence as usual.

'Yessir. I reckon it's all as dead as a Dodo. We got a government that's about put a stop to that sort of thing. What's more, public opinion's dead against it. And besides there's more equal opportunity today than when I was a kid and that's a fact.'

Dunwood stared around over open sights looking for opposition. There were murmurs of approval so he switched on the ill-fitting mask of extreme modesty. 'Sir,' he appeared to suggest with a mild smirk, 'would have to fight his way out of that bleedin' lot.'

'Sir' seemed to be considering his reply; in reality he listened to the almost audible acquiescence, thinking how easily men accept canned ideas without a tin-opener.

'How many children do you have, Corporal?'

'I thought you knew, sir. Two boys.'

'Clever?'

'Both got their eleven plus.'

'Good. Might even go to university.'

'I hope so.'

'Why didn't you send them to Eton?'

'Couldn't afford it.'

'Where's the equal opportunity?'

'Well . . .'

'Why d'you suppose Eton and the rest are so expensive?'

'Because they're good schools.'

'You mean they give a better education than a Secondary Modern or a Grammar School?'

'No!'

'They must do. Wealthy parents aren't so stupid as to throw money away on their little ones when they can get the same value for nowt.'

Dunwood began to flounder; Wyatt did nothing to save him.

'Expensiveness, Corporal, spells exclusiveness; in the long run that has nothing to do with ability and everything to do with opportunity. It's as true for today as it was for yesterday. University, yes. Teachers, scientists, journalists, barristers; they're all needed to strengthen the middle order of batting – I even know of a brilliant refuse collector who took a first at Oxford. But brilliance won't get your lads into the places that really matter because the System is highly selective – it has to be, or there'd be no such thing as a System which is the secret chamber of immortality within the pyramid.'

'Pyramid?' the Corporal looked perplexed, Wyatt seemed to ignore the question and pressed on with one of his own.

'If you were introduced to the Queen what would you do?'

'Stand to attention and salute.' Dunwood had no doubt about that.

'Why should you?'

'Why – well – well, she's a woman.'

'Do you come to attention and salute your wife every time she addresses you?'

General laughter swept Dunwood's answer out of existence; even Jennings relaxed long enough to grin.

'Respect, sir,' Private Jones volunteered.

'Respect is something you *earn*. You don't give it away to every Tom, Dick and Harry you happen to meet. But why show more respect for someone we don't know than someone we do?'

'Because she's the Queen,' the Corporal did what he could to climb back into the ring.

16

'And what does that mean?'

Dunwood stopped climbing.

'You see how difficult it is. We accept so much, take more than half for granted, never stop to ask why things should be as they are. Is it any wonder they remain the same? And would it matter at any other time?' He paused at the window, studying just long enough to take in the dreary scene, then turned.

'I mention the Queen because she happens to be the very apex of a pyramidal structure which went out with the ancient Egyptians. A democratic monarchy is as impossible as a pyramid balancing on its summit.'

'Then why does it exist, sir?'

'Why? Well, Private Kemp, someone once said, "It exists because no one quite knows what to do with it." I suppose he was thinking of a whatnot bequeathed by an ancient great-aunt. You saw bits off it, scrape away the varnish, give it a coat of paint, try to convert it into a birdcage – but, whatever you do, it's still a whatnot. Well, we started to discuss class distinction and now we're on to the monarchy. Does this mean there's a connection, Corporal?'

Dunwood was delighted at being consulted. 'No, sir – not under a Labour government.'

'You may be right. Let's have a look and see. Who is the Fount of all Honours?'

'The Queen.'

'And what does a true Socialist think of the Honours system?' Dunwood thought about this while Wyatt continued. 'You say the Labour government sets its face against class distinction. Let's forget for the moment that the Prime Minister, true to his middle-class nature, venerates royalty in general, and Her Majesty in particular. As a Socialist does he abolish the Honours List or tinker with it as a sop to the Left Wing? Does he hesitate to create peers? Are his Honours Lists shorter than those of a Conservative PM? Does he wear his Coronation Medal on every possible occasion or does he keep it locked up in a drawer at Chequers? Now we're coming to it. Do you honestly think that a newly created Labour peer considers himself to be a member of the working class?'

'But nobody talks about class any more,' Dunwood protested.

'Corporal.' Wyatt paused to stare sadly at the exasperated NCO. 'There was a time when nobody dared to use a certain four-letter word describing a certain natural function, but it didn't stop them doing it.'

It was some time before Wyatt could continue.

'The words are still used, the idea still exists. Read any journal, listen to any TV pundit discussing the social scene, open a Hansard at random; more often than not you'll find it's a Labour member who refers obliquely or directly to class distinction, antagonism, conflict. The PM himself talks of a middle class . . .'

'But . . .' Private Kemp began.

'There are no buts! Do you really believe Wrigley could have condemned the present strike unless he had a thoroughly middle-class mentality! His every action and utterance implies an acceptance of a divided society. It exists. Why else an "old-boy" network? Why else an Establishment? Why else a supra-national System grafted on to the Rose and Crown? Why else does a retired colonel complain if plans are put forward to build a housing estate bang next door to his pseudo-Tudor flop-house in Camberley? Why do residents protest against hostels for unmarried mothers? Class divisions? Perish the thought – as long as the lower orders keep their place.'

'Difficult to put a finger on it, sir. It's all mixed up nowadays.'

Private Jackson said little; he was the most politically conscious of them all. His father had fought Midley for the Communists years ago and proudly saved his deposit.

'It is – and all for the wrong reasons. It's a middle-class fashion to be Socialist, and the done thing to be a Tory if you're part of the "I'm alright Jack" lower class. When you've got everything that's supposed to be worth having, car, TV in the bathroom, a veneered cocktail cabinet and five shares in ICI then you've arrived – in time for the party representing true blue chip living – especially if it doesn't cost you a penny . . .'

*

'In a word, Jackson, you and your comrades were being deliberately incited to indulge in subversive ideas against the monarchy.'

'You asked me what he talked about. I'm telling you.'

'At any rate you were influenced?'

'I saw his point.'

'Which was?'

'That a combination of Establishment, Monarchy and Government as we knew it, creating a divide and rule atmosphere by a subtle manipulation of class prejudice, no longer provided an effective political system for a fifty-million complex called Great Britain – if it ever did.'

Counsel drew breath and wondered if he had underestimated the insignificant looking ex-soldier.

'So you acted on the assumption that Wyatt and a handful of malcontents could do better?'

'The results speak for themselves.'

Mr Featherstone was profoundly thankful for His Lordship's observation that it might be a suitable moment to adjourn for lunch.

2

But in the sober comfort of his chamber at the Lords, red robes shed, the bewigged mask of Rhadamanthus laid aside, he felt less like lunch, more like an old man, tired and disillusioned by the business of sitting in judgement on a world he could no longer understand. A discreetly desiccated sherry did nothing for his digestion, little to soothe his turbulent state of mind. He sipped, sighed and settled deeper into his chair, eyes carefully avoiding the mass of transcripted evidence skyscraping on the desk before him. His head ached abominably, all those damned lights flooding the scene – *lux legis, lux televisionis* – a chill memory still lingered in his bones of Thames-smelling draughts. Of all places to choose for a trial – be damned to tradition. A great medieval barn ... Hartfish again. The man was a shyster, a St Audrey's man, a ringmaster of Laws ... and there was nothing that he, the Lord Chief Justice of England, could do about it. Hartfish was powerful, suddenly very powerful. Not forty-five, and Attorney-General already. His Lordship had watched him rise from a nobody to an eminence. There was nothing he had asked for from the Government in the way of extra-legal powers that had not been granted him. And his Lordship was powerless to object in the name of Justice or anything or anyone else. He himself had been lucky to escape from the business unscathed. Not that they could touch him, of course; but there had been criticisms ... the legal profession had closed its ranks and there was little they could do but mutter 'reform'. After all, the Lord Chancellor, his old friend since Eton, had stated publicly that 'the Chief Justice had admirably fulfilled a delicate mission by continuing in office through the dark days. Whatever the system obtaining, legal or illegal, law and order must be maintained. It is as essential as the uninterrupted operation of the gas, electricity and water supply.' His Lordship felt a little better. He even felt prepared to face the world, lunch and whoever it was knocking at the door.

But it was Hartfish; his appearance was in every respect an unpleasant surprise. Those peculiar spectacles, the student's pallor, immaculate lawyer-black suiting gave the Attorney-General's features a sinister cast. He hunched his way through his profession like an undertaker contemplating revenge. His manner was deceptively deferential.

'Well, John?'

His Lordship bridled delicately.

'I do wish you wouldn't preface every chance medley between us with "well John".'

Edward Hartfish smiled, sat and made a mental note to forget on the next occasion, while remembering to pour himself a large drink from the decanter.

'You sound *distrait*.'

His Lordship gestured irritably. 'You were in court this morning.'

'Well?'

'Then you heard that fool Featherstone make a complete hash of Jackson's cross-examination.'

Hartfish left his glass in mid-air, a deliberate pause conveying astonishment, the eyebrows suitably arched. 'You're worried about the small fry?'

'Jackson isn't small fry. He played a significant part in the uprising.'

'A lot of people played a part of one kind or another in what you call the "uprising".'

His Lordship strove to ignore the implication. 'I cannot indicate the gravity of the whole affair unless it's clearly demonstrated that all active conspirators are equally culpable.'

'Is that your brief from above?' The spectacles glinted, the Attorney-General's lips showed a tendency to smile.

His Lordship swallowed the insult because it could only be an ill-bred joke. 'I subscribe,' he muttered stiffly, 'to the somewhat old-fashioned theory of an independent judiciary.'

'Really?'

Hartfish appeared either to consider the idea novel or unimportant. But his spectacular rise to power was due in part to just such an example of the triple *entendre*; an ability to leave two impressions in the mind whatever he said while producing a third, like an uninvited conjurer materializing the unwanted rabbit at an inconvenient moment.

His Lordship sensed the menace behind the one questioning word. 'Really?' And with lawyer-like acumen he stared up at Hartfish from the bottom of the trap. Only a mocking smile illuminated the Attorney-General's unspoken question. 'If the judiciary is as independent as all that, why did you implement Wyatt's illegal decrees?'

The Lord Chief Justice kept silence, except for a small voice of hatred damning the sallow little lawyer to hell.

Hartfish sipped his sherry. He would have preferred an Amoroso.

'I agree with you about Featherstone.' His tone suggested a nurse dealing with a fractious child. 'But it has its purpose. I thought you realized. Part of the grand strategy. Featherstone bungles the preliminaries, increases the defendants' confidence.

Then I take over, take them apart and leave them,' he smiled gently, 'to your tender mercies.'

'Machiavellian tactics!' His Lordship complained. The smile disappeared like a well-trained animal.

'Possibly – but they work – twenty-three convictions to a single acquittal so far. The last thing the caretaker government wants is a blanket judgement. I know as well as you do these men aren't a pack of ignoramuses, Jackson proved that this morning, but by the time I've done with him and the rest of them the fiction will read that they could be nothing else. We *must* establish that one man only had the brains, energy, drive and capacity, was solely responsible in the long run. If not, what happens? Every Tom, Dick or Harry will consider himself a potential thinking machine able and willing to follow in Wyatt's footsteps.'

'A life sentence on the ringleaders would be enough.'

'No! This is more than a question of ringleaders. You don't seem to understand, John. It's not this or that man who's standing trial or undergoing examination. It's man – mass-man, that's why I demanded a mass audience – the gogglers themselves are on trial.' He stared through His Lorship and far beyond to a vision that only a Torquemada could understand and rejoice at. The spectacles glinted with yellow fire ... 'I'm wrong,' he said at last, 'it's the pretensions of mass-man that are on trial.'

His Lordship stared at Hartfish. The room was comfortably warm, but an icicle seemed skilfully to be trepanning his skull ...

All units were alerted and ordered to resynchronize operations due to the alteration of Objective One's schedule. The major parts of Wyatt's plan had to coincide. A difference of seconds could mean a snowballing measure of failure.

Wyatt had foreseen the possibility and underlined it at every briefing to decrease the danger of overspilt tension. Simply a matter of putting the clock forward; no need for panic. Even the one-man units in the public gallery queue were in contact with Cencom, every one equipped with micro-receivers.

Amateur photographers carried the same apparatus in converted Yashicas. They moved elsewhere 'snapping' other points of view till the new time came for action.

Jennings parked the car less conspicuously and the two men settled down to wait. The sergeant rested the evening paper against the steering-wheel and read in silence for all of five minutes. He jerked to startled attention when Wyatt spoke.

'Worried, Jennings?' It was a simple question of interpreting the drumming of fingers on a steering wheel.

'I was thinking it's tough luck on Baynard – he's got a watchmaker's job.'

'That's why he got it – impeccable timing. He'll cope.'

'What about the lads in the queue? They'll be inside by the time we count down.'

'Your memory's going to the dogs. A party of civilian friends are backing up to help the Smith Square boys. I don't think they'll be needed, but we might as well be on the safe side.'

'Ah – the blokes in Lyons.'

'Blokes? That's no way to describe a trade union convention having an innocent cuppa before lobbying their MP.'

'I wouldn't mind a cup myself right now.'

'I'll stand you one if we pull this off.'

'Nice of you,' Jennings grinned. 'And if we don't?'

'Why then I imagine the State will provide you with free tea and evening cocoa for the next seven years or more. In the meantime have a cigarette instead.'

The sergeant relaxed and fumbled for his matches.

Eyewitness description of events by Mrs Emily Finn for a snap TV line-up of 'Those Who Were There On The 23rd':

'It must have been a tremendous experience, Mrs Finn.'

'Oh definitely.'

'What happened in fact?'

'It all happened so sudden.'

'Yes, of course, but what did you actually see?'

'Not very much really. I remember Big Ben struck four and then someone looked out of the window and said "ooh look". That was all. "Ooh look" he said. I remember that distinctly because he was wearing horn-rimmed glasses.'

'Yes. And these men – the soldiers – you actually saw them storming the entrance?'

'Not really. As I say it was all so sudden. There was a lot of shouting and I thought it was a demonstration – y'know, Cornish Nationalists or something.'

'What – what impression did all this make on you at the time?'

'Well I don't know really.'

'At any rate it was exciting.'

'Definitely. But I'm afraid I'm not really interested in politics and that sort of thing.'

'But this is after all in the nature of a revolution. Presumably it means something to you that you were on the spot actually witnessing an historical event?'

'Well I wasn't really . . .'

'But . . .'

'Me being a bus conductress our bus was finishing the run to Victoria, so we weren't on the spot really. I just happened to hear this bloke shout "ooh look" as we turned out of Whitehall and, of course, I looked out of the window . . . not so much on the spot as on the move you might say – still history's the same really isn't it? Always on the move – no fare stages . . .'

The item above was in fact deleted from the programme 'Those Who Were There' and is now in the BBC's Documentary Film Archives.

PARLIAMENTARY DEBATES (HANSARD)

House of Commons. Official Report

Wednesday 23rd October

3.49 VIETNAM

Mr Doubleday (by Private Notice) asked the Prime Minister if he will state what is being done by Her Majesty's Government to bring about a peaceful solution to the problem of Vietnam in view of the declared intention of the American Government to extend the conflict into the neighbouring territory of Cambodia.

The Prime Minister (Mr Kenneth Wrigley): I do not think it would be opportune to say too much about this matter until we are fully acquainted with all the facts and relevant circumstances. I would prefer to wait for fuller information before saying anything further.

Mr Winslow: Is not the fact itself disturbing enough to invite comment?

The Prime Minister: I ought to remind the Hon. Member that comment is out of place until we can be sure that facts are not being confused with informed opinion.

Mr Alby: President Johnson himself made the statement concerning America's future war aims in Vietnam. The statement was reported in *The Times*. Is the Prime Minister doubting the President's veracity or *The Times*' accuracy?

The Prime Minister: Neither. But a bare statement of intention is of no value until we know the reasons on which it is based.

Mr Alby: I take it you are saying we will prevaricate and blush with maidenly shame before yielding to yet another advance by our American Uncle? (Cries of 'withdraw').

Mr Loftford-Smith: This is a most improper slur on our own good faith and that of our American allies. If the Prime Minister cannot keep his supporters in order . . . (Opposition laughter)

Speaker: The phrasing was perhaps a little indelicate . . .

Mr Alby: Very well. I will rephrase the question . . .

Lieutenant Baynard commanded the storming party assigned to Objective One.

Three minutes to four: while the Labour MP for Chichely North dutifully leaks information to a lobby correspondent on likely abstentions in that evening's division, two Army type dual purpose trucks cruise into position. Observation units covering the route from London Airport report by simple code to Baynard that the Daimler with motor-cycle escort, shadowed at regulation distance (25 yards) by an SB Ford, will enter the Mall at one minute past four.

The Lieutenant swore a little, convinced that history should take place on the hour, and tersely acknowledged the message. He glanced into the nearside driving mirror to check that his Number Two was bumper to tail and directed Jaggers to drive around for a couple of minutes in less frequented side turnings. He calculated ninety seconds to rejoin the mainstream and 'break down' at the Northumberland Avenue traffic lights from which they would keep the objective in view.

He checked his Browning for the last time, slipped it into his pocket and smiled wryly. Jaggers missed very little.

'Feeling happy?'

'I was just thinking – wait till my old Mother hears about this.'

'Wait till a lot of people hear about it, my wife for example. I know what she'd say – eight years away from a pension and now look at you. Well we'd better laugh now before we start worrying.'

'It'll be easier than you think.'

'With forty of us?'

'I mean the whole operation.'

'Oh yes,' Jaggers dripped sarcasm. 'Two hundred against fifty millions.'

'The longer the odds ...'

But tension stifled small talk and they drove on in silence ...

'One minute to four, sir. We'd better start giving your Ma and my wife something to talk about.'

They jerked to a halt seconds before four. The lights were at green. Forty men in the two lorries tightened their grip on revolvers and sub-machine guns while the following traffic built up into a respectable and orderly queue. A bus slowed smoothly and came to rest as the lights changed, the driver poked his head out of the cab window and shouted vulgar advice, best described as ex-army. Baynard stood by and held his breath till he was red in the face simulating a junior officer embarrassed by the incompetence of clots under his command. Jaggers played the second lead credibly, gazing at the gleaming interior of a beautifully tuned engine with an 'I-can't-understand-it' expression of astonishment.

'They're on the way – now!' The words ducked and draked across the static of their RT but they had already seen or sensed the approach of Objective One.

Jaggers gave a cheerful thumbs-up sign to a mildly interested police-constable crossing the road and both were in their seats before the lights changed back to red. Not that it mattered. The sergeant had eased the truck over the line for a classical head start.

The play-acting was over.

They gave ten seconds to the long black saloon flying its proud little pennant, by which time the discreet Ford had also passed. Its three occupants hardly gave the army wagons a second glance as they trundled into position close behind them. It all hooked up so naturally that Baynard nodded once abruptly in approval. They reached the point of no return at a steady twenty miles per hour.

Tiny things. A couple stop to stare. A mother points to the car telling a small child something, the child waves without interest. Leaves falling from the trees and Victoria in the distance, disapproving in stony silence . . .

He could see a small crowd clustered round the open gates, anxious to witness a footnote to the scrap-book of history, unaware that they were about to occupy a paragraph.

Tourists naturally, and obviously a fanatical fringe of Loyalist Royalists missing no opportunity to demonstrate their soul-sick subservience to the princely smile or a queenly flick of the finger. A retired MBE from Croydon decorated for his services to drains was often to be seen at the gates with his portable gramophone, playing a scratchy 78 of the National Anthem as the cortège swept majestically by. He would stand stiffly to attention in bad imitation of the two redniks on guard duty.

Down the Mall and round the island dotted with sightseers. Like a man drowning in the Rubicon, Baynard had time to wonder why a man should be standing before the palace playing records . . . Before the guards frozen into an attitude of 'present arms' could show surprise they were through.

Curiously, none of those on duty at the Palace or concerned with the cavalcade itself thought it of any consequence when they were followed into the forecourt. Doubts began to filter through as the column passed beneath the portico leading to the inner courtyard. There was no time left for them to crystallize. The royal chauffeur's evidence on these crucial moments appears to be the most reliable. It was 'all over before it began', he told the preliminary Court of Inquiry:

I brought the car to a halt at the main entrance, yes it's right opposite the archway – exactly between the double columns. Very few of the staff assemble to wait on Her Majesty. In any case this was a routine journey; seeing Prince Richard off at London

Airport – a family affair – and back again. I only remember seeing Cuthbertson the head footman and the Duke's valet. Cuthbertson was waving frantically and shouting something. I thought he'd gone mad. By then, of course, we were in the Quadrangle.

Oh yes, I certainly did see the army trucks ... in my mirror as we drove down the Mall. No it didn't strike me as any way strange – not, not even when they passed through the gate. In my job you concentrate on getting the passengers from A to B. I was too busy bringing the Daimler in for a three-point landing to think about them. Besides the security men deal with that kind of thing. Not that I dreamed they had anything to deal with. Looking back I still find it hard to credit ... well because you don't think of that kind of thing happening.

After we stopped everything happened so fast I saw nothing very clearly. I heard Cuthbertson shout 'Stay in the car, Ma'am!' Oh yes, I was very concerned for the Queen's safety but it's difficult to know what to do in the circumstances. I remember glancing over my shoulder, it isn't done normally. His Highness seemed to be trying to open the door ... No, the outriders had left us at the gates. They returned minutes later but it was too late ... the SB men left their car and tried to form a screen between Her Majesty and the – the assailants. There wasn't much they could do against forty well-armed men, if they fired then they'd have been fired on in return – the Queen might easily have been hit. I did hear two shots – one of their men hit Sergeant Spears in the arm – no, I don't know if he fired, he might have done. I was already being herded up the steps by a sergeant and four men, Cuthbertson and the valet with me ... No, nothing was said.

I had time to see an officer open the nearside car door and motion the Queen, Prince Philip and Prince Charles out. Yes, he had a revolver in his hand. They were completely surrounded by men in khaki.

I heard a short burst of firing as we went through the door. The squads of men began rounding everyone up they could lay hands on. We were all taken to the Throne Room. They even got the staff out of the Palace Post Office in there – yes, everyone from the Comptroller to chambermaids. Thorough? Well I remember Cuthbertson saying either they knew someone who used to work there or they had a plan of the place. He told me the late Queen Mary got lost there once ... It was a thorough search all right.

From Baynard's preliminary statement:

Our orders were to shoot only if necessary. Most of us carried revolvers, the others – one in five – were armed with sub-machine guns – only those experienced in their use were issued with subs. They're touchy things.

The men were split into ten sections of four men each; they all had assignments, such as closing gates, sealing off all entrances; one section occupied the post office, another dealt with the Security Branch officers. But that was later. Our first task was to throw a cordon round the Queen and her family. Actually I was a little surprised that their bodyguard fired – in the circumstances. They must have been aware of the risk. As you know one of our men was wounded – he happened to be in line with Philip . . .

They behaved extremely well, were perfectly composed but said very little. He stood quite calmly, hands clasped behind his back, watching security men and a few odds and ends being rounded up. He might have been watching demonstrations at an exhibition.

The Queen wanted to know if something could be done for Spears. I assured her all arrangements had been made for dealing with emergencies. That's all she said as I recollect.

I don't remember exactly who lowered the Royal Standard – someone in D section probably. Is it important?

My immediate task was to conduct them to the Bow Room . . . because it was close to the grounds . . . I led the way and they followed – yes, they were surprised, I think, that we should know the geography of the palace so well. The Queen asked if the children might be sent for. I told her she was at liberty to ring for them. By then one of our men was on the switchboard.

Regina *v.* Baynard. Featherstone QC cross-examining. Second day.

'So after a period at University you drifted into the Army?'

'There was no question of drifting. I joined in the starry-eyed belief that it was an honourable profession and a damned sight more interesting than teaching.'

'What were your political convictions at that time?'

'I had none, none that tied in with the Lib-Lab-Con trinity.'

'An objective interest?'

'Yes, but ineffectually so.'

'Until you met Wyatt?'

'Yes.'

'When did you first meet him?'

'Soon after I was commissioned. I joined my regiment at Tasworth in '64. March.'

'Were you aware of his existence at any time before that date?'

'Yes. I knew he was highly regarded as an expert on tactics. In fact he spent more time travelling about the country as an instructor than he did at barracks.'

'Most convenient. So eventually you made his acquaintance in the course of your duties; in the officers' mess and so on?'

'I did.'

'What was your earliest impression of him?'

'The same as my last – he was an incredible man.'

'Incredible . . . what exactly do you mean by that?'

'He was a whole man, a man of integrity.'

'Integrity! Really?'

'That's what I said.'

'We'll come back to the question of his "integrity" later. Am I right in saying that you became friends within a short time of your posting?'

'Friends – I'm not sure.'

'You became his right-hand man didn't you?'

'It had nothing to do with friendship – friendship doesn't cover a relationship with a man like Wyatt . . . I'm sorry I can't explain further.'

'Are you suggesting yours was a Socratic master–disciple relationship?'

'There were no emotional overtones if that's what you're getting at. He simply radiated a peculiar sort of influence . . .'

'Authority?'

'It was more than that . . . others felt it too – I'm sorry, I can't explain . . .'

'You had many opportunities for discussion did you not?'

'Yes.'

'No doubt he talked a great deal and you listened.'

'To some extent that's true.'

'Politics only?'

'Everything under the sun. His knowledge was encyclopaedic.'

'You said yesterday that you were eventually converted to his radical views ...'

'I said I was soon convinced that his ideas were fundamentally sound.'

'Could you have arrived at his viewpoint without his help?'

'I – I don't know.'

'Let us go back to the occasion of your first visit to the London headquarters ...'

From Wyatt's journal dated April 4th:

Drove to the London headquarters with Baynard. Lieutenant French and Gaynor were already present. This surprised and perhaps impressed him. I know he has a great regard for French. Many of the area leaders were there – Morrison and his wife also, of course. It was an important meeting. I announced that action could not be delayed much longer. They gave unqualified support to my proposal that active planning should commence at once.

Wrigley's victory in the last election is a determining factor. In my view the Tories have finally abdicated responsibility once again, and once again the Socialists will inherit a mess armed with a hairless broom and a bucket of slops.

In six months they will be discredited, mainly because Wrigley is an Establishment man at heart. His devotion to the Queen is convincing proof of the fact. I believe he has cast himself in the role of a latter-day Disraeli to her Victoria. For the rest, Rhodesia will be settled to the white extremists' satisfaction, the unholy alliance with America will be strengthened and strong measures for economic recovery are almost certain to be introduced at the expense of the working population. He is the most dangerous politician this country has ever produced.

After the meeting I asked Baynard if he was prepared to join us. He accepted without hesitation.

'And from that moment, you, as an officer in the service of the Queen, conspired against her and the country you were pledged to defend?'

'Nothing of the kind. We conspired in the interests of our country. We fought a bloodless battle for our country. Our actions throughout were motivated by a standard of values un-heard of in this country's political history for a very long time. We considered the monarchy and still consider it to be a mere Punch and Judy show manipulated by a bunch of shrewd and unprincipled operators. Pledged to defend the Queen – the King – the country? If a third world war broke out tomorrow – I will speak! If it broke out tomorrow the armed forces would still be defending the vested interests they died to defend in '14 and '39!'

3

While Scotland Yard tries to make sense of garbled and in-coherent phone calls, refusing to believe any of them, in the few precious seconds it takes to convince them that the im-possible has happened, a handful of men in Army uniforms are taking up their positions in the Palace of Westminster. The initial rush carries all entrances without difficulty. Not a shot has been fired. The few police on duty outside are over-powered by nothing more lethal than surprise. The first phase is over before startled passers-by can reach a phone-box. At the third stroke it will be four one and ten seconds ...

The womb of the Mother of Parliaments is approached by a long cool hall lined with Pop political figures of the past, turned to stone by the critical gaze of history. Those who have business in the Chamber itself or want something or wish to protest or complain continue straight on into the great Gothic-ally arched Central Lobby from which passages radiate like spokes in a big wheel ...

Wyatt and his followers press forward shedding men here and there to deal with a bewildered opposition. Nothing is left to chance. Every man knows his position and what he has to do. The operation proceeds rapidly in a strangely muted silence still too sacrosanct to be broken. The desk sergeant is herded with distinguished visitors, stray MPs, lobbyists and ushers into a corner. One man with a determined expression and a

Thompson, its muzzle waving like a hound sniffing the air, is enough to keep them in order.

The diminishing party halts for a moment. Wyatt glances briefly at Gaynor, his second-in-command, who informs him all units are reporting back: 'in position'. A quick check on the number of effectives surrounding him. Fifteen as planned. So far so good. He glances back at the entrance. The civilian party has arrived to reinforce their rear. No shots, no sound at all except the ring of heavy boots on the patterned floor. In front of him a gust of laughter ... an Hon. Member humouring the still unsuspecting House ...

This was the moment that mattered. The swing doors ahead were the last physical obstacle. Everything now depended on Wyatt; his followers, knowing this, kept their eyes on him. Now or never he must carry them through. He was conscious of an open-mouthed constable, the grey hairs and gilt badge of an usher, and a woman having quiet hysterics behind him ...

Three steps to the doors ... each one seemed to add an inch to his stature. Supremely confident he flung them back and there, shining in gold lustred contortions, the lion and unicorn of England, another myth, crowning the dais on which sat the Speaker of the House of Commons – silently and eloquently dumbfounded.

As Wyatt strode forward, Gaynor and three men deployed to the right, Turner and three more to the left or Government side of the House. The Captain closely followed by Jennings approached the Speaker's chair. Others took up their positions at the entrance behind the dais. In the visitors' gallery a dozen tourists covered the whole chamber with automatics.

Fortune favoured posterity that afternoon. The official shorthand writers took the situation in their stride and continued to report the proceedings. Like recording angels they may have felt they were witnessing judgement on those who had tortured the language into an unrecognizable, unreadable mass of stale verbiage.

The innocent members of the public, realizing they were in no danger of being massacred wholesale, stayed to see a trailer that promised to be more interesting than the current film.

From the notes of Joseph Parsons, official shorthand writer to the Commons:

... if you accept that there has been an abuse of ...

Mr Houghton: Mr Speaker – there appears to be a disturbance of some kind in the outer vestibule ...

Something seems to be wrong – Houghton is staring towards the doors, Wrigley and several other members of the Government are on their feet and – my God ... men are pouring in ... soldiers – and civilians too in the 'public' – standing and waving guns – there are – there are machine-guns in the House – guns ... what's happening? There's complete pandemonium – Williams next to me is shouting something but I can't – everyone's standing now, the noise is terrific. Commander Welling (Con. MP for Hoxley) is protesting to an officer – he's – he's trying to pull the gun from his hand ... a Sergeant pushes him – sends him reeling – my God this is fantastic – I can only be dreaming. The din is tremendous.

Soldiers appear to be covering every exit, a woman has fainted in the gallery and the comedy in any situation – Williams next to me crouching behind his desk and missing it all. The first shot! a Sergeant fires over the heads of a small group of Opposition MPs who might have been about to rush the doors. They sit down. An officer, tall and very erect, I can't see his face, seems to be ordering the Speaker to do something – I'm not sure – but the Speaker sinks deeper into the Chair, he grasps the arms so tightly I can see his knuckles shining curiously like large pearls.

– This is sheer nightmare – this is October 196–.

Evidence given to the court of Preliminary Inquiry by Mr John Crowleigh, Joint Under-Secretary for the Home Department:

I recollect very well my thoughts at the moment of impact, so to speak. I was listening to the usual point of order argie-bargie without much interest and thinking about Alby's declared intention of attacking Government policy on the economic front on a motion for adjournment. Matter of urgency, he considered – very rare and not likely to succeed, but dangerous if you have Prime Ministerial pretensions. Carpers don't inspire confidence.

Still, if he meant to call down the heavens he was wonderfully anticipated. Just then there was a slight disturbance at the entrance and the insurgents were there. I remember glancing automatically at the House clock, one of the few advantages of over-indulgence in detective fiction. It was a minute after four. The place bristled with rather unpleasant-looking machine guns – sub-machine guns I think you'd call them. Quite frankly no one knew how to deal with so unprecedented a situation except by bellowing and, in some cases, inadequately flourishing order papers.

I'm sure an organized movement could have overwhelmed them – we were four hundred odd against a mere dozen. It's easy to show courage after the event I suppose, but looking back it seemed to me that we were caught rather like flies in amber, in the dictatorial groove of tradition, paralysed by this novel departure from the rules of procedure. I mean, if the Speaker had calmly given a ruling that in his opinion the business constituted a breach of privilege and Joe Bloggs MP had moved that it be referred to the Committee of Privileges we'd have all known where we were. As it was I heard cries of 'Strangers!' which struck me as being superfluous in the circumstances.

Instinctively we looked to Wrigley. As the leader we were thankful perhaps that it was for him to make some sort of stand. It was a collective realization I think because the House quietened down a little. Wyatt appeared to be arguing with the Speaker. I saw Wrigley hesitate then edge his way along the Table; he said quite loudly and distinctly: 'What the devil do you think ...' he got no further. Wyatt turned and said quietly: 'Sit down.' No great power in his voice but tremendous authority. It was an incredible confrontation: the Prime Minister and leader of the country by the will of the people – and this unknown usurper.

I know people are blaming him now, but what else could Wrigley have done? He was faced by armed and desperate men – he himself was menaced by a sergeant brandishing a revolver – what could he have gained by making some kind of mock heroic gesture? No one else did. Politicians aren't martyrs by nature. So Wrigley sat down, and that simple act, with all that followed, has undoubtedly cost him his political career.

Police Sergeant Newstead, desk sergeant at the Lobby entrance, before the Court of Preliminary Inquiry:

Resistance was impossible for a very good reason. Everyone recognized an organized attack when they saw one. We never expect to deal with anything worse than the odd crank who scatters a few leaflets on to the Floor from the Public Gallery. I mean this is England, you don't dream of an armed attack in Westminster at four in the afternoon, so no one's prepared for it. From their point of view it was a walk-over.

Extel 4.03 :

... $\frac{1}{2}$ Consuls $2\frac{1}{2}\%$ $37\frac{2}{5}$ $+$ $\frac{1}{16}$ – Stores steady – Industrials cautious – Disturbance reported House of Commons ... unconfirmed reports – attack on Royal Family ... repeat reports unconfirmed – attack on Royal Family.

Interrogation of Lieutenant Slingsby by Sergeant Lingfield of the SB:

Come on now, John, why not make it easier for yourself? Let's go over it again. The attack takes place at four o'clock – right? And it all hinges on the Royals being back in the Palace at that time – right? We can assume Wyatt knows certain facts about a departure – every fool knows Prince Richard was going off for a Caribbean trip – no secret about that was there? But it wasn't known the Queen was seeing him off – and it wasn't public knowledge exactly what flight he was going by was it? Wyatt had to know – right? What's more he had to know days in advance ·· I mean even a three-pip genius couldn't be that flexible could he? Now John – someone tipped him the wink didn't they? Someone at the airport or in the Palace – or someone somewhere else? Oh, I will John – I'll find out. That's what I'm here for – and that's what you're here for. Being one of the top boys you must know something ... all right – let's see if this reminds you ... sorry to have to lean on you, John – against my ethics – but we've got to know ... now let's try again – sure you can have a drink – later. You say Wyatt settled for a four o'clock deal – very convenient – put the Press all ends up till he was ready for 'em – but four o'clock or thereabouts couldn't be his choosing could it? I mean he had to *know* their movements spot on hadn't he? And no one said a thing – wasn't even in the *Gazette* till the morning. Now, John – who told him? Take you're time – we've got all night ...

'Mr Speaker, will you be good enough to leave the Chair.'

The little man in black knee breeches, gown and extravagant wig showed no fear. He merely felt a trifle ridiculous. It was as though he'd been called from starring in an Aldwych *Hamlet* to play Widow Twankey in a third-rate pantomime. He was sure of his lines but what of his position?

'There is no authority for such an order!'

'Mine will suffice.'

'I – I shall need more than that.'

'You will leave the Chair.'

Mr Speaker glanced uneasily about him. An army revolt ... or had he fallen asleep to dream he was Speaker Lenthall? He tried again: 'Only the Queen ...'

'The Queen is in protective custody.'

'What!'

The House had forced itself into a state of unnatural silence. It heard the Speaker's loud exclamation and leaned forward reactively, straining to hear, to understand what was happening. The Speaker turned pale, stared with comic disbelief at the intruder who had ordered the Prime Minister of England to be seated and now commanded him to stand. Erskine May himself would surely have been at a loss ... he could only snap back at these sudden dogs of war with a single word: 'Nonsense!' The House held its collective breath, inadequately prepared for the worst. Wyatt raised his voice to a parade ground degree of penetration.

'I repeat, the Queen is in protective custody.'

Parsons' report continued:

He replied, 'I repeat, the Queen is in protective custody.' For a moment no one seems capable of taking it in – not even mouth-opening surprise. It's too big. One shock then another have numbed the senses – as though a nerve gas had been introduced into the Faber ventilation system spreading paralysis. A great sigh like a plea for Habeas Corpus on All Souls' Day, and they can only stare at the captain of apparitions. They stare silently – it's uncanny ... the Speaker has risen with some dignity, though the wig is slightly askew; his hands tremble but the voice is clear enough.

Mr Speaker: What – do you hope to gain by this demonstration which is as ridiculous as it is unseemly?

Officer: You will know in good time. I must ask you again to leave the chair.

Mr Speaker: You will have to carry me bodily from this place.

Captain: I've more regard for my dignity than you have for yours. If you're so attached to it you may remain until the call of Nature carries you bodily to another place.

Mr Speaker: This is a lawful assembly ...

Captain: You are at liberty to step down and remain in the Chamber or leave as you wish. I will say nothing until you do.

The Speaker hesitates, clearly the situation is one of the stalemate. He confers with the three Clerks who may advise him to suggest that a Member moves the formal adjournment of the House. I don't see what else can be done in the circumstances unless Mr Speaker invokes SO 21. The Captain stands calmly waiting, he seems curiously isolated from the throng ... the Clerks retire to their seats ...

Mr Speaker: I must remind you, the Queen's authority rests in this house.

Captain: The evidence?

The Speaker points a trifle dramatically to the Mace. The officer glances at it and appears to smile.

Captain: Another tribal custom, the medicine stick, powerful ju-ju. It's time we grew up and left tradition to enjoy its darkness in peace.

The Speaker: (outraged) It's the Queen herself you insult ...

Captain: Then let it speak for itself!

He gestures sharply to a soldier standing at his side. The man, a typical looking NCO, crosses swiftly to the Mace and almost immediately Serjeant at Arms appears and places himself squarely in front of the soldier. He makes no attempt to draw his sword, thank God, as I for one would be disposed to laugh – anything to ease this unbearable tension. The Sergeant waves him away with an automatic, but Sergeant at Arms courageously makes no move, only places a protective hand on the Mace. Loud exclamations as the NCO pushes him violently and he staggers as far as I can see into a group of Members standing beyond the Table. The first blow has been struck in God knows what cause; the Mace has slipped from one of its hooks ... the ... well! the soldier removes the ancient symbol of Royal authority and has flung it through the Lobby entrance. The metallic clatter mingles with horrified cries of 'Oh!' from various parts of the House. It is as though a light has gone out.

Officer: So much for the Queen's authority. Will you now stand down?

It seems an age before the Speaker replies.

Mr Speaker: I propose to retire until such time as the forces of law and order are able to clear the House and its precincts of Strangers.

Strangers! Having coined the classical understatement of this century the Speaker retires with his dignity more or less intact. No directions or suggestions to the Members though; the three Clerks hurriedly confer as they gather up their papers, suddenly they dissolve into a looking-glass picture of unreality: three crows playing cards. Robbins exits with Temple after throwing a withering glance at the Captain. Filmer remains, no doubt to keep an eye on things, and record the decisions of the House – if any. A few MPs follow them out.

The Conservative Member for Darnley is shouting something to the officer. I only catch the word 'fool!' The officer appears not to hear. He ascends the Speaker's dais and turns to the House. I imagine he ... but an incredible thing happens ... the Opposition Front and Back Benches have risen almost as one man. The soldiers, and there are civilians too now, are waving their guns as though rehearsing a field of fire. But there is no attack – only a sound of singing. The Leader of the Opposition is half a beat behind Mr Higgs, the Hon. Member for Loxlade in singing the National Anthem; the rest are joining in ...

'Happy and Glorious ...' The whole of the Opposition is chanting full throated as a gesture of defiance ... it ought to be impressive ...

I thought so ... the Government side gets up too. They have no choice. Embarrassment is apparent but this is hardly the time to show a lack of patriotic fervour. Mr Wrigley, the first on his feet, is singing lustily. There are tears in his eyes ... One feels that the whole performance is a gesture of indecision. No one is sure how it will end ... so play for time ... six Labour MPs remain seated. They will be remembered no doubt.

The Captain meanwhile sits in the Speaker's Chair. His bearing is calm and surprisingly dignified. All eyes are attempting without much success to remain ahead; but one senses they are straining to observe his reaction. While they moan loyally on he remains impassive, strangely a part of and yet apart from his surroundings.

'Er – this is the BBC Home Service ... in five minutes' time – that's at four-thirty, all BBC Sound and Television services including the World service will carry an important announcement. Listeners are asked to stand by ... meanwhile here is a recording of Tchaikovsky's "1812" overture played by ...'

A tinge of anxiety in the announcer's voice was excusable in the circumstances. From where he sat he could see a khaki-clad figure perched incongruously on a table corner in the sound control room. Martin Buckley had never before read news or made announcements with one eye deflectively aware of a nasty looking revolver vaguely pointing in his direction. It was even more compulsive than the red second hand of the studio clock sweeping away the remains of the twenty-sixth minute after four ... was that damned plate-glass separating them soundproof *and* bullet proof?

Broadcasting House gave Lieutenant Slingsby and his party very little trouble. The coach-load of 'troops' drove into Portland Place a few seconds before four. They showed no sign of urgency as they climbed out under the indifferent surveillance of their commanding officer, lounged about in bored contemplation of the London scene until a radio message flashed tersely from Objective One: 'Go ahead.' Suddenly the tension snapped into place trigger-tight. The coach carrying six of their number drove round to the rear of 'Objective Three', while the main party approached the main entrance. Franks, the commissionaire on duty, eyed the group with non-commissioned disapproval – very slovenly – boots unpolished – civilian haircuts ... what was the Army coming to? He even had time to wonder why they were there – instruments and all. Nothing about a band practice or broadcast on the day's schedule. He saluted the young lieutenant with nostalgic precision, but looked a trifle concerned.

'Afternoon, sir. Didn't know there was a rehearsal due today.'

'There isn't.' Which was what the ex-sergeant thought and he looked even more concerned. The revolver was something of a surprise too. 'For all I knew it might have been Candid Camera' was the disloyal thought confided to an avid Mrs Franks much later. The bandsmen were opening their instrument cases.

*

Baynard stood with his back to the portrait group seated almost out of sight in the pillared recess of the Bow Room. From his position at the far left he could gaze out of a great crimson-curtained window and still keep them under observation by reflection. His orders were to allow the Royal Family a maximum degree of privacy consistent with strict security. There was therefore, no question of letting them out of his sight. He found the situation too real to be embarrassing, too overwhelmingly enormous for petty emotions. Niceties of behaviour had no meaning – just as the room itself he felt had no meaning or purpose except as a place of detention, a way of reaching the garden when necessary. Cold silence could no more fill its magnificence than the most animated conversation. There was little to be said on either side. He for his part would reply briefly if spoken to; they he imagined, were absorbing the shock to delicate sensibilities as best they could. Meanwhile, the ragged silence reminding him of doctors' waiting-rooms; behind him a child stage-whispering 'Who is he, Mummy?' The Queen's reply was low and inaudible . . .

He concentrated on the view – no, the word was too small for the prospect before him, just as the desk on his right was too small for the room itself. Hard to realize they were no more than a rifle shot from the hub of London. Baynard smiled, remembering the backyards and dustbins of boyhood where grass was a miracle. And somewhere over there was a lake . . . six hundred rooms – and beyond the lake seven thousand homeless men, women and children. Perhaps, after all, there was a touch of unreality. Any minute now he would hear from Wyatt; he wondered how things were going with Slingsby, French and the rest of them. His thoughts began to dissolve into speculation: the possibility of a counter-attack before they could consolidate? Unlikely – the risk to Her Majesty was too great. For no very good reason he tried to imagine Victoria standing where he stood now – looking out over the grounds . . .

An irate voice broke into his thoughts.

'. . . precisely what your intentions are?'

Baynard turned quickly, instantly alert, like a sentry caught dozing: 'I beg your pardon?'

The Duke had taken a step forward, his chin aggressively elevated: 'I am asking what you intend to do with us.' He spoke quietly as not to alarm the children.

'You will be informed in good time. Meanwhile you have my personal assurance that no harm is intended to your family – or yourself.'

'In that case, Father, I don't see why we shouldn't walk out of the door and ask the first person we meet to ring the police.'

Baynard smiled good-naturedly at the Prince's brave flow of words. At that age heroics are more important than a firm grasp of realities.

'Unfortunately the first person you meet outside will be an armed guard. He has orders to shoot on sight anyone other than myself who attempts to pass through that door.'

'Then we'd better stay here,' the Queen replied.

'That would be the more sensible course, madam.'

He noted that she still wore her outdoor coat. So much the better.

The silence was taken up where it had broken off. He half wished they would make a fuss, do something erosive to their superb dignity; but they were resisting in their own defenceless fashion – a well-bred dumbness against an intrusion of ill breeding. He could hear the Queen playing some childish word game with the smaller children, having dismissed the fact of his existence. Glancing at his watch he was astonished to find that only four minutes had passed from the moment of entering the room. Jaggers should appear soon. He suddenly remembered a minor detail of his instructions.

'If you should require refreshments for yourself or the children you are at liberty to order them.'

The Duke opened his mouth to speak then glanced at the Queen and kept silence.

'Thank you. We will think about such matters when this little unpleasantness is over.'

Jagger's arrival curtailed another bout of silence. Baynard took the tape-recorder from his sergeant who informed him that no counter-moves of any significance were developing. He closed the door and with elaborate care placed the machine on the desk, turned to the group. They eyed him with detached interest, mildly curious perhaps about the latest in a series of events . . .

'Madam, it's my duty to ask you to be good enough to record a message of assurance to the British people. We consider it vitally important that it be broadcast at the earliest opportunity.'

The Queen looked surprised, but said nothing.

'At this moment,' Baynard, striving for a matter-of-fact tone, continued, 'our forces are in effective possession of the Houses of Parliament, Broadcasting House and the Tower. Most important of all, as I think you must realize, we control the Palace.'

'A revolution,' the Duke murmured.

'We're hopeful that it will be bloodless. Success depends on one thing only – your custody. So if you have any concern for those you are pleased to call your subjects you will record this appeal and we shall, as I say, arrange for its immediate broadcast. If you refuse we cannot possibly guarantee the prevention of at least a minimum of bloodshed.'

'You're holding us as hostages?' For the first time the Duke looked concerned.

'That's the very essence of our plan,' Baynard replied.

He made no effort to disturb the profound silence that followed. At that moment, he recognized the Queen was truly alone; a regiment of Privy Councillors could have done nothing for her. There was only conscience and the inherited sense of duty which had taken root and become a part of her. At that moment, nothing and no one else would matter. She stroked the hair of her youngest child with a stranger's hand. Baynard waited.

'If I refuse . . .?' she asked at length.

'We shall continue on our course whatever you decide. My superior was anxious only that you should be given an opportunity to allay public concern for your immediate safety.'

'Who is your superior?'

Baynard handed a typewritten sheet of quarto to the Queen

who hesitated, then took it and read slowly to the end. She looked up and stared beyond the officer ...

'Wyatt ... there was another Wyatt – a long time ago.' Abruptly she returned to the now of things: 'I would like a few moments to discuss this with my husband.'

He thought rapidly, reasoned that he could safely leave them alone; two of his men were on the terrace, the doors were guarded, and it could do no harm. Time was still on their side.

'Very well. I'll return in three minutes.'

He left the room briskly. Not until he was outside did it occur to him that rounding up history could be a trifle wearing.

4

'This is the BBC World Service from London. Here is a special announcement. At approximately four o'clock this afternoon Army contingents with civilian support occupied the Palace of Westminster, Buckingham Palace, the Tower – and the headquarters of the British Broadcasting Corporation. There has been no loss of life and the public is assured there is no cause for panic or confusion. The Revolutionary Council will justify its action as and when the situation is finally consolidated. Meantime the people are requested to stand by for further important communiqués and announcements on radio and TV.

'This communiqué is issued by order of the Revolutionary Council over the signature of its Chairman, Captain Richard Wyatt. Scheduled programmes will resume as advertised, but listeners are reminded that these will be subject to immediate interruption in view of the circumstances.'

An agitated Director-General had raced to BH summoned by an equally agitated telephone call. His secretary shrilled hysterically that there were soldiers ... one of them was holding a gun to her head ... he assured her gently that she was imagining things and made a mental note to send her off for a week's leave – conscientious and overworked ... a male voice intruded, 'Your secretary is correct up to a point; I'm not pointing a gun anywhere – but I think you'd better come all the same.' The DG stared at the telephone as though it had suddenly grown a head. 'Who's that?' 'Listen in to the Home or Light on your way,' the voice continued. 'It'll put you in the picture.' The voice rang off and within twenty minutes the DG was engaged in the most extraordinary conversation of his life with a self-possessed Lieutenant Slingsby who appeared to be in command of the *al fresco* situation. The conversation was taped at the DG's insistence.

'Now will you kindly tell me what this is all about?'

'We're taking over control, surely that's obvious?'

'Control of what?'

'The country.'

The DG glanced round him feeling obliged to convince himself that the surroundings at least were familiar. He bitterly regretted the inadequacy of his reply. 'What for?'

'Our movement,' Slingsby explained, 'is anxious to see a more responsible and representative government in power ...' he smiled suddenly. 'Aren't you?'

'For the moment I'm more concerned to discover how you think you can get away with such outrageous ...'

'That's our worry. You need only concern yourself with your own position as Head of Broadcasting.'

'My authority isn't as absolute as yours appears to be!'

'For all practical purposes you are in control.'

'Well?'

'You must therefore consider your organization and your good self temporarily at our disposal.'

Maniacs! Raving lunatics the lot of them. The DG could only assume a mass escape from a military asylum if such a place existed. For no very good reason he found himself thinking of the War Museum. Wasn't it the original Bedlam? – and where the devil were the police? He could only play for time and humour the man who switched from gravity to good humour like a day of April showers.

'You're an extremely cool customer ... very well – assuming that I'm at your disposal ...'

'Temporarily, that's the key word. A matter of an hour or so. After that, I'm instructed to inform you, you're free to resume "normal transmission" in every respect.'

'What!'

The nonplussed Director-General was scarcely aware that Slingsby read from a sheet of paper in his hand:

'You may invite any member of any political party to discuss, criticize or comment on our actions. You are at liberty to transmit programmes on sound or TV concerning the coup without fear of censorship or other restrictions. You may conduct interviews of the public in the studio or in the streets.'

'Can you afford to be so sure of yourselves?'

'That also is our worry.'

The Director-General frowned. For the very first time it dawned on him that this was no lunatic; he was in deadly earnest, and something big had happened – was still happening.

'Are you saying that we're free to treat all this as just another of the day's events?'

'I think I've made myself clear.'

Judging by the DG's expression the clarity was unilateral. He was struggling now to keep in step with the march of events. 'I take it,' he spoke slowly in a voice cross-hatched with sarcasm, 'that this freedom which we already enjoy is conditional?'

'Nothing impossible – certainly no more than would be asked of you under the former administration – perhaps less.'

'Former!'

'Communiqués, decrees and announcements of a general nature to be carried on your news services. Captain Wyatt also requests one period of fifteen minutes preferably at a peak hour to make his statement of intent.'

'One period?' the DG was visibly giving up the struggle.

'You're at liberty to refuse ... you seem surprised.'

'I ... is that all?'

'As far as we're concerned, yes. Any questions?'

'There are bound to be counter-moves, you realize that?'

'We haven't gone to all this trouble simply to be thrown out almost before we're in.' The Lieutenant was grinning now – quite cheerfully.

He pushed an untidy swatch of black hair back from his brow and waited for further objections.

'You'd do well to seriously consider your position young man – police reinforcements are on their way to my certain knowledge . . . I'm thinking of the staff.'

The 'young man's' smile disappeared leaving a sombre smokiness about the eyes.

'I seriously considered my position a long time ago and I know exactly where I stand and what I'm doing. I'm not concerned about the police and you need have no fear for the people in this building. Two minutes before you arrived I received a message from the Palace.'

The DG tried hard to appear unconcerned. What in God's name had happened at the Palace?

'Message?'

'A recording in fact. It was made by the Queen. Her Majesty signified her willingness to broadcast to the nation.'

'Her Majesty! You mean . . .?'

'Yes – that's what I mean. You'll be good enough to have it broadcast immediately.'

The Director-General stared at Slingsby for a long drawn-out moment . . .

Ten minutes later Outside Broadcast Units were racing to the various scenes of the Great Takeover. Far from panicking, the British public, or as much of it as had returned from the day's labour, sat phlegmatically glued to its TV sets with a vague sense of pleasurable anticipation that only a World Cup match or the odd Mystery Playhouse could normally arouse. Revolution on Channel One would make a nice change.

Meanwhile the DG consoled himself with the dubiously pleasing thought that the BBC had stolen quite a march on the other crowd, albeit a forced march.

Parsons' report continued:

4.45. The situation is quite incredible. Either this man is mad or too clever to last. For example, Members are coming and going with as much impunity as they did at a minute to four. Imperceptibly, though, the House is filling up as the news no doubt spreads. One assumes either that they're confident of rescue – though surely something would have happened by now – or they remain out of purblind curiosity.

This chap takes one's breath away – a sort of James Bond gone wrong. Supremely indifferent to the hostile glares, the stupefied stares of the Westminster Hundreds, he sits now at the apparently more convenient Clerks' Table signing orders as they come to hand, listening to reports from uniformed orderlies and civilians who approach in an almost constant procession. His sergeant stands nearby keeping an ear to a pocketfone and both eyes on the House.

I'm not sure he isn't deliberately keeping them waiting. Williams next to me has overcome his fears by the way and scribbles frantically to make up for lost time. One can visualize the placard round his neck bearing the words: 'No Book of Memoirs to Support Me.'

A soldier, crash-helmeted, clatters in wearing boots surely soled with cement, and still the heavens refuse to fall as he strides beyond the sacred Bar to the officer, salutes and delivers a message. The officer smiles as he reads, then turns to the Sergeant who listens in to the RT device. Whatever the officer has said brings a cheerful grin to the NCO's face, he nods and appears now to be relaying a message. The Members watch all this activity with a collectively glum expression. Almost immediately a civilian enters carrying – I think it's a portable radio, a powerful looking instrument. He places it on the Table, an incongruous object between the filigree dispatch boxes – but what does incongruity mean at this moment in time and space? The officer glances at his watch, while tension in the House begins to rise once more. Something's afoot, that's obvious – the atmosphere is electric – bizarre – there are really no words to describe it as we all wait for God knows what.

Suddenly at a sign from the officer the radio is switched on. What else can happen now? A long, uneasy silence, an exchange of apprehensive glances ...

'This is the BBC World Service from London ... Her Majesty the Queen.'

One of Wyatt's strongest supporters had planning and executive responsibility for Operation Whitower (Plan A). Lieutenant French also commanded the largest mixed force engaged in the coup. Its size was hardly surprising since his objective was the Tower of London.

The defence of London's great fortress appears to be something of a formality, but French and his followers had no reason to assume that their attack would be met by a display of ritual defiance. Unlikely a posse of 'Beefeaters' charging with swinging halberds. The Fusiliers in residence are not lead soldiers, nor are their rifles. More important, an efficient alarm system links the Tower with Scotland Yard. There are Crown Jewels to be considered – let the Yeoman warders take care of History. At the almost impossible hour of four after noon on the 23rd all the advantage French could unreasonably hope for was the element of surprise. Never since the days of Fosse and Bailey had the Castle been captured.

Wyatt's choice of French for a difficult assignment was both typical and a tribute to qualities in the Lieutenant unrecognized or undreamed of by his brother officers from the CO down to the latest subaltern. Soured, it was rumoured, by a brief and broken marriage, French at thirty-five soldiered on, maintaining an almost unbroken silence harnessed to a reserved even surly disposition to the world at large. Appearances perhaps were against him; he had the eyes and complexion of a gypsy – was in fact nicknamed 'the Gypsy' at mess time – and a deep distrust of humanity characteristic of the Romanies, who have their reasons; so perhaps had French, but he never mentioned them. The majority dismissed him as stupid, the younger, more pretentious officers labelled him as a boor and left it at that. And since taciturnity is socially and promotionwise disadvantageous in the officer class, French's destiny appeared to be determined until the day came when he could retire even further into himself.

Wyatt had had little to do with French, knew that he performed his duties meticulously, guessed that he commanded respect even the affection of his men. Their conversation outside of military necessity was of no consequence until a few months prior to the coup. One evening Wyatt called at his quarters. French was courteous but showed no surprise at the unexpected visit. His expression remained unchanged as the

Captain without benefit of preamble talked of his plans, described the organization slowly built up over the years, invited him point blank to take a key role in the venture.

The 'Gypsy' listened in silence and made no immediate effort to break it when Wyatt finished.

'You know nothing about me,' he said at last.

Wyatt glanced down at the worn volume of Montaigne's Essays lying open on the table. 'I know the value of the sword,' he replied. 'To hell with the scabbard.'

For the first time in Wyatt's experience French smiled, no more than a reluctant movement of the lips at the Captain's woeful misquoting of old Michel.

'Very well,' he replied. And that for the moment was all.

By four o'clock the number of visitors to the Tower had created a minor record for the time of year. Most of them from coaches which parked on Great Tower Hill. After a quick cup of tea in the café across the way, they paid their one and six-pences and passed group by group through the Middle Tower, across the causeway and beyond the grey grim Byward Tower into the main complex. Bored sentries recognized 'foreigners' making the most of a package tour. A constable idly guessed at a union outing; a woman in the café said later she thought they were schoolmasters. And a Yeoman Warder would testify that he'd kept a particular eye on two drunks 'in case they caused trouble'.

For two hours they drifted along, in groups, singly and in pairs, while three lorry loads of uniformed men cruised care-fully from the East to time their arrival for four ... at five minutes to zero nearly two hundred men were distributed with pinpoint precision throughout the Tower precincts; a few queued for the Jewel House, more snaked through the cramped exhibition of Fusilier history. All were deeply interested and discreetly armed.

The warders are impatient, five minutes to closing time and there are still stragglers; former Warrant Officers themselves they summon up rusting tones of command, 'Come along now, please!' The stragglers make a reluctant move as the museum guides begin to lock up for the night. At two minutes to four suspicions begin to grow ... the last of the law-abiding citizens are already at the main gate – that's better – they're beginning to move now – 'Lock up the ravens, Charlie!' Suddenly the two dormant 'drunks' start a brawl under the arch of the Middle Tower – attention is diverted, a footguard resplendent in nylon bearskin wonders what they're on about as a constable goes into action. The Chief Warder considers calling the Major and decides he can handle the situation. He turns to watch the coach parties, laughing and carefree streaming towards Byward past the Traitors' Gate ... glances at his watch – thirty seconds to go ... the drunks sober up in sight of the Law ... French is in the first lorry as it turns into Great Tower Hill, his driver accelerates suddenly, races to the entrance closely followed by two more Army trucks, past the sentry, his face set in the mould of a question mark, and through the Middle Tower, scattering warders, police and their own followers. The coach-drivers across the way crash gear their vehicles into action and race to block the entrance.

In ten minutes it was all over. More effective arms were distributed from the luggage compartment of the coaches as the 'visitors' streamed back unhindered. No resistance was offered at the Middle Tower, no time even to set off the alarm circuit. No opposition from dumbfounded Fusiliers faced with Thompsons. Guides and warders stare in astonishment at modern automatics ancient with menace.

All those taken by surprise assumed that left-overs from the Great Train robbery were gunning for the Crown Jewels ...

Back to pin-pointed positions, men fanning out in all directions: St Thomas's Tower, Develin, Constable, Flint, Boyer and Beauchamp – history was being occupied by unknowns, The Bell Tower, Martin, Broad Arrow, Brass Mount and Legges, centuries trampled underfoot as guns were hoisted from the New Armouries to battlements – trained from the North and West casements, guns everywhere while flintlocks and back-swords slept in the White Tower. And French was there – at the closing of the gates – checking fields of fire from the ramparts, superintending the evacuation of staff, warders, all who had no business in a fortress flying Wyatt's standard of rebellion.

In less than half an hour the Tower was a stronghold once more, a petrified corpse resurrected for a purpose every one of its blood soaked stones might recognize. The 'Gypsy' flashed a curt message to Wyatt: 'Mission accomplished'. For the first time the Tower of London was in a state of siege.

And so was the communications centre at New Scotland Yard.

Effective occupation of various strategic areas no more constitutes a coup than the swallow makes a summer. Any brilliant fool can promote a rising and push it successfully to a short-term conclusion. If he cannot weld the separate elements of his conspiracy together he will either be compelled to surrender – or be crushed. The forces of reaction may be stupefied, but they are not stupid. They will quickly recover from the first shock, collect scattered wits, rally all available opposition and mop up the separated groups of dissidents piecemeal and at leisure.

Wyatt's solution to this problem of unification centred on the Queen herself. The voices of Authority had proclaimed her special position so long and so persuasively they could hardly deny it to her now. In custody she strengthened his own hand and paralysed the strong arm of his opponents. 'Spiking the enemy's guns is a military extravagance if they can be turned against themselves,' as Schliessen once said.

To the citizens of Great Britain, the Lords and Commons, and peoples of the Commonwealth, I am asked to inform you that I and my family are safe and well. We are given to understand that no action on our part can influence the course of events with which many of you will by now be aware. The underlying purpose of these events will be made known to you in the very near future.

That we are in custody is an undoubted fact, and I am requested to make it clear that our continued safety depends on your acceptance of the new situation and of those responsible for its creation.

It is evidence of the nature of those who have seized a measure of power that my request to add a personal footnote to this statement has been courteously granted. I would like to say this:

I ask nothing for myself, I should be unworthy of my position and the trust I have held for so many years if I urged you to refrain from actions inspired by loyalty which might conceivably endanger my person. But I am sure you will understand the dilemma of a Queen who is also a mother – and I can only beg you for my children's sake to remain calm and patient. This may after all be no more than a shower and not the storm that destroys all things.

Silence.

Wyatt showed no sign of elation; but that postscript was beyond what he could conceivably have hoped for. By allowing the Queen to add a tassel to the rope Baynard had taken a gambler's risk and drawn an ace more than he needed. The Captain instructed Jennings to transmit a single word to his second-in-command: 'Congratulations'. He turned to face the House, groped for the mood of a concourse uneasily banded together in united opposition, and read in its collective expression an accelerating upsurge of irresolution, a swift-flowering recognition that this was no sporadic outburst of insurrection after all. The ground had been cut from under their feet, and those of the forces of law and order; and they were falling into the devil of a hole ...

So Wyatt rose, knowing the conspiracy was welded indissolubly, that he and his followers were now inviolable. Gazing round at the crowded chamber he felt a sudden and overwhelming contempt for these bit-part politicians who had fought for crumbs of power knowing they would be used by their masters as whores are used by pimps. At the nation's expense they had nibbled at the nation's problems with the delicacy of mice and fought like rats over a point of order. Whores at least were professional. It was time to kick them back to their constituencies ...

'I'm not going to take up too much of your time – or mine. For many years it has been increasingly obvious to more people than you or the opinion polls seem to be aware of that this country's affairs have been passed from one set of incompetents to another. There's no doubt that the system has benefited property speculators, building tycoons, bookmakers and organized crime; there's no doubt that under the system both parties have succeeded in running the country into the ground with the gay abandon of two frustrated spinsters daring their all in a cosy game of Monopoly.

'That you act with a cynical disregard for those you represent is the measure of your dishonesty. That you assume public apathy to your actions is total shows a blindness to reality suggesting outright stupidity.

'I am here to tell you that the country refuses to be led by the nose from the Right, by the hand from the Left. It is prepared to march forward in step with the times with whoever is prepared to give effective leadership. The House is no longer an effective instrument of government. Consequently it's my pleasurable duty to inform you that from this moment you no longer exist. You are free to leave.'

Three minutes passed before the uproar subsided. A movement among the Opposition members incensed by Her Majesty's coercion and further infuriated by doubts cast on their sacred right to govern (at a time of their own choosing) threatened to overwhelm the small group of men surrounding the Speaker's Chair. Reinforcements moved in and persuaded them to retreat. The noise was deafening and for some time it was impossible to distinguish the roar of a dozen voices demanding the right to be heard. At length, and by common consent, the Floor was granted to Wrigley.

The Labour leader rose, waited for absolute silence then slipped effortlessly into his pseudo-Churchillian role. He stabbed a shaking finger at the latest of a long line of critics.

'I command you, in the Queen's name, to stand down and leave this House! By your uniform you appear to be an officer in Her Majesty's Service; if that is so you have stained the honour of your regiment and of the Army itself. The only honourable action you will ever again be capable of is prompt surrender to lawful authority. Your words and deeds are treasonable to the will of the people, the power of this Parliament and the person of Her Majesty whom you are pledged to defend.'

Wrigley paused dramatically and listened with his mind's ear to the effect of his words on those around him. Things were going badly for the PM as usual. Only that morning he had stared at the findings of a Public Opinion Poll on his personal popularity with something like the horror of a man who stares at a mirror and sees no reflection. If he could retrieve this impossible situation and restore the Queen – then surely everyone would love him ... like a man drowning he saw in a fleeting pale pink vision, Meaker the Opposition Leader thanking him with tears in his eyes on behalf of a grateful country 'for delivering our beloved Queen'. Warmed by the thought he sought for an appropriate full stop.

'You may rest assured,' he continued, 'that we will spare no effort to root out the subversive organization of which you no doubt are an insignificant underling.'

Wrigley resumed his seat with the air of a pudgy St George who knows how to extinguish fiery dragons with a bucket of water. The House gave him an ovation that set the pale pink visions dancing once more and it was observed that Dunne the Foreign Secretary (known affectionately by his detractors as 'UnderDunne') looked quite sulky.

Wyatt waited patiently while the Members made a noise then deigned a casual reply: 'None of us can doubt the meaning of "subversive organization". The House and the country are aware of Mr Wrigley's mastery of McCarthy-type smear tactics. Shall we ever forget how he won the Seamen's strike! I acknowledge, however, his courtesy in addressing me with the synthetic venom usually reserved for those on the Opposition benches.'

They made two mistakes: first they stayed to satisfy their curiosity when dignified withdrawal might have cleared a way for strong counter action, and having stayed, the Opposition showed their delight at Wyatt's spirited rejoinder. Certainly it was a weak reaction, the pale reflection of a wintry smile, but the fact remained, they had identified themselves with Wyatt's sentiments. The scene had all the appearance of a debate in progress.

Wyatt continued: 'The unfortunate gentlemen responsible for Press coverage of debates in the Commons may like to save me the trouble of informing their editors that a Press conference will be held in the Chamber at seven o'clock this evening. You may now leave.'

The permissive words barely concealed an order. Quite suddenly the scoundrel was busying himself with other matters. For all the further notice he took of the Members, they might not have existed – and, of course, they didn't as far as Wyatt was concerned. In half an hour the womb of Government was barren. The last Member to depart (the ex-shop-steward, now ex-Con. for Wolsely East) had to be assured by Wyatt himself that his salary would continue to be paid for the time being.

5

Traffic grew to unmanageable proportions. All streets leading to the 'rebel positions' were choked with a rising tide of transport. Thousands of people surged into the Mall eager to witness incredible events, so many doubting Thomases anxious to see for themselves, to put a finger on the raw trouble spot so they could affirm with grave conviction 'Though strange, 'tis true.' While secretaries, typists and clerical officers streamed truantly from Government offices to congregate wide-eyed in Parliament Square, a few millions joined the early crush to get home and watch it on 'telly'.

The police, uncertain of their role in the changing circumstances, lacking precise orders from above, stayed passively alert. They found it beyond their powers to gauge the general mood of the people, and if the news of revolt was more than rumour, if the sudden crowds were on their way to a popular rising, buses might well turn into tumbrils and heads, their heads, could be among the first to be paraded down the Strand on the sharp end of a businessman's furled umbrella. So they waited uneasily and looked on non-committally. To his subordinate, a wary sergeant patrolling the entrance to the 'Ladies' in Oxford Circus was heard to say: 'It's all these holidays abroad. Too many people go over there these days, bring back Continental ideas – you wait, once we're in the Common Market there'll be revolutions every other Sunday ...'

It was the silence of the people that the lower ranks of Law and Order found so ominous, or at least vaguely disturbing. A constable on duty in Trafalgar Square stated at the Police Inquiry that he had been literally forced in the direction of the Palace by converging throngs. He continued:

I attempted to restore some sort of order at the Admiralty Arch. Traffic was ignoring all signs and lights: in five minutes there was chaos. The congestion was so great it could only inch its way forward until it had to come to a dead stop. What with pedestrians mixed up with transport and drivers who just abandoned their vehicles, trying to get to the Palace in front of everyone else, I decided it was hopeless and let the tide take me with the lot ... No I don't think I could have fought my way clear – the Mall was packed – all going one way ... Yes I heard the news half an hour before on Patrol Officer Phillock's receiver. Just the news ... we received no orders.

What struck me was the way everyone around me took it. Very calm ... I remember thinking 'Typical British, taking it just as it comes, show up better in a crisis than any other time.' Then I thought a bit more and wasn't so sure. There was something unnatural about that silence ... Expected? Well, it's hard to say what I expected, some character raising a laugh maybe or shouting 'Down with the rebels!' that sort of thing – but there was nothing to speak of. Only a sort of excitement – held in – like kids being taken down Regent Street Christmas time.

These were golden moments for the high priests who interpret the will of God knows what in those mini-temples stuffed with transistors, printed circuits and neon tubes. Crash programmes were arranged in minutes as OB vans raced to the trouble spots. There was so much to do they hardly knew where to start.

Radio and TV interviewers were soon in action; they

handled their little black microphones like missionary priests fondling sacred phallic symbols, thrusting them at the masses and insolently demanding a brief prayer to Saints Cathode and Transistor.

Westminster. 5.30:

As I speak Big Ben is striking the hour of decision across London, a London torn and ravaged by the dark forces of rebellion if not revolution. A vast concourse of the people is milling around me. Following Her Majesty's dramatic speech the whole world must know that in one incredibly brief hour the Queen has been made a prisoner in her own Palace and the House of Commons treated with a disrespect unknown since the dark days of Cromwellian tyranny.

Yes – rebellion, and it's happening here and now – this is Great Britain, and the crowd you see is British. A Queen imprisoned, Her Parliament shattered and the people stand firm – no sign of disorder or panic. A few are reading the paper – they could be in a bus-queue ... perhaps they think – some are chatting in subdued tones as though their neighbours may be members of whatever organization has planned this fantastic coup. That's the question on everyone's lips – 'Who is responsible? Who is this man Wyatt? Is he really an Army officer, or a civilian in disguise? How far is the Army itself involved? What other, perhaps more powerful and sinister elements are behind this the greatest take-over bid in our history?' No doubt we shall know the answers to these questions in due course; meantime the people as always must wait. And they are doing just that, patiently, expectantly, knowing that any rash action on their part could well snap the slender thread by which the sword of Damocles is suspended above the head of a queen.

It seems that the MPs are leaving by another exit. Yes ... my information is that they have been thrown out. Mr Wrigley left with his PPS and several members of the Government after a few words with a Police Inspector. Meaker, Grammond, all the familiar faces we know so well have departed like evicted tenants, their expressions ranging from bewilderment to restrained anger. A few MPs have left and are still leaving by the entrance we're now covering. It's strange but true that no cheers of sympathy have been raised for any of them – the people are no doubt stunned by events as we all must be. Ah! There now, coming through the archway is Frank Rhodes, one of Wrigley's ablest supporters – you can see him as he climbs – he's climbing on to a bench and appears to be making a spirited speech – his voice booms across the crowd's heads and I can just make out the odd phrase – 'no effort spared ... the perpetrators ... I myself ... will take command ... security forces'. You probably heard that – a lone voice in the crowd yells 'Well get on with it then!' ... otherwise there seems to be no reaction ... he stands and stares at the crowd for some moments ... and descends from his makeshift platform a bit embarrassed I feel, makes his way as best he can through the silent crowd.

Er – two soldiers guard the entrance, you can see the sub-machine-guns in their hands; the only sign of violence discernible from where I stand. Of course, there may be tanks just round the corner – no one can be quite sure what forces this man Wyatt has at his command ...

A sea of faces, and there are more I'm told, pouring down Whitehall and along the Embankment in a constant flood. And now there goes one of Her Majesty's Ministers almost unrecognized, jostled by a crowd which shows its annoyance as he pushes his way out. Somehow he symbolizes the present plight of MPs who having been returned to the Commons by the people are now being returned to the people by the Commons.

From interviews recorded at Aldwych, Kingsway:

'This is London – the very heart of London. I'm standing in one of its busiest thoroughfares not two miles from the scene of today's tremendous happenings. There's only one way to find out what the man in the street thinks about it all – let's take a look at John Citizen's reactions.'

'*Excuse me, sir*, would you be prepared to comment on the situation?'

'Well, obviously it's the work of Communists. I've been expecting something like this for a long time. Country's going from bad to worse – not surprising if the worst takes over, is it?'

'What do you think should be done about it?'

'Done? Er – that's for the police and so on to decide. It's not my job. And that's what I pay my rates and taxes for, isn't it?'

'Excuse me, madam ...'

'Oh I think it's shocking – shocking. Our beloved Queen in the hands of those bloodthirsty gangsters. To think that I once stroked Winston – her horse you know – with my own hand. It's shocking!'

'I wonder if you'd care to comment ...'

'It's a bloody good thing. Dunno why someone didn't think of it before.'

'But we're now without an effective government.'

'We've been without an effective government ever since I can remember and I'm pushing sixty.'

'Excuse me – you've heard the news I suppose?'

'Yes. Can't be much worse off than we were before, can we?'

'Excuse me ...'

'Yes you can put this on record. There's only one way to deal with this latest crime wave. Catch 'em quick and bring back hanging!'

'Do you feel that this is ...'

'Certainly ... no I'm not a bit concerned. If my wife and kids were beaten up by thugs would she want to know what she could do for me? I'm not important to her so what's she supposed to mean to me? As for the politicians they're always saying they'll fight for the people – well now they've got something to fight about. I did my lot in the last war – now on I fight for the wife and kids. Oh you think I'm being unpatriotic? No you didn't say it in so many words – well I'm unemployed – had a good job till the Socialists came along with Pay Roll Tax and Wage Freezes, so I've nothing to thank them for have I? Let this bloke Wyatt have a go – he can't do any worse.'

'How do you feel about ...'

'If this man can pull the country together let's give him a run for his money. No, I'm not a bit surprised. Something drastic had to happen. Politics? Well I suppose you could say I was a Socialist till tea time.'

Naturally Sir John Blades, the Police Commissioner, sought guidance; the position couldn't be allowed to deteriorate any longer. The whole Force would be demoralized unless something was done quickly. Communications were breaking down under the weight of advice, sympathy, opinions, astonishment, anger and horse laughs being tendered, offered, expressed and suggested by citizens grave, perturbed, delighted, shocked and other ways affected but united in their determination to ring 230 1212 from all points of the compass.

He himself phoned Sir Thomas Motts, the Deputy Under-Secretary of State, who referred him to the Parliamentary Under-Secretary of State, who was nowhere to be found. He was more fortunate in cornering the Parliamentary Private Secretary, who informed him sulkily that everything was in a bloody shambles and he for one was going home. Try Rutgers. Sir John tried the Secretary of State's Private Secretary but he apparently was indisposed that day. Desperately Sir John went further down the scale. An Assistant Under-Secretary (FI) thought it was a matter for C Division. The head of C Division primly explained that whatever the circumstances he was responsible to the Permanent Under-Secretary alone. Had he tried him?

Sir John's suspicions concerning his blood pressure began to harden into certainty when a message arrived from Wyatt himself. He was requested to present himself at the Commons at the earliest opportunity.

'Requested! Infernal cheek! What am I, Saunders, eh? A bloody errand boy – him! requests!'

But after two minutes of reasonably coherent reflection Sir John wondered if perhaps it might not be the very ticket. He, in person, would go to the House, not at Wyatt's summons, but by his own volition. If no one else bothered it was his plain and personal duty to go across the road and arrest Wyatt on the spot. Any fool was entitled, indeed required by law, to arrest a traitor *nil obstat*, no need for warrants or any other fol-de-rol. He would go. And afterwards ... he almost fell asleep dreaming of the glory that would be his – the nation's saviour – Earl of ... time to think about that later ...

Minutes later and flanked by Chief Inspectors Jepson and Fleming, Sir John shouldered his way through the crowds, and arrived at the St Stephen's entrance sourly ignoring a posse of saluting constables roused from their masterly inactivity. The three men were met by a lieutenant and two privates who escorted them in silence to the Chamber. Sir John paused as they reached the sacred portals of the nation's forum. Surely not . . . he glanced at his companions, they remained impassive.

'In here?' he forced himself to sound credulous. The officer nodded as guards pushed open the doors.

There was nothing more impressive in the scene revealed to Sir John and his aides than Wyatt himself. The Captain sat at the Clerks' Table and could still dominate the elegantly homely grandeur of a little 'talking shop' which would fit comfortably into the State Banquet Room at Buckingham Palace and with room to spare. Its very emptiness emphasized his unique position. Uniformed men and civilians milled around on the sacred Floor: there was much coming and going, a great deal of purposeful bustle – but no confusion, no voices raised in argument or even command; only, as far as Sir John could see, a smoothly functioning organization, a mood of quiet determination predominating in every expression – nothing to suggest success for his mission.

Wyatt stood and smiled encouragingly: 'I've been expecting you. Glad you could come. If you care to take a seat you've a choice of about three hundred and fifty.'

'We'll stand.'

'Strange,' Wyatt continued. 'Few people realize half the sitting Members were standing most of the time.'

'I'm sorry but I haven't come to discuss Parliament's seating arrangements!'

'Oh? – What have you come to discuss?'

'Nothing. It's my duty to place you under arrest.'

The few men standing nearby grinned and waited for Wyatt's reply.

'Are you intending to read the Riot Act, Commissioner?'

'I don't think that'll be necessary – the Statute of Treasons covers your case well enough.'

'Very well – arrest me.'

'I beg your pardon?' Sir John seemed not to have heard.

'Come now, Commissioner, surely if I'm to be arrested I'm the one needing the pardon. You've done your duty – so much for the formalities. Shall we now deal with the realities?'

'I – I don't think you quite understand –'

'Commissioner, I don't have time to waste.' He turned to the lieutenant. 'Gaynor have three chairs placed for these gentlemen.'

Sir John glared at Wyatt and did his best not to believe the evidence of his stricken ears. To be treated by a – by a – like a ... like a ... then suddenly his blood-boiling anger simmered down to tepid resignation. What the devil! he'd done his best. Hardly expect the man to come quietly when he'd gone to all this trouble – not his job to fight the Army ... he felt slightly shaken. It wasn't the interview he'd had in mind. The chairs were placed. He sat, thankful for some real support.

'I sent for you,' Wyatt continued, 'as a matter of courtesy – and necessity. Naturally, although our position is secure, we'd prefer to continue knowing we had your whole-hearted co-operation.'

'What!' Sir John's eyes threatened to roll from their sockets.

'Perhaps that is asking too much. Let's just say your co-operation.'

'Do you imagine – seriously imagine I could cooperate with traitorous criminals –?'

'Yes.'

The Commissioner glanced at his subordinates, who were staring studiously into the upper regions of the House. He computed feverishly to select the only possible answer but Wyatt gave him no time.

'It's a question of law and order isn't it? Are you a servant of the Queen, the Crown or the public? Either you remain in office – in public office – or you step down ...'

'Whatever I did – half the Force would resign!'

Wyatt leaned forward and spoke softly, his voice hardly carrying to the others ...

'Funnily enough, Commissioner, it's my opinion this country could rub along very well with only half the present Force. There's also no reason on earth why crime shouldn't be halved. Everyone from overworked judges to underemployed sociologists has been missing the point for years. Crime's been *allowed* to increase by successive governments, because only by maintaining a swollen police organization can we have the reality of a Police State . . .'

'That's ridiculous!'

'Is it? People once said phone-tapping in this country was an impossibility. Is it? Is it ridiculous, Commissioner, or is it the thin end of a rather nasty looking wedge? The man with a bugged telephone isn't a criminal, he's usually an outspoken public figure who dares to depart from the norm – watch him! Universal finger-printing! Is that to make criminals ridiculous too – or is it the back-door method of scaring people into uniformity? I say again, Commissioner, there's no mystique about reducing crime and you know it.'

'Even supposing that were true . . .'

'In my book it's true! We've already solved one crime, Commissioner, we've destroyed the permissive attitude of the State towards crime. And with or without your cooperation we can now prove that crime really doesn't pay.'

'I shall refuse . . .'

'I said with or without your – personal – cooperation. If you refuse I shall appoint some ambitious member of your organization in your place.'

'Do you really think –?' the Commissioner was left holding another torn thread of the conversation.

'I have the names of three members of "A" department who are in this movement up to their necks.'

Sir John kept silence, but frowned at his companions, speculatively. They had volunteered to accompany him . . . after all, he might be of more use where he was, might still play a glorious part in Her Majesty's restoration – later. Resignation wouldn't get him far, but sticking to his post, against the odds . . . perhaps not an earldom but – ruefully he thought of Grace – she'd never forgive him for passing up an opportunity that would've occurred to her damned intuition in a flash.

Cruel dilemma! The choice between Queen and country . . . having to his own satisfaction given a convincing display of a man wrestling with his conscience he glanced up to find Wyatt's eyes fixed on him with more than a suggestion of amusement. The damned scoundrel was laughing at him! Might almost have been reading his thoughts. But it was such a friendly smile that Sir John, to his infinite surprise, as he very nearly explained to Lady Grace much later, found himself baring his teeth in response. Nervous reaction, of course ... The Chief Inspectors continued to inspect the view above their heads ...

'And Her Majesty?'

The police officers looked grave at the indelicate reference to *habeas corpus*.

'Will be treated with exemplary courtesy.'

'I mean –'

'We're as concerned for her safety as we are for our own.'

That, thought Sir John, was plain enough. Wyatt had not only put the case in a nutshell, he also managed to convey that the subject was closed. Without formalities the three men rose and began to take their leave. At the door Jepson turned and for the first time appeared to notice Wyatt. The eyes were cold as the clink of handcuffs; there was a sinister quality in his tired almost bored tone.

'Sir John would no doubt have added, if he'd remembered, that while we'll do everything compatible with the safety of Her Majesty we cannot give you or your confederates any guarantee – accidents do happen.'

No man living enjoys being carefully measured for a coffin; but Wyatt smiled pleasantly enough: 'Sir John is sufficiently experienced to know he doesn't need to state the obvious. That's possibly why he's your superior.'

Jepson blinked, but said nothing. I will, he was thinking, take care of you personally. Curiously, he was the first flesh and blood enemy Wyatt had made in the last couple of hours.

The advance guard of technicians were already paying out cables and wheeling in their TV impedimenta as the police chiefs left the building. Invited to televise Wyatt's first Press conference that evening, both BBC and ITV had found the morsel too succulent to resist.

This is a CBC all American newsflash: we interrupt our scheduled programmes, sound and TV, to bring you the following newscast. Revolution struck with paralysing swiftness at the heart of the United Kingdom just over an hour ago. In London the Queen and her family are under house arrest, the House of Commons is in occupation by rebel units of the Army and other major points have been invested. Barricades have been thrown up from Whitehall to Wapping as fighting spills over into the streets. Casualties are described as heavy. The situation continues confused, but first reports leave no doubt the rebels are in temporary control. Further information will be screened and broadcast on all stations as received. Meantime over to Washington for official comment on the big situation ...

This is Paris. We interrupt our programmes to acquaint our listeners with the latest news from England. At approximately sixteen hundred hours this afternoon an armed insurrection succeeded in gaining control of the capital. After three hundred years of stable government the UK once again finds itself in turmoil. Our information is that units of the Armed Forces are holding Her Majesty Queen Elizabeth under close arrest ...

The Russians made a primly correct announcement of the facts and continued with an Oistrakh recital. If there had been a Communist rising they wanted nothing to do with it for the time being.

Rerun of a hot-line conversation between the President of the United States and his Ambassador in Great Britain:

'What the hell's going on over there?'

'That's just what I'm endeavouring to ascertain, Mr President.'

'Cut the diplomatese and give me the facts – plain, you all American!'

'Well – their Army's flipped – no one knows how much – it may be nothing, it could be corporational. They've taken over –'

'I know all that! What's the angle?'

'Just an old-fashioned power push I'd say.'

'But who's behind it?'

'That I wouldn't know Mr President.'

'Then find out. Keep an ear to the ground, boy – that's how to grow a basket of information.'

'Very good, Mr President.'

*

Moscow: Top priority coded instruction to Gorjinsky, London:

Find out political associations Wyatt. Act strictly in accordance with protocol. Defer contact Wyatt until further notice. Condemn uprising as work of bourgeois reactionary malcontents – also until further notice.

'He's coming! The man responsible for this fantastic coup is leaving the Commons with his principal officers – none of them above the rank of lieutenant as far as I can see. Detachments of troops attempt to keep back the crowds but reporters are pushing forward, dozens of them, almost surrounding him – batteries of cameras – the whole panoply of publicity for this, the sudden man of the moment. Viewers may just be able to see Wyatt himself in the top left-hand corner of their screen – he's only yards from the statue of another soldier who made headlines three hundred years ago – For a possible on-the-spot interview over to John Tallent . . .'

'And the chances seem pretty slim of speaking to the man of mystery – this Captain who has leapt incredibly into world prominence as the man most likely to succeed by toppling a government and a throne – a situation unparalleled in our history. The police . . . the police are actually helping to hold back the crowds! Well this is . . . you can see them even if you don't believe it – they're helping the troops to clear a way to his car! This in itself raises the question – how extensive is support for the rebellion? No one seems to know . . . and people are – the people are cheering him! Well . . . I'm doing my best to reach him – hopefully – for a few words, but it's no good – there are too many . . . does anyone know where he's –? Buckingham Palace – you probably heard that – someone in the crowd suggests Buckingham Palace – we shall see. For the moment then as Wyatt is driven away, there's nothing more we can tell you from here – except that as you can see, the situation is under control and the crowds remarkably orderly in face of this bombshell. So over now to Buckingham Palace, where Thomas Marlow will describe the scene . . .'

'Thomas Marlow speaking from the Victoria Memorial outside the Palace. It's a grey home for Kings and Queens, there's a grey crowd all around me, it's a grey autumnal evening and there's rain in the air.

'It's a grey day in our history, splashed with khaki and the steel-blue glint of guns ... almost six o'clock and our information is that Wyatt is on his way. Speculation is rife and non-stop. Why, we're asking ourselves, is this man able to operate with so much freedom? Why does he ignore the power of Press and TV? Censorship is an indispensable must in all revolutions or rebellions and yet TV at least is under no such constraint. "Say what you like – do what you like – there's no censorship." That's Wyatt's first official pronouncement. Well, nobody likes to feel ignored, but, however odd it may seem, it's at least reassuring ...

'We understand that Wyatt has arrived at a rear entrance to the Palace, and in fact it'd be impossible for him to approach by way of the Mall ...'

6

'Is that you, Fred?' the wispy voice of the wispy little woman peeling potatoes in the kitchen, half an eye almost rounding the corner to watch TV in the sitting-room, could hardly have reached Fred as he slouched into the flat closing the door with a to-hell-with-the-neighbours bang.

She wiped damp trembly hands on her nylon apron and went fluttering next door, trying not to notice where his labourer's boots had printed ghost-grey footmarks on the carpet.

Milly gazed vaguely at the morose figure slumped deep into the moquette armchair. She'd always been a bit vague. Worse, they said, since she'd married Fred.

'... heard the news, Fred?'

'Stuff the news!'

It was a real bad attack of the miseries. The job most like – all those niggers on the building sites – that was the trouble with 'em. And Fred was cut out for something better. She stood a little behind him looking down, a picture of love, pity – and helplessness, then remembered what she wanted to tell him.

'They've captured the Queen.'

'So?'

'I – I just thought you'd be interested.'

Their meeting at the Palace was an Englishmen-meeting-by-chance-in-the-desert affair. Jubilation would have been out of place and there were hurdles still to come.

'No trouble getting here?' were Baynard's first words.

'None.'

The Lieutenant gave his leader a brief account of the operation as they walked through the Marble corridor; he watched Wyatt striding along the palatial passage completely unaware it seemed of the high magnificence surrounding them. Only when they came to a mirror-glassed entrance to an enormous room did Wyatt break off his own synopsis of events at the House to look about him with a fractionally raised eyebrow.

'Why are we up here?'

'My temporary headquarters – the State Dining-Room – I thought you'd like to see it.'

Wyatt studied the overblown opulence, the vulgar ostentation reminiscent of a giant pre-war teashop and assumed an air of amazement.

'Temporary headquarters – delusions of grandeur and we've hardly started.'

Baynard smiled. 'I saw it at an auction and couldn't resist it. Impressed?'

'Oh yes – I'm impressed.' Wyatt thoughtfully approached the eight yards of dining-table (a further nineteen leaves increase its length by fifty-seven feet) at which Baynard's men were already working on preliminary inventories, listing household effects for crating and packing ... members of the staff in everyday uniforms of gold-braided dark blue battledress were cooperating with the dazed expressions of sleep walkers ...

'Yes,' the Captain repeated, 'I'm impressed – that people pay five or six pounds a week for the privilege of living in a room covering less space than this table. Three fire-places Harry, and OAPs still die for lack of warmth – and while Wrigley plays his nasty little fiddlesticks to throw men out of "non-essential" jobs, two hundred men and women are essentially employed to take care of one family – in one house ...' he smiled with a winter touch at Baynard. 'Do you want any more impressions?'

Mildly Baynard accepted the mild rebuke knowing it was deserved, knowing he still fought a strict Catholic upbringing in which inflated pomp had been lauded at the expense of reduced circumstances. He turned the Captain's footsteps in another direction and they walked in silence for a while. Then Baynard smiled. 'I wish I could've seen Wrigley's face.'

'You didn't miss much ... how are they taking it?'

'As you'd expect – with dignity on purple silence – we might not exist.'

'No more do they exist for us – except as pieces taken in the game.'

'We've accounted for a hundred and eighty-six of the staff so far.'

'Give orders for them to be paid off – every single one.'

'I've asked for volunteers from the personal staff.'

'How many?'

'A dozen came forward.'

'Six will be enough.'

'I thought we'd give the rest twenty-four hours to pack.'

'That'll be enough. What about personal effects?'

'I've two men working on that. I'll submit the lists when you've finished with them – they're in here.'

They stopped at the doors leading into the Bow Room. The Captain turned to Baynard. 'I want them out of here by seven.'

'Right.'

Baynard knocked perfunctorily, opened the door, introduced Wyatt and left.

The Queen stood at a window with the Princess. The Duke sat by an ornate chimney-piece chatting to his eldest son hidden from Wyatt by a large screen. The other children sat midway between the two groups looking through a picture book. Their sudden silence was a gesture of protest at this fresh violation of privacy, but all Wyatt saw was an ordinary family drawn together by extraordinary happenings. He addressed himself to the Queen.

'I regret any inconvenience to you and your family, madam. We shall do our best to make life as easy as possible in the circumstances.'

The Duke regarded him with mild curiosity.

'You realize the penalty for your actions?'

The Queen remained silent.

'You'll be glad to know that your message to the people had the desired effect. There has been no bloodshed – no spontaneous uprising.'

She turned and stared through him.

'Are you being deliberately offensive?'

The Captain's expression was as impassive as his reply. 'Perhaps you'll be good enough to explain your meaning.'

'I mean that I'm accustomed to being addressed formally.'

'The custom is dead.'

'My subjects . . .'

'Subjects are necessarily those in subjection, which suggests servility – let's say they were victims of historical non-necessity.'

'May I ask what you intend to do with us?'

'You will be transferred to the Tower.'

The Duke involuntarily rose to his feet, glanced at his wife, but managed to reply calmly. 'You wouldn't dare.'

'You'll be comfortably housed and given a small staff to attend you. Visitors will be allowed . . .'

'But why the Tower?'

'Nothing sinister. It's a natural stronghold for my forces and it's a defensible position with maximum security. There may be rescue attempts – and we can't afford to lose you.'

'This is monstrous!' the Duke blurted out.

'It is also a fact.'

'You'll never get there! You'll be mobbed before they allow Her Majesty to be treated so – so damnably.'

Wyatt crossed to the window and stared up at the misted sky.

'As an experienced pilot you'll recognize that the helicopter has its uses.' He turned to the Queen. 'Lieutenant Baynard will discuss details of your transfer. You'll be given a list of personal effects to which you may add as you think fit. You may choose a maximum of six from your personal staff to accompany you.'

Wyatt left the room abruptly, unaware that the Duke was speaking. Nothing could be heard above the insistent clatter of whirring blades as the helicopter settled gently on the lawn beyond the terrace.

Ten minutes later Wyatt left the Palace after a brief conference with Baynard. The crowds watched and waited in the light drizzle now falling; they and the millions anchored to TV sets were to wait another half hour after his departure before they saw the helicopter soaring above the Palace to set a course towards the darkness gathering from the East.

Pantechnicons were being loaded under the harassed supervision of the Deputy Palace Superintendent while queues began to form for the latest editions of the evening papers.

At a little after six that evening certain gentlemen met at Bookers to discuss the day's events.

Bookers in St James's is a political club; a Wolfish establishment devoted to the principles of its founder who had lost principles, fortune and all in the political cockpit of his day. The grimy portrait of 'Pistagen' Wolfe still hangs in the Small Card room, a painted symbol serving as a lasting example to succeeding generations of members to whom he was and is affectionately known as 'the Dirty Picture'.

The club deplores the present and extols the past, damns the hoi-polloi and everything Left of Right Centre, spending time, energy, wit and invention on the problem of holding back the rising waters of the twentieth century. It was the proud boast of every member that he could smell a Radical, i.e. a Conservative left of centre, at a thousand yards and blackball him at five hundred.

The best of everything belonged; Generals, tycoons of industry, lords spiritual and temporal, QCs and Judges, the best sort of rakes and dissolutes, the bluest-blooded homosexuals; everything that is inherently committed to preserving the *status quo*. Strong socialists have been known to weep at the rejection of their application for membership. On the surface therefore, the outcome of that momentous gathering in the hallowed Card room (where Wolfe himself had once vomited into the old oak ballot-box) seemed to contradict all the cherished ideals of its members. But any such reflection does little credit to the serpentine sagacity of men who feed the nation's power lines from an eighteenth-century generating station designed by Kent.

There were five men at the meeting; five of the most powerful men in the land. Collectively they formed a kind of unofficial Cabinet to which the Jacks-in-and-out-of-office paid slightly more than lip-service, a lay Conclave concerned with intrigue and policy-making at the highest-level; it was the very sewer of the political system with its countless gratings leading into every private or public place of importance, a dark thoroughfare that made the so-called Corridors of Power seem like disused back passages ... it was known to very few people as the 'Cabal'.

The long thin figure of Sir Aubrey Minter stretched comfortably in Sheraton seemed welded to the seat as the chairman and director of a dozen industrial companies, co-chairman of the Affiliated Industrial Employers and senior partner in a firm of Merchant bankers should be.

Lord Wynlose of the cherubic smile was considered to be the best Judas in the business. A champion of the Socialist ideal, he had, in the intervals of drafting Labour manifestos and generally advising the political machine on election tactics, made himself a millionaire by judicious sorties into the Stock Market. He currently advised the PM on country-running and relayed to the Cabal the benefit of his inside knowledge. It was perhaps the Cabal's best-kept secret that he had infiltrated the enemy's territory in depth without losing a shred of his Conservative convictions. Wrigley rewarded his adviser with a life peerage – for services to charity.

Martin Rigg, the third member and trouble shooter of the

group, sat staring at the Reynolds portrait of their bloated founder with an expression of profound distaste; a shrewd politician in or out of the ring, with a religiously flavoured intolerance that gave the Cabal a badly needed tinge of moral purpose. Distaste is perhaps a milk-and-water word to describe Rigg's near permanent expression; almost everything and everybody nauseated him – from plastic to 'niggers'. As for the electorate … in fact he was wondering at that moment what would happen if the Cabinet Minutes fell into those dastards' hands. Some of the things he had said when in office about the moronic public … and niggers … and Jews … and, of course, there was Field-Marshal Lord Douglas Compton-Douglas, PC, GCB, GCMG, DSO, MC and God knows what other old iron collected in a lifetime of self-grooming for the position of number one soldier hero of the United Kingdom. Lord Compton-Douglas had every reason to be thankful for the Second World War.

He strode about the room as if it were an officers' mess, not too rear of and not too near the battlefield. His lordship disliked elegance – comfort and elegance, the twin tap-roots of decadence, as he never tired of intimating with parade-ground subtlety in the Lords, were sapping the nation's fibre. Having modelled his persona on the public's remembrance of his spartan campaigning days, he could hardly intimate otherwise.

So the Field-Marshal glared at the chandelier because he dared not enjoy its glittering frivolity and paced furiously between the Adam chimneypiece and the window that billowed out over St James's like a foretop sail, wondering why that damned old fool couldn't hurry himself and be punctual for once at a time of unprecedented crisis.

Silence shrouded their mixed feelings; one of the unwritten rules of the Cabal forbade speech of any kind until all members were present.

Five minutes passed before a querulous voice beyond the shining mahogany door foresounded the arrival of the 'damned old fool'. He was certainly old and almost as certainly damned, but the Earl of Langley was no fool and Compton-Douglas knew it. At eighty-four he could still put God's fear or the

Devil's into many who considered themselves unassailably powerful, immeasurably indispensable and inordinately influential. A word from Langley had sent many reputations to the political Carey Street and few of those could name their principal creditor. His power was virtually indefinable but it should be sufficient comment that he had been unofficial, unconstitutional adviser and confidant of three-and-a-half monarchs, an office hallowed by custom and long usage. It was a Langley who suggested that the regicides should be dug from their graves and hung at Tyburn, and from the funeral of the Commonwealth to the present day a long line of Langleys had provided the private eye, the sensitive ear, and an expedient loyalty to kings and queens. Curiously, as the Monarch's power diminished, the Langley influence increased. His grandfather had read the signs and warned the fourteenth earl accordingly: 'Mark my words, Edward, the throne'll end up as redundant as a close-stool – but we'll keep it anyway – when that happens jobbery's dead and long live snobbery – but it won't do the Langley's any harm ...' Events and the sixteenth earl had proved the old man right – until now.

There were no preliminaries, the conference began with Langley's entrance. Seniority and Burke's Law gave him the first opening, 'He's a clever blighter whoever he is.'

'Should go a long way if the going's firm,' Wynlose murmured.

The Field-Marshal snorted like a war-horse with Bertrand Russell in the saddle. 'When we've finished congratulating the swine perhaps we can usefully consider the situation!'

'And how to deal with it no doubt?' The old Earl scratched himself gingerly before collapsing into a chair by the window. He seemed more interested in what was going on in the street below than in Compton-Douglas's abrupt retort. 'Naturally! what else are we here for?'

Nor did he pay close attention as Wynlose, the group's acknowledged fact finder, gave a detailed account of all that had happened, including his own ten-minute discussion with an agitated Prime Minister.

'Lost his head has he?' Langley half stated. He rubbed the

side of a long, pointed nose as another man might rub hands together to show satisfaction. 'I always said when it came to a real crisis we'd see what he was made of.'

'Not much he could do in the circumstances,' Wynlose observed mildly but watchfully.

'*If* such a thing had happened while Winston was alive he'd have told this Wyatt to go to hell *and* he'd have had the Army, Navy and Air Force mobilized by now. Only a lily-livered bunch of adulterated Socialists could've allowed a handful of men to hold the country to ransom in this manner.'

'If it is a handful,' Minter said.

'Of *course* it's a handful!' Langley made no attempt to hide his contempt of anyone who thought otherwise. 'The whole operation – methods, approach and so on – points to a few.'

'The point is,' Compton-Douglas barked: 'What's to be done?'

'Nothing.'

The four men stared at the ancient Earl as if he was mad out of season.

The Field-Marshal was the first to find his voice – not that he had ever been known to do more than mislay it briefly. 'Nothing! D'you realize they have Her Majesty in custody and intend carting her off to the Tower of which I'm the bloody Deputy Constable. My God! if something isn't done and soon I'll form a squad of picked men and go to her rescue myself!'

'Steady, my dear chap. Don't assume the country will go on thanking you forever. And if you want the blasted Garter that much you might remember that no one in authority will thank you for putting Her Majesty in even greater peril than she is in now . . .'

'He wouldn't dare!' Minter was indignant.

'Wouldn't? What other bargaining power has he got?'

'Security'll have to be tightened drastically after this,' the Field-Marshal mused. 'I shall press for an augmented Corps of Gentlemen at Arms.'

'Shall we come to the point?' Rigg spoke for the first time; acid tones etched the silence with words. 'The country's in the grip of an unprecedented catastrophe and all we have so far is a suggestion that we do nothing and Douglas seems to be living in a chapter of *The Three Musketeers*. This isn't a royalist romance.'

Compton-Douglas bristled, bridled and barked his way out of the ambush. 'Well what do you have in mind – if anything?'

'It's quite simple – we return to the Commons and continue the business of governing as if nothing had happened.'

Langley chuckled quietly to himself.

'Dunno why you all let yourselves be kicked out in the first place.' Minter growled, but Rigg was ready to snap at all-comers.

'D'you think I didn't urge our people to stand firm? If we hadn't made the confounded mistake of starting the Anthem . . .'

'What,' asked Minter, 'had that to do with it?'

'Good God man isn't it obvious? The boy stood on the burning deck chopping firewood – it was the wrong gesture at the wrong time – we bloody well sang ourselves into defeat! I told Enoch we should've rushed 'em.'

'Why didn't you then?' Compton-Douglas demanded with a touch of malice.

'D'you think some of us didn't? They actually fired a shot – what could we do?'

'Such a splendid opportunity you missed, Rigg. A martyr's death – burial in the Abbey and your statue well to the right of "Dizzy's".'

Langley was enjoying the whole thing hugely. He smiled and nodded to himself and once or twice cast a glance at the meaty portrait of old Wolfe as though sharing a secret.

'When you finish seeing the funny side of this situation you may care to offer some practical . . .'

The smile disappeared abruptly and the old man's reply be-headed the Field-Marshal's sentence with axiomatic finality.

'We do nothing!'

No one spoke. They simply waited. Either the old boy was growing senile or his cunning was beyond the comprehension even of this informal committee of devious Ways and dubious Means. So they waited while he snuffled and fidgeted and watched the shadows gathering in St James's. The words came slowly when he did speak; they had taken on an odd quality of detachment, as though a message was being transmitted by generations of Langleys, guardians still of the holy *status quo* . . .

'This man is a scoundrel – but he's done us all a favour. Nothing could have worked better to take the hoi-polloi's piece of mind from our present situation. Wrigley should go down on bended knees and give thanks for this Wyatt. So should we. The people are sick to death of us – all of us. Edward'll realize it before I tell him if he's any savvy at all. Besides, the Socialists were mucking up everything as usual, another six months and either they'd be begging us to get back in the saddle – which we wouldn't want because we'd have to take unpopular measures ourselves, or we'd be faced with a National Government and we all know what that means.

'Along comes Wyatt and does our job for us. He'll do it badly and he'll be got rid of – we can leave that to those in Labour . . . what happens then? If he fails they'll blame the Socialists for letting him in – they'll turn to us – and we establish ourselves even more firmly in the saddle – have to take unpopular measures won't we? Can't have such a thing happening again . . .'

The old man paused and stared at his hands, brittle as twigs. They flexed and reflexed strangely . . .

'Clay in our hands . . . we can mould them in any damned image we choose – thanks to this gift from the gods . . . we've got a bogey-man you fools! They'll burn him in effigy every 23rd of October and give thanks for Monarch, Parliament – us! anybody who delivers them from the evil of having to think it out all over again. And you want to destroy him before he scares all the little ones in the dark half to death. We do nothing – let him have his day, month or year – then we'll think about lighting the bonfires . . .'

7

Ravens fluttered nervously as an alien clatter swept away the cobwebbed silence, croaked themselves hoarse as they pavanned among the rebel garrison watching the great red helicopter hover bird-like and slowly drop. It landed on Tower Green, not far from the Scaffold site, an old and rare place of execution.

No salutes, no guard of honour, only an untidy group of soldiers and French, the new Yeoman Gaoler, holster unbuttoned, motionless, hands clasped behind his back. Even as the Queen descended the steps with her family he made no move ... the Duke paused, gazed round at a scene going grey with mist and autumnal gloom. He seemed almost to be reading a parallel with the past.

'This way.' The tiny group looked uncertainly at the commander of the Tower as he indicated an L-shaped house tucked Tudoresque into a corner of the Green. Uncertain, and too dazed perhaps to understand what was happening. But there were no concessions in French's tone of voice.

'Your immediate luggage should be here soon. Two of my men have instructions to give you any assistance you may require till your servants arrive.'

That was all. He turned away abruptly, neither expecting nor receiving a reply, and they followed him along the neat cobble-stoned path to the old house from which Lady Jane had walked to the very edge of the axe . . . now, the air was damp as a sexton's brow, scarcely carried the mournful lowing of tugs from the river. The younger prince tripped and almost fell. A member of the rebel escort involuntarily stretched a hand to support him – but the Queen was there first.

She looked pale but composed as she paused for a moment on the threshold of the former Resident Governor's house, which curiously is better known as the Queen's House.

*

Instant historians still pose the question: why did Wyatt summon a Press conference *before* making his declaration to the country? Surely, they argue, no self-respecting revolutionary would expose himself to a journalistic inquisition until he had advertised and justified his seizure of power to the nation at large?

Letter dated July 7th 196– to the poet and novelist, Paul Morrison, one of the chief conspirators:

Of course it's a gamble! But what if the Press does ask any one of a thousand damaging questions which only one in a million of the population would think of – can our position be any worse? Either we're accepted from the word 'go' or we're not. No half-measures – damaging questions are irrelevant so screw courage to the sticking point and remember this – the people are natural iconoclasts if someone is prepared to play the agent of destruction in their name. Therefore we don't have to excuse what will already be acceptable. Of course I shall explain what we intend to do – but not by way of a statement. I'm sorry but your idea is unsound. Any attempt to justify our position would suggest the craven attitude typical of a Party Political broadcast.

You'll remember I said at our last R— Street meeting, the people are sick and tired of being button-holed in their living-rooms by greasy, sanctimonious 625-lined political hucksters trying to peddle damaged goods. So – no playing for sympthy – as for those thousand damaging questions – the trick is to be ready with a thousand and one answers.

I shall be in Yorkshire for the next fortnight – an opportunity to look into the Leeds group – their area leader appears to have an attack of stage fright ...

The House filled and spilled over with Press representatives, national and provincial, and every available London correspondent of a multitude of foreign papers, long before the conference began. Maintenance men had abandoned the air-conditioning plant and gone home – the atmosphere was stifling. One or two female reporters fainted in the heat of the moment aggravated by TV lights warming the scene into high definition.

Excitement mingled with conjecture, theories tangled with

anticipation and curiosity dangled from slender threads of disbelief. Extreme heat melted the welter of words into a Babelis-
tic cacophony. Few of those present could believe they were
invited to the funeral of Monarchy and democratic government by an unknown body-snatcher . . .

'At four o'clock this afternoon the Revolutionary Council
took certain measures considered essential to save our country
from irretrievable ruin.

'We're not here to excuse ourselves; our actions require
none. I will state our case and our cause and our intentions
plainly and I will take nothing but the will of the people for
my judge. To our accusers I have this to say . . . in the people's
name I here publicly accuse the major political factions of
criminal negligence in the conduct of the nation's affairs. They
have failed the country, mishandled its resources, misled the
electorate with false promises, failed from moral cowardice
to take desperately needed action and so led the State blindfold
to the very brink of ruin.

'Britain today is a land without purpose, without hope, without a will of its own. The political system creating this state of
affairs has much to answer for.

'Our aims are few: abolition of the Monarchy, the establishment of a republic, a thorough reconsideration of our insane foreign policy and the introduction of a constitution to
be submitted by referendum to the people, a constitution
guaranteeing true political representation in place of the
spatchcock system reeking of illegality that we now abolish.'

'Anything else?' Wyatt caught the anonymous shaft of irony
in mid-flight.

'We consider the Church of England sufficiently buttressed
by investments to have both visible as well as invisible means of
support. A State religion is an insult to God himself unless he
is a politician. We shall see to it.'

'After three hundred and . . .?'

'After a thousand years if necessary! The Church of England
was established by the stroke of a pen – and it can be dis-
established in exactly the same way. If you must protest then

for God's sake find something more worthwhile to defend than the brainchild of a blue-bearded, pox-ridden, bloody-minded Tudor tyrant!

'You may now ask your questions.'

This was the latest danger point – the testing time for Wyatt, his ideals – and his followers. The few men about him looked more anxious than he felt. From now on, the script would be unrehearsed ...

The questions came thick and fast, tripped over each other and were scattered out of all recognition. After a period of confusion the first accusation badly disguised as a question was permitted to *The Times*:

'You miss the point entirely. However much you may charge the politicians of any party with criminal negligence – you are the usurper. The fact remains and always will, they are chosen by the people and you are not!'

There followed a long silence – too long many believed. The feeling grew that Wyatt, confronted with the fact of his 'vile treachery' had suddenly collapsed ... then Wyatt spoke – quietly, forcing the majority to lean forward to catch his words.

'I admit that I am a usurper – but it is an essential part of my case that the whole system, from the resident of Buckingham Palace down to the six hundred political yokels who lay about this Chamber, constituted a usurpation without parallel anywhere in the world.'

He waited for the dynamo hum of excitement to die down ... 'Let me ask *The Times* representative a few simple questions. First, what is democratic government? Let's be quite sure about this – democratic government ... well?'

'Government by and for the people – what else?'

'What else indeed. Did we have it?'

'Of course we did!'

'Rubbish! By whom is power exercised in this country?'

'By the Executive of ...'

'Wrong! By the Queen in Parliament – well?'

'Strictly speaking – yes.'

'That's to say by the Queen acting with Lords and Commons?'

'. . . yes.'

'Is the Monarch elected?'

'She succeeds –'

'According to the Act of Succession?'

'Well?'

'An act passed by a few privileged landholders and never repealed, questioned or challenged till now?'

'Why should it be?'

'I'll tell you . . . if the Monarch is an indispensable third of a truly democratic, that is, representative government – she should be democratically elected! But the Monarchy is hereditary – entailed to infinity! It is not elective – the will of the people is *not* consulted – whole generations unborn are subject to a fixture who has no more right to govern . . .'

'She does not govern – she merely . . .'

'She merely receives half a million pounds a year to flourish a few signatures . . . in the name of Prices and Incomes is that or is it not a physical partaking in actual government? . . . so much for anomaly number one – a so-called democratic Monarch foisted on the people . . .'

'The Coronation?'

'Two thousand distinguished guests bawling *"Vivat Regina"* does not constitute an election! I say again the Queen is not Queen by the will of the people – how can she be since they are never asked!

'Anomaly number two – Queen, Lords and – well – what about the Lords? Do they sit in their gilded cage by the people's express command? Are they entitled to robe themselves in ermine and vermin by the will of the people? Tell me – who votes for the Lords at a General Election? But if they're not voted in – how in God's name can they be representatives of the people!

'Tell your readers this: two thirds of our system of government based on a phraseological Queen in Parliament was nonrepresentative – and if this is true of the Lords and Monarch it must also be true of the Commons.'

There were loud cries of 'No' and 'Nonsense' but the Captain sailed through them without a pause.

'Nonsense only because you and the multitudes beyond these four walls have been conditioned to believe in the sanctity of Trinitarian democracy – Queen, Lords and Commons; but if you believe in the Trinity – you cannot take Son and Father without the Holy Ghost – if there is no Son and Father – where is the Holy Ghost? I tell you solemnly – the British people have been the victims of the most exquisite constitutional hoax ever devised in the annals of Politics.'

TV cameras recorded every reaction, every expression of professional observers who were themselves observed ... the effect of Wyatt's arguments was writ large in their faces and faithfully transmitted to the unseen audience. Wyatt, listening to the freshets of excited chatter, knew that his gamble had paid off. He waited with quiet confidence for the unimportant questions to come; the foreseeable future had been taken care of.

The Birmingham Post: 'I don't argue with your logic because the constitution never claimed to be founded on logical principles. But what can you hope to do about it?'

Wyatt: 'I'm not concerned with an "illogical" constitution, my purpose is to expose a system based on fraudulent practice. The people's dissatisfaction with the system proves they were aware, however dimly, of the fraud being perpetrated in their name.'

The Scotsman: 'Are you suggesting that the existing political parties were aware of ...'

Wyatt: 'Of course they were aware! Why else was so much emphasis placed on "party" strife, on engineered party clashes in Parliament and out of it? Why else was the two-party game played to the hilt except to blind the electorate to the really important questions?'

France Soir: 'I would like to know what you intend to do with the Royal Family?'

Wyatt: 'The Royal Family as you call it will remain in protective custody – for obvious reasons.'

'Their treatment?'

Wyatt: 'Treatment! At this moment, my friend, they are housed in better conditions than is one quarter of the population of Great Britain.'

The Guardian: 'How would you expect the people to react to this violation of Her Majesty's person?'

Wyatt: 'There is no question of violation. I have given the people my word – the woman is safe – only the Queen is dead.'

Daily Express: 'Suppose it's the will of the people that you set the Royal Family at liberty?'

Wyatt: 'Faced with a majority decision we should do so.'

'You seriously believe the majority is against monarchy?'

Wyatt: 'If the majority has a shred of self-respect it will prefer to be a majority of citizens rather than subjects.'

The Cardiff Herald: 'Would this be some kind of egalitarian society you're aiming at?'

Wyatt: 'If we destroy the Establishment – create a Republic – then we can hope for a ground base of equality. By abolishing all forms of official privilege from the Garter to the MBE ...'

The Daily Telegraph: 'But you can't do that!'

Wyatt: 'If a man is proud of working for the good of his country then pride is its own reward! Equality means nothing if we make honour and privilege the basis of a neo-class distinctive meritocracy.'

New York Herald: 'Your aims appear to have much in common with those of the Communists. Would you agree with that?'

Wyatt: 'I represent no party. Our strength lies in the fact that we are uncommitted. We are sick of parties – and we are legion ...'

The Daily Mirror: 'What about our relationship with the United States?'

Wyatt: 'It'll be to everyone's advantage if we succeed in saving our country from subservience to everything American.'

'Anti-American!'

Wyatt: 'If you ask from whom we have most to fear I would answer without hesitation – America.'

This produced a gasp of astonishment from everyone in the House. Treachery to the Monarchy, it implied, was hardly in the same class as this calculated insult to England's greatest ally. The correspondent for the *Baltimore Sun* jumped to his feet, white, shaken with anger.

'I somehow don't think you'll get the British to go along with that one!'

'Are you here to make statements or ask questions?'

'Very well! How do you suppose the British people will take this unprecedented attack on its greatest ally?'

'Ally! Is Europe the first line of American defence or the Rocky Mountains? Do you bolster our economy to support the Pound or the Dollar? The British people will thank God for losing an ally costing this country one thousand million pounds in arms purchases over the next ten years. We'll defend ourselves if necessary – regain a measure of self-respect in the process and to hell with America!'

'You've got a heck of a nerve!' The *Baltimore Sun* gasped and sank below the horizon stuttering incoherently. If hardened reporters and blasé correspondents had come prepared for shattering revelations they gave no sign of it. Pandemonium followed until they realized that no questions could penetrate the dinful scene.

The Indian Times: 'How widespread is your organization?'

Wyatt: 'It is nation wide.'

'No question of an Army coup then?'

'None at all.'

The Guardian: 'How do you intend to exercise power?'

Wyatt: 'With the aid of a council – the Council of Six.'

'Government is a complex business – how can a few men do the work of hundreds?'

'Detailed administration isn't our concern – we have the finest Civil Service in the world – it will keep this country going whoever is in power. Our purpose is to simplify the policy-making machinery for the time being – drastic measures can't wait on fools who believe time is on their side.'

'Are you seriously suggesting that you and your Council can run a country by inspiration and intuition where highly sophisticated politicians appear to have failed?'

'Are you seriously suggesting that any greater value can be placed on the political experience of a man who may be

Minister of Transport today and the Minister of Defence tomorrow?'

The questions continued . . .

When at last the men of the Press closed notebooks, pocketed ballpoints and shuffled off the Commons precincts they were almost in complete agreement about one thing: Wyatt was there to stay. Subconsciously they wrote the idea into their copy and that, from Wyatt's point of view, was a very good thing.

Observers of the October events consider Wyatt took risks of a kind only permitted to men of destiny. 'He saw his star in the ascendant and grabbed it before it got out of hand.' Possibly. But these romantic notions colour without explaining his chain of successes, every one of which could have been frustrated by the metaphorical whiff of grapeshot. His followers, better qualified to judge, discounted destiny, stars and similar bits of superstitious nonsense as mere extras who are paid for never appearing. At their trials they were to insist that his every move was calculated, every course of action based on a profoundly intuitive understanding of the country's mood at any given time. Wyatt's first TV appearance could have been a failure; instead it whetted the public's appetite for more. His subsequent speech to the nation should have destroyed good impressions: it was hard, uncompromising and unflattering to the prevailing national sentiment: smug self-satisfaction. An extract of the speech follows:

. . . Don't deceive yourselves; if you look for a Saviour to redeem the broken promises of former Jacks-in-office I'm not your man. If you even believe I care what you think of me you're wrong again – no man locks up a queen and kicks a few hundred of her loyal subjects out of bounds worrying about delicate sensibilities. What I am concerned about is what you think of yourselves. The politicians didn't care – the Wrigleys and the Holmes sat here just as I do now and told you what was wrong with the man next door – they didn't dare tell you what was wrong with you because that didn't bring in the votes . . . well, what did they say about your neighbours after their fashion? Workshy – every one of us must pull our weight – something-for-nothing-addict – no one owes us a living – expense-account man – time-sheet fiddlers – overtime crazy – strike-happy and I'm alright Jack? Not you, of course – the man next door. So what did you do – settle back comfortably, pour another drink and tell yourself 'it's not my fault – it's some-one else he's on about.'

I'll tell you this: We're all responsible for what this country's become. You, me and the man next door, as much as any politi-cian living. More! Because we gave them the opportunity to play at blind man's buff and count up our losses with matchsticks!

Revolutions only happen in countries going rotten to the core – decadence was the last prize we could hope for. Do you suppose therefore I'm proud of what I've done? You can take me for a power-hungry despot or you can take my word I saw for too long only drastic action could bring us out of a looking-glass world back to reality.

There can be no pride – only purpose – when mutiny breaks out on the ship of State. God knows we needed a captain – not a gilded figure-head stuck in the bows doing nothing but beauti-fully. We tacked from left to right under a succession of first mates drunk and incapable on Conference wine bottled in Brighton and Blackpool. The ship was adrift and most of the crew didn't give a damn – there were some who'd watch it sink rather than cross a demarcation line to plug the hole. But a few mutinied – because they cared for the ship – and they mutinied with nothing but a sense of purpose to get her back to port.

So we took over – and this is what we intend to do ...

A pub in Manchester.

The bleary-eyed individual glances round at his cronies, mournfully finishes his pint with a faint suggestion of the death-rattle.

'All very well,' he pauses to suck his lips dry, 'but he 'asn't said anything. I mean what's he going to do? Tha's what I want to know before I lay money on him.'

A morose little man with tired hair and dark fingernails watched TV commercials out of his eye's corner, managed with an effort to drag a fading mind from the dubious world of cat food ...

'Takes time don' it? Can't expect 'im to 'and it out on a plate in ten minutes. Only been going a few hours.'

'Well I'm not standing for it I can tell you that – ten Seniors Duffy and don' unwrap 'em will you, makes me feel a bloody invalid – I can tell you that – I'm not standing for it as the actress said to the bishop.' Whereupon the soldierly-looking member of the trio, ex-Eighth Army – blazer and badge to prove it – wheezed into his beer mug like a ruptured concertina. Then he frowned, realizing even his sparkling wit was out of place. 'I like things done proper and he's doin' it improper as the actress ... I don' know what he's done but I fought for my country – tanks – knocked out twice by Rommel's own ...'

They'd heard it all before so the bleary-eyed one chipped in with the first thing to hand.

'I say it don' matter who you've got in – Queen or no Queen, they all end up the same – out for 'emselves and nowt for us.'

'Aye – true enough,' said the morose one staring sadly at the emptiness of his glass, 'but there was somewhat about him I 'aven't seen wi' the others. Felt you could trust him if you know what I mean.'

'Oh aye?' the ex-Eighth waxed heavily sarcastic. 'I allus feel I can trust a chap who claps Queens in the Tower and puts the toe of his boot up a lawfully elected Prime Minister's soft spot *and* tells the MPs including mine they can go and get stuffed!'

'True enough,' the bleary eyes conceded. After a long pause he added: 'But he did it didn't he?'

'He did!' said the ex-Eighth ... 'Must've enjoyed it too.' He finished his beer thoughtfully and ordered another round. The others looked a little more cheerful as he added, 'I would've.'

8

The morning after – a time to take an attitude, an opportunity for the Press to guide opinion this or that way. So the workers in Peking chatter excitedly over news-sheets pasted on hoardings while a few thousand ideas away out of Town commuters discuss events in England with frank disbelief all the way to Grand Central.

In London nothing appeared to be different. People still escalatored to the tube and crammed into overcrowded trains to make the office, factory and shop on time – the same a.m. cavalcade across Waterloo bridge – the streets were swept, the milk was delivered and traffic jammed. They all had to live whatever else happened.

A small crowd waited in an uncomfortable knot outside Buckingham Palace, rewarded for their vigil by nothing more than a glimpse of large removal vans and a car or two taking volunteer staff to the Tower. They would stagger home at last with little to show for their loyalty beyond a cold in the head. The Footguards had been withdrawn, then remounted, then withdrawn with the final realization that they had nothing to guard. Now in the granite light of morning the Pimlico Palace had an abandoned air, like an old Opera House striving to recapture yesterday's positively last performance.

Rain fell in a steady drizzle, the knot of mourners contracted to a handful of fanatics. They stood out of hearing of the record turning scratchily on an ancient portable – the old man, thin as a winter branch cranked the handle, stood to attention, cranked the handle, stood . . .

A day of national mourning according to the *Daily Telegraph*. The 8.32 regulars from Purley and all stations similar unfolded their black bordered papers and were smitten by tombstone headlines carved in jet.

ARMY COUP TOPPLES GOVERNMENT
THE QUEEN HELD AS HOSTAGE

They turned to the 'leader' with regimental precision. It called down the wrath of God, heaven, Fleet Street and all the angels on the perpetrators of a 'vile treachery'. 'Could England ever hope to hold up its head again?' *Homo sapiens urbis* type 8.32 raised his eyes, glanced at his neighbour and out of the windows with no apparent difficulty. After breakfast, thoughts fumbled with the obvious fact that censorship had no part in Wyatt's vile perpetrations. Consequently, and unconsciously, they edged an inch or two to the side of illegality. They read dutifully – but remembered in their mind's eye Wyatt's appearance on television ... some newspapers missed the point by leaning too heavily on the absence of censorship.

From Brixton and Poplar, Hoxton and Shoreditch came the short-time travellers, flipping through the sports pages of the *Mirror*, chuckling at Andy Capp before turning to the front page.

OUR QUEEN ARRESTED!
ENGLAND IN IRONS!

Into the blood-soaked fortress of our darkest history came the pale figure of Her Majesty Queen Elizabeth the Second surrounded by her loved ones. Nothing in England's saga can surpass the tragedy that struck our Royal Family at four of the clock yesterday afternoon. No Marie Antoinette, no Charles I could have borne the anguish suffered by a Queen who believed herself secure from the brutalities of the past. Theirs was, after all, an age in which such things could happen.

What were her feelings as she passed the spot where so many of her illustrious predecessors had walked to their doom, walked to the black velvet beat of the muffled drum? What ghosts of the great rose up to torment her with their fate? How far did the shadow of the headsman stretch across her path? A Queen flouted, a Parliament routed. This is England. T O D A Y!

Someone it seemed, had burned the oil to its deadline; wrestled with Hyperbole – and lost.

In some such fashion the Nationals and Provincials dealt with the coup. Editors sweated like conductors gone mad with an unbelievable score on an incredible scale in the impossible key of H. They were too dazed to find some perspective for events daring to knock History out of orbit. Only *The Times* retained sanity enough to explore the implications of Wyatt's rebellion.

The impossible appears to have happened. After three centuries of comparatively serene government, Great Britain finds herself uncomfortably faced with a situation only expected of once-backward Latin American states and forward-looking African nations.

91

The events of yesterday, calmly executed in an atmosphere almost entirely lacking in panic, may testify to certain sterling qualities in the British character of they may not.

Either we are in the grip of apathy so powerful as to nullify our collective power of judgement and action, or our negative attitude has a more positive meaning, proving we are prepared to acquiesce in a crime against the Monarchy and the whole democratic system. It is too early to draw a parallel with the rise of Nazism, though total disillusionment with the prevailing forms of democracy is a would-be totalitarian's happy hunting-ground. Nor is it wise to be over-impressed by the seemingly genuine concern of one man for his country. World War II after all was the end product of one man's concern for a country.

At this stage all theory is in the melting-pot, but one fact has hardened and taken shape. A profound malaise affects the public to depths of which those in authority must have been blissfully unaware. The acceptance of violence appears to be a condition of our existence; the degree of violence is unimportant – though it is some consolation that no lives were lost – it is the acceptance that suggests symptoms of mental sickness on a national scale. We must bear in mind that some forms of insanity are incurable. If remedies exist they must be used sparingly and at the right time. For the moment we can do nothing. If Wyatt is a quack doctor, the patient will soon discover the fact for himself.

The minor incidents belonging to the early days were numerous. Most of them were forgotten or hardly considered at the time. Much that was spurious or curious appeared in the spate of 'personal reminiscences' published later. The charwoman's story, recorded at Mrs Dinwood's home in Lambeth, is a less typical but more reliable example of man-in-the-street reaction.

'Yes I suppose you might say I was there – that thing won't scratch the table will it? – you can see Big Ben from the upstairs back. Hubby and I watched it on TV of course – saw it all happening not half a mile from us and we just said "*Well!*" I mean there wasn't much else we could say was there? Always said the devil looks after his own but when it comes to cheek this bloke had his fair share – shutting up the Queen like that. I mean you wondered who'd be next, and

Herbert – that's my hubby – said if that's all the police was worth he'd appeal for a rate reduction would you care for another cup of tea? (Deletion) Well we knocked at Mrs Willis's next door and said have you heard? Mrs Willis don't miss much so it was a silly question really. Being a national crisis like we all four went round to the local – very select you know – all done up modern kind of thing and we had a gin and chat as you might say – of course I think Mrs Willis had the dead needle on account of me working at the 'ouse of Commons and being connected with politics in a manner of speaking. I do the Front Bench y'know – Labour, of course.

'We had quite a ding-dong about it believe me. One said one thing and Mr Willis said something else and eventually I said well it's for me to decide anyway and since we can't let the place get filthy I'm going in as usual. They tried to persuade me – said it was dangerous but once I make up my mind . . .

'Well I walked across the bridge like always – never forget it – that fateful day they said, course it was early next morning but still fateful – and perishing cold. Not a soul about except the Law – er – a constable in Horseferry Road. "Hullo 324," I said. "Still wondering what hit you are you?" "Still wondering who's side I'm supposed to be on," he said and wandered off past ICI. Looked for all the world as if he'd lost his special eraser they issue for notebook cleanliness . . . he was going the wrong way too.

'All the girls were there when I turned up. Having a right set-to with the guards they were.

' "What's on?" I said to Margot – her mother was a staunch Liberal – staunch – worked in the 'ouse before we was thought of – but wouldn't touch Lloyd George's seat for a pension . . . "They're saying we can't go in," she said. The soldiers or whatever they were looked a bit sharp but I reckon they was scared – fifty of us and only three of them never mind their pop-guns – we'd have made mincemeat of 'em if it hadn't been for the poor Queen. So I stepped up and had my say. "We've got a job to do and that's it," I said. "Sorry," one of 'em said, very polite – nice spoken, "we've strict orders not to let anyone in." "That's all very well," I said, "but what's the place supposed to be?" "It *was* the House of Commons," he said. "Right, well you won't find anything more common than us lot – MPs excepted – so you'd better have another think." Five minutes more of this and we were still standing there like love locked out and then a sergeant came along. "What's all the fuss, girls?" he said. "We've got work to do never mind who's the cockalorum," I said. I was just shaping up for a good old row and he says: "In you go then and don't forget to sweep under the stairs." Nice bloke he was, just like one of us, not a bit what the *Sketch* made of 'em – "blood dripping from their hands" and that. So he told us which rooms to leave alone there being committees at work. "Already?" I said. "That's right," he said, and in we went, no trouble at all. Are you sure you won't have another cup of tea . . .?'

Wyatt established his headquarters in the Prime Minister's room at the Commons. From there he could supervise the initial administrative work needed to push the coup through the next day. Between times he rested, ate a little, drank strong black coffee and read the teletype reports coming in from all over the reactive world. He dictated directions and memoranda, visited the working committees and found time to discuss progress with his immediate subordinates. Time too for receiving the odd visitors who appeared in the darkest hours; furtive men like Morgan – a true 'camp-follower of revolution'.

A knock at the door. Slingsby appeared.

'I've taken over liaison for a bit, Chief. Baynard's held up with the Publications Committee.'

Wyatt looked up from a desk piled with papers. 'I see. Something special?'

'Someone to see you.'

'Well?'

'Head of a political party.'

'Go on.'

'Gerald Morgan – founder and leader of the British Union of Socialists.'

Morgan, nondescript as a railway clerk, bustled in importantly carrying an empty-looking black brief-case. Wyatt remained seated.

'Something I can do for you?'

'I came to congratulate you.' His voice had the gritty texture of a street-corner ranter.

'At two in the morning?'

Morgan smiled carefully: 'We're busy men you and me.'

'I see – well that's very civil of you, isn't it, John?'

'It had to come,' said Morgan. 'We've always said it had to happen and by God you've done it. This country needs a lesson.'

'Yes?'

Morgan moistened a lip dried by the cool atmosphere. The meeting between gauleiters was going awry somewhere.

'I've come to offer you the services of my organization. You probably know, we've been on the battlefield a long time, tub-thumping for a new Britain – everything you said on TV we've been saying for years. We're strong – ten thousand odd members throughout the country. I'll be glad to put the whole set-up at your disposal.'

'In return for what exactly?'

'I assume our policies have much in common,' Morgan ventured.

'For example?'

Morgan ignored the question: 'Naturally there'd have to be discussions.'

'Let's discuss it now. You're offering me your support, I'm asking you on what terms?'

'Well, frankly, we'd expect implementation of our basic policies, but I don't see any difficulties there – as I say –' he paused and glanced quickly at Slingsby who had remained standing by the door. 'I like your methods.'

'What policies?' Wyatt pursued.

'Control of the unions, expulsion of all immigrants – a thorough clean-up of unwholesome elements in our society.'

'Are we discussing policies or fallacies?'

Morgan coloured: 'What do you mean exactly?'

Wyatt stood and walked round the enormous desk. 'Granted we got here by gun-flourishes – there we end. Then you crawl in and suggest we join forces to carry out your filthy racialist policies. What did you have in mind – concentration camps? If this country's sick – then you're a deathbed case! I warn you, any time you're found fouling the air from a street corner platform you'll immediately be taken in and brought to me – and I'll shoot you myself.'

Exit Morgan.

At two-thirty that morning Jennings prepared coffee for Wyatt and his two lieutenants, Baynard and Slingsby. Baynard ventured the question uppermost in their minds.

'How do you think it's shaping, Skipper?'

Silence. The stirring of black coffee, Wyatt seated in the half-light of a desk-lamp, head bowed over other thoughts or searching for the right words. They waited.

'Our enemies are doing nothing ... that's interesting.'

'The threat to the Queen ...' Slingsby suggested.

'I wonder.'

They glanced at each other, not understanding. He continued like a man absorbed in a private dialogue.

'The counter-measures are already under way. By now those powers behind throne and government have considered the steps to be taken. We don't need to worry about the corridors of power – corridors are for the couriers, the satellites, minions and twopenny mandarins. The men who matter, our real opponents, are elsewhere, cliques in club-rooms and discreet gatherings in country houses – an "old boy" network in gilded sewers ... they're grateful to us – we've given intrigue, their favourite word, a new meaning – they've considered their tactics – and they'll do nothing. They ride to hounds too well to rush their fences ...'

'You – don't sound very optimistic,' Baynard ventured.

Wyatt considered the possibility. 'It's a question of whether you want me to say what you'd prefer to hear – or what I think. Suppose I tell you we're surf-riding to success – all objectives gained so we can't lose? Believe me we can – especially if we underrate the opposition.'

'If it's been too easy it could be some kind of trap,' Slingsby suggested.

'No – there's no short-term trap; but it has been easy. That was inevitable – no one believed it could happen.'

'It's been worth it too – just for the look on Wrigley's face when we walked in,' said Jennings with a chuckle.

'It didn't look much better when he went over to Number Ten and found Gaynor in possession,' Baynard said.

The conversation continued light-hearted, but they were all desperately tired. Wyatt seemed to have forgotten their presence as he worked on through the subdued laughter. Jennings nagged at intervals: 'You ought to get some sleep.' The Sergeant had a dog's devotion for Wyatt.

A few minutes later he cut across the reminiscences. 'Harry, I want you to get on to Scotland Yard.'

Baynard looked surprised: 'Okay.'

'I want a breakdown of all reported cases of criminal activity in London between yesterday afternoon – four o'clock – and two this morning.'

'Will they give it to me?'

'Yes.'

Bewildered, the three men glanced their question at Wyatt. He took time off to explain.

'In an abnormal situation, natural catastrophe, overthrow of a government, social unrest, the crime rate tends to rise sharply – it's usually immediate too. Crooks don't wait on the event. If the figures we get are no worse than those I have already it'll tell us something about the situation.'

'You mean the criminal class takes advantage of turmoil – and if they don't – there's no turmoil?'

'That, Harry,' said Wyatt faintly smiling, 'is what I mean.'

Half an hour later Baynard returned with the figures. Wyatt compared them carefully with those he had and sat back at last with a look of satisfaction.

'No increase,' he announced briefly.

'Except in Westminster,' Jennings observed.

The Captain was too tired to understand.

'Breaking and entering a Private and a Public House,' Jennings explained.

Wyatt grinned. 'Now Sergeant Jennings has had his little joke I feel we deserve a couple of hours' rest to recover . . .'

Three-forty. A charlady clattered past Wyatt's room singing a slop top-twenty dirge with a gusto belying her fifty-eight years.

'Not so loud,' the guard whispered, 'the Boss is asleep.'

'Asleep is he?' she paused to stare at the closed door. 'That's politics for you,' and swept on her way bawling louder than before.

Hartfish surveyed the crowded courtroom with the satisfaction of a player counting the takings by the size of the 'house' on his first entrance. The routine evidence of witnesses could be boring at any time, more so after ten days' sitting. But interest had never flagged, thanks to his masterly stage management; he had overlooked nothing and nobody to make this the greatest trial of the century. Some say he reserved his most exquisite insolence for Justice itself – for the rest, all were equal in the sight of his vindictiveness. As the first witness of the day was called he noted that John already fidgeted with the pen in his hand – the Attorney-General noted everything.

Edward John Rankin, a distinguished-looking man of middle years, entered the witness box, was suitably awed by his novel and intentionally imposing viewpoint of the scene, and after preliminaries concerned with Almighty God, identification and so forth, waited for Hartfish's onslaught.

'Mr Rankin, you were at the time of the events of October 23rd last, Permanent Secretary at the Ministry of Fuel and Power?'

'I was.'

'Did you receive a communication of a somewhat unusual nature on the day in question?'

'I did.'

'Will you be good enough to tell the court what it was?'

'It was a typewritten letter, requesting Permanent Secretaries and heads of departments of all Ministries to assemble in the Chamber of the House of Commons at 10 o'clock on the morning of the 24th. It was signed "Wyatt".'

'When exactly did you receive this letter?'

'A minute or so before four. It was marked "urgent" so, of course, it was sent straight to my office.'

'What was your reaction to this improbable invitation?'

'Frank disbelief. My secretary suggested it might be a hoax and I was inclined to accept that as the only explanation – until I heard the news.'

'Of the Government's overthrow?'

'Yes.'

'Which you also treated with "frank disbelief"?'

'Naturally.'

'Naturally. However, you could not be expected to remain in a state of "frank disbelief" forever?'

'I made inquiries among my colleagues in other Ministries and found they'd all received this – this invitation. I also put through a call to the House of Commons' Exchange to see if the rumours could be substantiated,'

'And, of course, they were. What did you do then, Mr Rankin? I ask you again – what did you do then?'

'I – I went home.'

'You went home – to The Cedars, Tangley Avenue, Carshalton . . .'

'Yes.'

'Strange thing to do – in the circumstances?'

'What else could I do? Practically all the staff . . .'

'I'm not concerned with the staff, I'm asking if it is inconceivable that your position warranted your presence at a responsible post in a time of acute crisis.'

'Whatever responsibility I had for this country's fuel and power resources left me little authority for dealing with revolutions.'

'Surely your responsibility to your Minister was sufficient to keep you at your office until he had an opportunity to see you – to discuss the situation?'

'I stayed long enough to learn that the Minister himself had gone home – five minutes before. I really don't see what else any of us could have done.'

Hartfish allowed the laughter to die its own death. A little mirth oiled rusting attention in this period of legal doldrums. And there was the TV audience to consider.

'So you went home and watched the affair on your television set no doubt?'

'I – yes, I did.'

'What was your impression of all you saw and heard?'

'Is that really important, Mr Hartfish?' His Lordship tapped his gold Parker pen impatiently. The damned charlatan had no respect for the rules of evidence . . .

'With respect, my Lord, I'm anxious to know the witness's state of mind prior to the meeting in question.'

Without waiting for Sir John's views on the matter he continued: 'Shall I repeat the question?'

'No – it isn't necessary. I watched Wyatt very carefully – at the Press conference – and later. Although I considered the man had gone too far in violating the Queen's person – I felt his arguments from a constitutional point of . . .'

'Never mind his arguments.'

'Very well . . . I was impressed by the man's obvious sincerity.'

'Really?'

'I believed then and I believe now, that right or wrong, he acted purely out of concern for his country.'

Hartfish considered Rankin for a long, sinister moment. A witness ought to know better than that, he seemed to suggest – especially in times like these. The distinguished audience stirred like basking sharks scenting a drowning man. Merely a question how Hartfish would turn the matter to his advantage.

'Is that the reason you gave him your unqualified support?'

'No!'

'You mean your support was unqualified for other reasons?'

'No – I only – my support certainly was not unqualified.'

'You cooperated in expectation of some advantage – an increase of power perhaps?'

'Of course not!'

But the efflorescence of verbal fireworks had done its work. Rankin had unwisely spoken his mind. Sincerity, and integrity, were ugly words, capable of resurrecting other, equally fine feelings. By casting doubt on Rankin's integrity Hartfish had scotched the question of Wyatt's sincerity. Having brought his witness to heel the Attorney-General came to a point.

'At any rate, having previewed the man on your television set you felt disposed to attend the meeting to which you were invited?'

'It wasn't a question of disposition. There seemed no other way of assessing the situation, of deciding how much real power the man already wielded.'

Rankin's feeling was shared by his brothers in administration. By nine-thirty that morning the Chamber had filled with the higher echelons of the Civil Service. A secretariat in the galleries prepared to take notes.

They had time to debate the situation among themselves and the majority, including seconded officers of the Armed Forces, inclined to a wait-and-see attitude until Wyatt could outline his plans for a working relationship. The politicians were gone; therefore no authority existed other than Wyatt to whom they could appeal. They realized the country was in their hands subject to one man's doubtful authority. It was not a question of anxiety or elation – they were professional bureaucrats only vaguely concerned with political implications. But the inter-locked, inter-departmental relationship with a group of politicians had disappeared overnight and with the best will in the world they could not function without an ultimate authority.

Punctually at ten Wyatt appeared flanked by two officers and four civilians and sat at the Clerk's Table.

'I won't take up too much of your time, gentlemen. I hope there'll be opportunities for us to get to know each other in due course. Meantime, a matter of clearing away the generalities.

'You'll remember the Fisher Committee defined as one of the rules of conduct that a civil servant must give his undivided allegiance to the State. Kings, Queen, Parties, even Wyatts –

are of secondary importance. Whoever is in power, *de jure* or *de facto*, must accept that his position is secure only as long as the administrative machine functions smoothly.

'Accordingly you have a duty to continue serving the public no matter who takes overall power. Let's understand one another; I intend to govern – and I shall expect you to implement my policies, however unpalatable they may be to you personally. There must be less secrecy on the part of the Service and more cooperation. I shall appoint liaison officers to each department – they will act as intermediaries between the Council and the administrative arm. I promise nothing in return except non-interference in your internal affairs, a lot of hard work and the satisfaction of working for the country's good.

'It's for you to decide. You may resign, wait for something better while your absence creates chaos, or you may join us in a venture planned for no other purpose but to rescue this country from dying a slow and unnatural death. It's up to you gentlemen . . .'

'It is up to you gentlemen,' Hartfish repeated slowly. 'By that I take it to mean you had a choice; either you remained loyal to your Queen, to a lawfully constituted government not to mention the people, or you forswore your loyalty in order to serve the country through the medium of a traitorous criminal.'

'It's easy to see the issue in black and white at this distance of time!' Rankin blurted the words almost recklessly and with a moment to spare for repentance. These were not the days to protest too much. Retribution was taking strange forms . . . the newly established Control Commission could review his case, demote him still further – even retire him on a punitive pension – it was happening to others, 'collaborators' who had willingly gone all the way with Wyatt. The Commission left him in no doubt; his prospects depended substantially on his showing as a prosecution witness, but no one told him his pride would be pilloried. Just go in the box and tell them you were wrong – a public confession old boy – that's all the Pro-Go wants. A Home Office crony had done just that and got off scot free ... but no reservations, no arguing ... he must take care.

'I quite agree.' Hartfish was amiable, placating – inwardly he seethed. This fool's reaction was contrary to the agreement. Essential that all senior civil servants recanted in public. Their power must be diminished – they could never again be trusted. The power houses of Left and Right had never ceased to lay siege to the authoritarian stronghold of the Civil Service – not the least of its faults was its absolute incorruptibility. The decision to serve under Wyatt proved a god-sent opportunity to the champions of the New Democracy.

'But,' Hartfish continued, 'at this distance of time you no doubt realize your mistake?'

'Yes,' Rankin mumbled.

'You realize that a firm declaration of non-cooperation from you all would have rendered Wyatt completely impotent?'

'Yes.'

Hedley of the Foreign Office asked the first question:

'What guarantee do we have that the Queen's life is not imperilled?'

Wyatt knew that he had won them over to his side. Guarantees given and taken provide a basis for an understanding.

'You have my word the woman is in no danger while I remain unmolested. In time she will be freed with her family and permitted to retire into private life.'

'Having accepted the word of an obvious scoundrel you then proceeded to listen quietly as Wyatt outlined his plan for the country's rehabilitation?'

'I – we listened because –' Rankin almost continued to suggest that he, everybody, listened because they felt something had to be done. Men like the former Permanent Secretary were better qualified than most to gauge the extent of the nation's disrepair.

'... because once again we had to know what grasp the man had of the situation.'

'Can you explain what you mean by "grasp"?'

'No – that is, it isn't easy. It's the large view, the all-embracing view a man has of complex administrative machinery. If he has it he's a statesman – if he hasn't he's just another fumbling politician . . .'

'So you wanted to find out if you were dealing with a statesman before you committed yourself?'

Rankin gazed round at the distinguished members of the public filling every inch of available space. He saw nothing but hostility. The man was an obvious collaborator, and there were so many like him – ten years would be leniency . . .

'Before you committed yourself!'

Rankin . . . collaborator – forced himself to answer 'Yes.'

'And what was your personal impression of this so-called plan?'

'It – had much to commend it – or so it seemed.'

'Quite. You have, of course, revised your impression?'

Too much at stake to do otherwise, Rankin thought. But he hesitated.

'I'm waiting for your answer.' Hartfish looked angry, and stooped to whisper a few words to his junior.

'I – yes – I have,' Rankin agreed at last to the pre-cooked suggestion.

A few more questions concerning personal meetings between Wyatt and the Heads of Departments and Rankin left the witness box. The newspapers printed his evidence in full. No limit was placed on their freedom to comment adversely. An editor had been gaoled for 'supporting' Wyatt. The others excepting *The Times* took the hint.

Two days later the Control Commission received a communication from the Attorney-General.

The Commission immediately informed Rankin that his case was to be reconsidered.

A week later Rankin disappeared.

Not long after he was found in the river, suicidally wet.

9

Milly had always known it was there. She wasn't supposed to touch that drawer. Fred was very particular about it. She forgot one day – put his things away without thinking, the way one does, and there it was, under the pullover she'd given him last Christmas, horrible black thing next to a small cardboard box. Bullets she called them but the label said cartridges. She worried about it, especially with Fred keeping peculiar company.

'I thought I told you not to . . .!'

She never opened that drawer again – always meant to ask what he was doing with it in the house – but courage doesn't grow on trees.

As if things weren't bad enough. They were threatening to take away the carpet; then this Captain somebody and all that business about the Queen and now Fred acting strange and talking worse. Not that that was surprising. The world hadn't been as good to Fred as he deserved. Still he might've kept his job a bit longer. Especially now the baby was coming.

The imposing bulk of Sir Timon Marsh was as impressive in its own way as his Seifert designed office block behind Fleet Street. He dwarfed the well-built five-eleven of Baynard, who showed him into Wyatt's room and left the two men alone.

Marsh was a tycoon who did nothing in a hurry. He eased himself into a large armchair and for some moments nothing was said. Dynamic in their different ways they frankly summed each other up, Wyatt penetrative, Marsh speculatively from behind pebble-thick spectacles.

'Last time I sat here,' Marsh reminisced, 'I talked and Wrigley listened. I suppose times change.' His manner was easy as the second million, the drawling tones deceptively bland.

'You didn't come here to do a little name-dropping?'

Marsh checked visibly, then smiled with buttered-toast

warmth. As a man of business he liked the implied invitation to come to the point.

'I guess I didn't,' he agreed. 'Still I'm not so hard-boiled I can't appreciate the auspicious occasion – they don't come that often. Anyway I'm glad you could spare me a few minutes.'

'I don't spare my time to anybody. It's given freely.'

Sir Timon raised a hand in mock deprecation. 'Steady on young feller. Rule number one – don't give anything away – especially time. Bit of advice for you though I don't suppose you'll take it. Make 'em wait. Don't be punctual for appointments – don't see anyone on the dot. The way you've done things, you've got opponents. Well – nothing punctures opposition so much as keeping 'em hanging around. Time's what you do with it. God Almighty, you got the Houses of Parliament why not Big Ben too?'

Wyatt smiled and had no trouble liking the man.

'It's okay to smile at me, I'm harmless, but don't do it for everyone – slows your reactions, while you're pulling your face into shape for pleasantries the bastard's knife is half-way to your back – believe me I know and you'll find out – especially you.'

'I'll remember,' Wyatt promised, and waited.

'It's about this statement you just released to the Press this morning . . .' Marsh began.

'You're printing it?'

'Sure we're printing it – so will the others. You could recite "The Last Rose of Summer" backwards and we'd all print it – that's what power is about. No – I just want to know if you're serious.'

Wyatt looked puzzled.

'On the level,' Marsh amended.

'Didn't you watch TV last night?'

'I never watch TV.'

'Your man covered the Press Conference.'

'I never read my own papers.'

'As bad as that?'

'No – I only read the balance sheets – anything else I want to know I find out for myself.'

'All right, Mr Marsh, I'm serious.'

'That's all I wanted to know. Y'know I said to one of my editors: I thought I knew all about takeover bids but this is ridiculous. Course, I don't like what you did to the Royal Family – but funnier things happen these days. I guess your good fortune is most people know it and don't care any more.'

'What's worrying you?'

'It says here: "government by decree". Think it'll work?'

'For the time being.'

'A phased advance towards a Republic. Think they'll buy it?'

'Why should they? they'll get it for nothing – the Monarchy was costing them money.'

'Oh yes – I heard about your arguments – you swung a lot of people with that two-thirds non-representative line.'

'That was my intention.'

'I'll tell you what really worries me,' Marsh continued. 'You can make a Republic – take our titles away with a stroke of the pen – personally it won't worry me, I've got a better one.'

'The Overlord of Fleet Street.'

Marsh chuckled: 'Like most titles it does me too much justice – as I say, all this you can do – but can you give the people common sense?'

'You can give it room for manoeuvre. They've got their share.'

'So?'

'So if they're treated responsibly they'll react accordingly.'

'Trust the people. I hate to think how many politicians came a cropper on that one.'

'I'm not a politician.'

'Maybe – but man's a political animal –'

'That's the trouble, the people're tired of being treated like circus elephants, waltzing to the crack of a whip. Once in a while it gets beneath their skins, they turn and crush the trainer.'

'Where does that leave you?'

'When the clowns arrive everyone's happy.'

Marsh smiled: 'Well have a good run for your money. I just wish I had your faith in human nature – when I look at

people then think about politicians I'm glad I'm a newspaper-
man – and when I see myself in a mirror I'm glad I'll be dead.
What makes you think they'll read your decrees?'

'I don't. I just think they have a right to the opportunity of
seeing for themselves what we intend to do.'

'Hansard?'

'Have you ever tried to read Hansard?'

'I see what you mean. Government White Papers?'

'Too exclusive.'

'I don't want to blow a trumpet but we covered Parliamentary business pretty thoroughly in our big papers.'

'You were wasting your time. Mud-slinging and a level of
debate they wouldn't allow at the Mad Hatter's tea-party.'

'You win Captain – for the time being.'

He inched his way out of the chair, stood and gravely scru-
tinized Wyatt's face for a long minute, then grinned like a
heavily disguised Puck.

'Almost went out of my head. I meant to ask, what made
you quit the Army?'

'I was tired of giving orders. Why not ask me why I joined?'

'I'll wait for your biography. They'll write books about you
when you're dead – how about that?'

'You make it sound imminent.'

'Gamblers are bad insurance risks. Your dice are okay. But
dice can be switched . . .'

Marsh's strange, semi-transatlantic way of saying he was on
Wyatt's side.

Extract from daily report to Perrins of the Special Branch
by Detective-Inspector Walsh in charge of 'The Shadow
Squad':

Wyatt seldom moves out of the Palace precincts. He has been
seen once on the Terrace – could easily be picked off by a fair
shot with a telescopic rifle. He undoubtedly has a group of men
specially attached for duty as a bodyguard, but a Sergeant Jennings
appears to be the only man in constant attendance. More of the
Buckingham Palace garrison have withdrawn to the Tower.

Very few people have called on Wyatt so far. The most interesting of these was the United States Ambassador, who seemed anxious to preserve some sort of incognito ...

'You understand that this is strictly *ex officio*, Mr Wyatt. For obvious reasons I can't be seen to contact you in a capacity which obligates me solely to the Head of State.'

Wyatt thought about it. '*Ex officio* ... I'm afraid the distinction is too nice for me. Either you're here recognizing *de facto* authority or you shouldn't be here *de jure*-wise in which case I'm talking to myself and I don't have time for that.'

'Okay, Captain.' Jarman dropped the CD plates with relief, and became as unpleasantly expansive as an atom bomb cloud.

'I don't have any official briefing on how to go along with you – it's an incredible situation – incredible – but don't think we don't sympathize a little – revolution made us what we are today.'

In that case the sooner I give myself up the better, Wyatt thought acidly, and said merely: 'You have much to thank the English for.'

'How's that?'

'We set the fashion.'

'Oh, the Commonwealth. Well we've all grown up since then, Captain. Still – you're in and everyone has to rub along together best they can in this ole world.'

Southern fried with napalm jelly, you canting bastard.

But Wyatt only said, 'Well?'

'As I say, an incredible situation, so off the record I, that is the Administration would like some indication as to your policy *vis-à-vis* the United States. We'd like to assume as long as you're in the saddle *status quo*'ll be maintained.'

'Don't you read the newspapers either, Mr Jarman?'

'The Press Conference? Sure we know what you said – but no one takes it seriously in Washington I assure you.'

'Oh?' For the first time since it all began Wyatt found he was worried.

'Part of the established procedure. When irregulars knock off a régime like you did they've got to have an Aunt Sally – and Uncle Sam fills the bill – rouses the worst in people – makes 'em feel like li'l David mixing it with Goliath and you're in. You can rest assured Captain we understand and we don't hold it against you one bit.'

'Go on.'

'Well – er – as I said, we'd welcome an indication that in fact we can count on a continuation of good relations.'

Wyatt fought to hide his anger, wondered if the day would ever come when a man's words would be taken to mean exactly what they said. He damned all double thinking double dealers to hell as he answered.

'Your Administration must be very worried.'

'I don't get you.'

'Not only the first, but also a great foreign power, making what – unofficial soundings? Either the President is just curious or very anxious –'

'Wait a minute –'

'It isn't the soundest policy, Mr Jarman, to seek assurances from a shaky administration unless your own happens to be in an equally shaky condition.'

Jarman sat back and exhaled a long stream of air through twitching nostrils. 'Boy – you take my goddamned breath away! You're talking about you and LBJ in the same mouthful. I reckon you've got it coming – boy you sure got it coming. The United States! Here you railroad in – not even a general – just a plain ole ornery captain from God knows where and you're telling me! th'representative of the United States of America ... you who put that poor little woman and her kids – do you know they're saying *prayers* for her in Washington? and the Government lawfully elected by the sacred will of the citizens of the United Kingdom – and now here you come lousing everything up just when ...'

'Just when you thought you had us where you want us?' Wyatt inquired.

Jarman pressed his lips to near invisibility. 'Then you weren't kidding last night?'

'Kidding the British people went out with the Monarchy.'

'And the arms deal?'

'Off.'

'You won't find it as easy as that!'

'Easier than sweating to find a thousand million for a pile of sophisticated junk.'

'Sophis...? What about the Alliance?'

Wyatt rose to his feet as Baynard appeared by prearrangement.

'You'll be informed in due course,' he replied.

Jarman also stood. He made a poor effort to keep his temper.

'You mean you intend to make a decision *before* informing the President!'

'First the British people, then maybe the President. And you're at liberty to inform Mr Johnson that if he dosn't like it he can fly here for once and argue with me.'

'Let me tell you, the British people won't stand for it!'

'We'll see.'

'This is unheard of!'

'That, Mr Jarman,' Wyatt concluded, 'has been the trouble. Good day to you.'

Baynard straightened his face in time to open the door as the enraged diplomat turned and strode out like a rumble of Texas thunder.

Preliminary report on Wyatt prepared by the Special Branch. Filed October –th.

Richard Antony Wyatt, born London, 17th October 1924. Only son of Jennifer, née Morgan and William Richard Wyatt. William Wyatt was called to the Bar in 1909 at the age of 23, practised in London till the outbreak of World War I, a brilliant career predicted. Joined Inns of Court Regiment November 1914. Wounded at the Somme, mentioned in dispatches. MC 1916. Head wounds in January 1918. Returned to England – long period in hospital. Salesman 1919–1925. Established small toy-factory in 1926 which failed in 1931. Wife died in 1932 and he appears to have taken to the road with his son. Known to have worked in fairgrounds for the next five years. Set up as a fair booth proprietor in 1936 – travelled all over the country. Wyatt apparently assisting his father until called up in 1943. Education sketchy but considered 'knowledgeable' according to WO records. Drafted into commando-training course and took part in Normandy landings. Father killed 1944 – flying-bomb incident. Demobilized in 1947 with rank of acting Sergeant. Cambridge University on a Service grant, studied Social History, left abruptly after two terms without giving reasons. No record of employment, but known that he joined various political societies usually resigning membership after a few weeks. No known political affiliation to date. Rejoined Army in 1949. Recommended for officers' course and passed out top of his group. Records state splendid tactical grasp. Commissioned with — Regiment. Served in Korea, decorated for bravery; refusal to wear ribbon taken as personal idiosyncrasy. Subsequently served at home and abroad, gazetted Captain 1958. Exemplary conduct. Special features: his present commanding officer seems to be pro-Wyatt. All officers with knowledge of Wyatt remark his eloquence. Quiet and pleasant spoken, but effective when discussing politics. At such times he was able to command everyone's attention in the officers' mess. As one major put it, 'this was remarkable in itself'. No evidence as yet of women in his life. Has been heard to describe himself as 'an incurable bachelor'.

This is the Home Service BBC Radio 4 with the six o'clock news and Radio Newsreel. First the news:

The Right Honourable Mr Kenneth Wrigley is to broadcast to the nation in three hours' time.

Contrary to expectations, the Bank of England did not have to intervene today to support the Pound following yesterday's events. The Pound in fact closed steady and at one time moved to a new high at 2.42 before dropping to 2.39 $\frac{7}{16}$. Official observers consider that this indicates a policy of wait and see, both at home and abroad. The major banks report that cash calls have shown no abnormal rise and prices on the Stock markets fluctuated marginally though Gilt-edge and War Loans showed fractional losses.

Britain's representative at the United Nations flew home today for talks with the leader of the Revolutionary movement. He told reporters at Kennedy airport he was 'absolutely convinced' that common sense would prevail in the near future and that he would return as representative of a restored Government and Monarchy.

A protest rally is to be held tonight at the Central Hall in Westminster. Several eminent personalities are to speak and the occasion will be televised tonight at eight o'clock in place of scheduled programmes.

Neither MPs nor leaders of the two main parties have been available for comment today. It is thought probable that their individual views will wait upon Mr Wrigley's statement.

The Archbishop of Canterbury has called for a Day of National Prayer on Sunday. He himself will lead prayers for the Queen's safety in St Paul's.

It has been 'business as usual' in London today. One foreign visitor described the atmosphere as reminiscent of Britain in 1940. 'Tense, expectant, but cheerful.'

Throughout the day crowds thronged the approaches to the Tower of London to catch glimpses of soldiers patrolling the ramparts. Six girls from Australia have vowed to remain on their knees in prayer until the Royal Family is safely delivered . . .

Early this morning a woman wrapped herself in a large Union Jack and leaped from the observation platform of the GPO Tower. Before officials could prevent her she fell to her death screaming 'I am a victim of Communism'.

World reaction continues to suggest a feeling of stunned surprise tempered by cautious interest or outright condemnation of Captain Wyatt's seizure of power. The question everyone asks is 'what will he do now?'.

Radio Newsreel this evening is mainly concerned with Commonwealth reaction but first a report from Michael Audley in Washington . . .

Martin Rigg sat in a secluded corner of the main smoking room at Bookers and eyed Langley with studied, almost insolent disdain. He tapped the report which His Lordship had conned with some care between snuffles and returned to him.

'Where are we then? In the hands of a fairground entertainer and you say "do nothing".'

'I do and I say it again if you wish. Country isn't falling apart, even the police have to admit that – by the way has Wrigley seen this report?'

'Naturally. He asked the SB to prepare it.'

'Did he now!'

Rigg fixed a balefully suspicious eye on the old man. 'Well, I assumed – didn't he?'

'No, Martin – I did. D'you suppose Wrigley would think of doing such a thing? How d'you know he's seen it?'

'I rang him to see what sort of line he intends to take. He said he'd just received confidential information that could be the end of Wyatt the moment it's made public.'

Langley looked pleased with himself. 'True to form – he'll fall right in ... and you'd have done the same given half a chance. While we're on the subject don't get thick with the Socialists – ostensibly this is their problem – they were in office – they got kicked out. Let 'em find their own way back – if they can.'

'This is a common cause –'

'Common fiddlesticks! I tell you it all works in our favour if we keep our heads.'

Rigg thought sourly, and that's how your blasted family's stayed the course for four hundred years.

Langley was chuckling like a skeleton in the larder. 'Given anything to see his face when this Wyatt ... only yesterday was it? Reminds me of a little horror at Eton. Finch-Fellows – yes – Finch-Fellows – eating ice-cream or something of the kind – along comes the head boy and takes it away – worth it for his expression ...' Langley almost choked on the puerile recollection then lapsed further into a seventy years old dream ... 'and here I am, and poor old Double F blown to God knows where at Le Cateau half a century since ...' then abruptly: 'Mark my words, Wrigley'll show his ineptitude all over again, "we are in the hands," he'll say in his best grammar school tones, "of a fairground entertainer". Won't be able to resist it – but the people will.'

Rigg fretted visibly: 'You seem anxious to strengthen Wyatt's position!'

'Why not? Let him command the heights – He'll fall that much lower in the people's estimation.'

'– country's in the hands of a fool!' Rigg spat the words through a Scotch mist blown from a perpetually wet mouth: 'only a lunatic could allow his opponents complete freedom of the mass media at this stage.'

'Only a fool would take advantage of the fact.' Langley spoke above Rigg's head, finished his brandy and wondered if his cold had really passed away.

Somewhere in the Kremlin a dozen sober-suited men sit in rigid silence at the long mahogany table, they sit with the strange immobility of hungry mourners waiting for the will to be brought in and read. A few are fingering the typed reports before them with infinitesimal movements, others stare straight ahead as the Chairman comments at great length on Wyatt, circumspection and the need for purity of thought to promote true revolution.

'. . . unless it is based on strong ideological principles in accordance with Marxist-Leninist theory, revolution so called is mere rebellion – a Menshevik spark of discontentment carrying within itself the seed of extinction. Our responsibility at large is to the Workers' movement, not to bourgeois reaction to a pseudo-socialist conspiracy . . . with the glorious exception of Cuba – doctrinal revolution died in 1917. The October tocsin sounded across the world, calling on the great middle classes to double their defences – the result is that a people's uprising will never again be possible among the older nations. Had this Wyatt been a true man of the people, he must inevitably have been crushed; but he appears to be tolerated. In view of the overwhelmingly bourgeois composition of Britain's population this is suspect . . . we must conclude that the event has no great significance in itself and consequently cannot affect the international scene . . . if we are satisfied beyond doubt that we are witnessing a drastic redrafting of bourgeois pretensions, then this Captain Wyatt cannot hope even for a measure of moral support from the Soviet Union.'

The Chairman, secure in his middle-class income, assured of

his middle-class privileges, would doubtless have been surprised to learn that Wyatt neither expected nor hoped for help from anyone.

10

Builders' lorries were converging on Regent's Park. Foremen were already on the site poring over plans of a cage-like structure – a simple enough job – it could be run up overnight. Bound to keep the animals awake though. What was it for? No one knew – Wyatt's orders . . . let's get on with it then.

Pender headed a group from the Home Office, Collet of the Lord Chancellor's Office was there with his subordinates. Ubiquitous Treasury men represented the nation's purse-strings, the Lord Chief Justice felt it his duty to hold a watching brief and surprisingly, the Police Commissioner had decided without too much heart-searching to accept Wyatt's second invitation. With secretaries, reporters, foreign observers and the public who were freely admitted to all meetings the House appeared quite respectably populated. Far more so, *The Times* political correspondent observed, than on the occasion when the 'former House of Commons debated the extremely important question of its own procedural reform. 25 members were present.'

The Decree Concerning Crimes and Penalties had been read by Wyatt; he had carefully explained each point. His audience was impressed though obviously not to the point of total acceptance. There would be protests and reservations. He showed little anxiety as he sat, less, certainly, than the members of his Council. This was the régime's first administrative venture. Some of them felt his plan was hasty and ill-considered. If the bureaucrats and other lawfully constituted bodies refused to implement his decisions – their decisions – the result could be disastrous. But Wyatt was as a firebrand to a sack of woodshavings; he had long since burned their objections to useless cinders.

'We cannot succeed if we dare to attempt seven-league strides in carpet slippers!'

Remembering the scorn in his tone, they waited, hoping he could do as much with men like Pender and Collet, men entrenched behind the ramparts of their own judgement and experience. They had to trust in Wyatt. There was no alternative.

'It's all too simple.' Collet spoke first.

'Premature,' the LCJ rumbled.

'And too severe in my opinion,' Pender added.

The Police Commissioner said nothing.

Wyatt sat back in his chair, hands resting on the table before him, and stared up into the limitless reaches of the mind's capabilities.

'God save us! Too simple ... as though we were searching for a complicated solution to a basically simple problem. Premature! Are we desperately in need of means to reduce an appalling crime rate or shall we leave things as they are, procrastinate? Too severe! Either we demonstrate that justice means what it says or it is nothing!'

He stood suddenly, dominantly, his eyes blazing like lasque diamonds. And his followers began to relax a little.

'What in God's name do you want; more and more prisons – to hold more and more criminals – to create the need for more and more reform? Do I have to tell you the situation is so desperate there are men *waiting* to go to prison – it's our national housing problem with its system of priorities all over again – farcical!

'Too simple ... but I tell you the Ten Commandments are still worth more than fifty battalions of psychearchs who have murdered the very concept of good and evil. Whether hell or heaven exist I've no way of knowing. But this much I do know – we are all of us, guilty or innocent, good citizens or bad, lost in a purgatory of uncertainty.'

They continued to listen ...

This is the Home Service BBC Radio 4. We now repeat the statement made earlier this evening by the Right Honourable Kenneth Wrigley on our Television service ...

'I want to talk to you tonight about the events of the last forty-eight hours, a period surely without parallel in our history. Y'know, it's hard to believe this is Great Britain in 196–, hard to believe this old country of ours should be in the hands of organized thugs doing their best to turn back the clock a few hundred years. A queen – our Queen – in the Tower, a Parliament dismissed, by what? A mere fairground entertainer masquerading as an Army captain, decking himself out as some kind of latter-day Cromwell, like a third-rate actor striving for external effects. This fugitive from a world of roundabouts and coconut shies, doesn't, it seems, like the way this country is run. So he flourishes a gun and says: "I'll run it my way." Well, I've got some news for this Captain Wyatt. If he thinks he can push this country farther and faster with a gun in its back – he's got another think coming. There's only one answer to discontent with a government – vote for another party. Behaving like those South American states where coup succeeds coup, where all appearance of democratic government is illusory, is not our way – and never will be.

'You're probably wondering why the Government – my Government – doesn't do something. I wish I could give you some assurance, some measure of comfort. But ours is a cruel dilemma. Any precipitate action on our part could endanger not only Her Majesty's life but that of her entire family. Wyatt's only bargaining counter, his sole claim to power, is through her, as he well knows, and we dare not act while she remains in rebel hands.

'Meantime my advice to you is to go about your everyday affairs and obey only the laws made in accordance with custom and the Constitution. Have nothing to do with the so-called decrees issued by the rebels. They are not worth the paper they're written on. And pray. Pray for the safety of our Queen who even now suffers for her people, for you and me.

'If she is watching or listening, in that cruel house of sorrow, I send her the only message permitted to me. Be of good heart; these dark days will have an end, and you will be restored to your Crown, your Throne, and ever more securely to the deep and abiding affection of your loyal subjects.'

But the session at Westminster continued far into the night – long after Wrigley had said his prayers and retired to bed. Wyatt seemed inexhaustible. He argued and elucidated with superabundant, almost demonic energy. Hour followed hour as he countered objections: the filming, the barbarity, the feasibility of labour camps; cut through obstacles, ridiculed pleas for more time to prepare legislation. And yet, as time sifted through to ante meridian, the audience, undiminished, caught fire from his burning enthusiasm. Men who had started cold with opposition grew lukewarm by degrees, reaching boiling point almost as he expounded ideas with a fervour that surprised even his own followers. Something of the pioneer spirit sent new blood coursing through old and cynical arteries long since hardened by 'impossibilities'. The Lord Chief Justice himself spoke equivocally of 'legal buccaneering' with the ghost of a glint in his eye.

'This business tomorrow,' he inquired. 'How do you hope to persuade Justice Bourne that your experiment's worth a trial?'

'Don't worry about Bourne – I'll persuade him,' was all Wyatt said.

In the end they accepted his proposals, set deadlines of mere days to settle a thousand and one administrative details and agreed that quasi-legislation should be retrospective. All-out support from the Police Commissioner through to the Treasury was implied or promised by a nod, and while the presses were throwing off the last copies carrying news of Decree One, many officials returned to their offices with oil still to burn, determined to get the great experiment off the ground ...

'WYATT ISSUES FIRST DECREE.' 'THE CREEPING SHADOW OF THE REPUBLIC.' Murderous headlines meant to send shivers down the backs of aspiring middle-class readers. But the *Daily Compress* had chilled the spines of the faithful for so long that the collective backbone was now as frozen as Twit's Green Peas and twice as impervious.

The morning air was alive with excited speculation. 'Crimes and penalties – putting them in cages. Well I never! Who'd've thought of that one? It's different – might work. Worth a try. And what about France, eh?'

Wyatt had given them crime and punishment as *hors d'œuvres*. They swallowed the delicacy and were ready for more. Britain was happier than it had been for a long time. Even Fleet Street was cheerful. With sensational events in full spate came an insatiable demand for news. Sagging circulation figures soared and Wyatt's administration was paying standard rates for the publication of the decrees ...

New developments. 'France,' screamed the headlines of late London editions, 'gives qualified recognition to Wyatt.'

'Last night the Élysée issued the following communiqué. The President of the French Republic has indicated his readiness to acknowledge Captain Wyatt's administration. The President doubts the wisdom of allowing a major Power to remain diplomatically quarantined for more than a few days having regard to the present international perspective.

'While reserving the right to withdraw recognition in the event of failure to honour obligations and trade commitments already agreed, the President wishes it to be known that he warmly applauds the avowed intention of Captain Wyatt to steer a great ship of State back into the High Seas of Destiny.'

'Damned, infernal nerve! Still living down Waterloo with his cheap jibes!' While Rigg and many others fumed at his latest expression of *entente* cordiality, Langley nursed another cold in his Jacobean bedroom. As he sipped camomile tea and nibbled a dry rusk he chuckled over *The Times* report.

'Calculated – very shrewd – very.' Again the Earl cackled like the snapping of kindlewood: 'One soldier to another. Destiny!' His rheumy eyes narrowed to gaze up at his father's portrait on the opposite wall. The fifteenth Earl stared back, his frown of displeasure seemed more pronounced than ever. Langley stuck out his chin.

'Don't give a damn what you think Pa – we do nothing. It's cheap and it pays.'

Then he sneezed three times in rapid succession.

*

Two in the morning. Why should he come home at two in the morning? Milly Lavery forced more washing into the Machinomatic, far more than was good for it. She never could understand why it always broke down. Things shouldn't break down while you're still paying for them. Afterwards was different. He definitely opened and closed that drawer before he undressed and got into bed. Definitely! She switched on and listened vaguely to the humming of the motor ... He looked worried this morning – read the paper more than usual ... something clicked in her mind as the washing machine choked on its overload and slowed to uselessness. Of course! All that excitement about whatsisname. Right worked up about it last night Fred was. Knew a lot about politics did Fred – what was it he belonged to once – some Labour thing – Union of – the English Union ... he'd have been a smashing politician given half a chance – Alf Pearson was a member too – used to be. She remembered how the pair of them sat up half the night discussing politics over their beer and how the Jews and niggers ought to be thrown out of the country. So there was nothing to worry about; like he told her – he'd been having a chat over at Alf's place about Captain whatsisname.

She sat down for a quiet cigarette and wondered whether she needed to go out shopping after all.

Early editions of the London evening papers for October 25th carried the following:

Police are investigating the shooting of a night watchman on the premises of Ludlow and Co., an engineering firm in South London. Detectives keep watch at the bedside of 59-year-old George Crabtree who was shot and severely wounded when he disturbed two intruders in the accounts office. A member of the firm said today they might have got away with three hundred pounds, certainly not more. Meanwhile the police believe Mr Crabtree may be able to give a description of the gunmen when he recovers consciousness.

He seemed to glide through the corridors of the Commons like a dark Dominican friar hurrying to Compline; his dark angular features might have been the work of a medieval stonemason. Bourne J. graced the Bench with the dignity of an Inquisitor, but one no longer warmed by the fires. He was typical of those professional men who retire as far as possible from a world in which they are still forced to labour. A cold fish, many considered, but a fine judge. He followed Baynard into the room and experienced a rare moment of surprise. Face to face with the usurper he instantly recognized something of himself.

'Sit down, won't you?'

Long after Baynard withdrew, the Judge, ignoring the offered chair, stared with undisguised frankness at the man before him, as though questioning in depth a witness's credibility.

'The Lord Chief Justice called on me this morning. He seemed most impressed by your performance.' The words were cold and distant as an east wind in Siberia. Wyatt ignored them and came to the point.

'I asked you to come because I want to talk about Simpson.'

'So I was informed. I made it clear that I could do nothing not consistent with my position as a member of the Judiciary – whoever is in power.'

'That's natural enough. My concern though is for Simpson and the country at large.'

Bourne J. nodded: 'Then I suppose we can be said to understand one another.'

'This morning you'll no doubt sentence this man to life imprisonment for the murder of a police officer.'

'No doubt.'

'Do you consider the sentence effective?'

'It's – inadequate.'

'I said effective.'

Wyatt saw the cold grey eyes flicker and narrow. Again the Judge contemplated this phenomenon who levelled Parliaments in minutes and cross-examined Her Former Majesty's judges in almost the same breath. Quite suddenly he turned to the chair and sat.

'No, Captain Wyatt. It is not effective.'

'Presumably because it neither deters nor reforms?'

'Quite so.'

'Merely postpones a troublesome problem for a statutory term of years?'

The Judge almost smiled. 'You could put it like that.'

'Are you one of those who thinks he deserves a more severe punishment because his victim happens to be a police officer?'

'The police have a difficult task –'

'So do old ladies or children when it comes to resisting violent assaults.'

'Your conclusion?'

'There's no such thing as a more deserving victim. They all end up dead or raped, or injured in mind and body.'

A long pause before Bourne inquired: 'You're asking for Simpson to be made the subject of a test – an experiment?'

'We have to begin somewhere.'

'By degrading Simpson?'

'No ... by deglamorizing crime.'

The Judge was clearly startled into awareness. Those three words illuminated the whole of Wyatt's meaning – shed light on the purpose underlying his first decree. Simpson was merely the example. Floodgates of perception opened and the possibilities offered by Wyatt's solution poured through.

'I see ... this decree – it's clumsily worded.'

'The man who stops to polish his armour during the battle will never polish it again ...'

'I could refuse to be a party to your intentions.'

'Then I'd have to set up a tribunal – and that would be illegal.'

Both men dared to smile imperceptibly.

'Perhaps I may be permitted to ask a question or two?'

Wyatt nodded, knowing he'd gained the day.

'How powerful are you?'

'I'm here.'

'But for how much longer?'

'Who can say? The Administration is on my side out of sheer necessity – the people are with me – out of curiosity.'

'And you want me to give a demonstrable lead to my profession?'

'I want nothing that cannot be agreed between men above considerations of self-interest.'

Not another word passed between them. Only the long searching stare from one grown a little warmer by curiosity and a few degrees of understanding. A lesser man than Wyatt might well have doubted the Judge's intentions. After all, he'd not said, in so many words, that he would implement the provisions of the Decree.

Reuter report, 25th October: Several Latin American states including Brazil, Uruguay and Chile have signified their intention of according recognition to Wyatt's régime. Reliable sources consider certain remarks of ex-Prime Minister Wrigley in his national broadcast are responsible for this decision.

The Lord General strode about Wyatt's office like a runaway tank. Clad for the occasion in the grandest uniform he possessed, every medal and order he could lay hands on dripped from him like tired leaves on a dried-up birch tree. Wyatt watched with undisguised contempt as the jingling general worked himself up to an all-out offensive.

'Intending to abolish titles are you? Damned three-pipped whippersnapper! Try taking mine away from me! Fought for it – my country's thanks for helping win the blasted war. Don't think you'll get away with it. A word from me and the Army'll make mincemeat of you. My name still means something y'know!'

'Your name,' said Wyatt, 'doesn't mean a bloody thing. Your title means even less, however impressive it may look on a company prospectus. The only thing the public knows about you is that you're a rather stupid little man who makes rather stupid statements in the Lords about everything under the sun except the subject of your right to waste everybody's time simply because you put a division or two in the right place at the right moment. Fought for it! Did you bleed for it Lord General – or did you buy your title with other men's blood? Don't prate to me about your fighting exploits! Get back to your television audience and tell them the truth about war –

make them hear the sickening squelch of a bayonet in the guts – make them smell the burning flesh in a knocked-out tank – make them hate the sight of you for being a part of the whole rotten business – when you can do that Lord General, you may just be worth one of those medals – for conspicuous humility.

'Now I advise you to get out before my sergeant sets eyes on you. He fought under your command . . .'

The Lord General went home and sat for a long time, staring at the unfinished manuscript of the third volume of his memoirs.

The court sat at half past ten. Ushers were hard put to it to silence a buzz of conversation rising from the stalls to the gallery. Word had spread that Simpson was to be the first subject of Wyatt's decree. While lawyers argued the consequences, reporters devised a tic-tac system to transmit the sentence even as it was being prononunced. No one who knew Bourne the judge could really believe him capable of straying from Law's lane. Messengers were ready to carry the verdict to other courts, and few judges that morning gave undivided attention to their own proceedings until they knew the outcome of the test case, or 'Bourne's tribulation' in the words of legal wags.

The prisoner was a lean, thirty-eight-year-old individual of no fixed address, a former member of a 'protection' gang living parasitically off the gambling clubs and betting shops of West London. The facts were brutally plain; defence was a mere formality. He had shot and killed a constable while resisting arrest, and stood now to hear sentence passed. Nothing apprehensive and all studied nonchalance, ignorant of decrees, he knew only that he could expect the 'lot' which is life, which isn't bad at the current rates of exchange and a sight better than topping. So he waited for the inevitable, wondering if he was getting enough from the *Sunday Sludge* for a story like his, while 'Bourne yesterday' did his little patter.

'. . . in sentencing you to life imprisonment –' the Judge paused for a negligible second, aware perhaps for the first time in his judicial career of the court's profound attention.

'– I would be acting according to the law as of yesterday.

But times and circumstances change. It is not for me to question the wisdom or validity of the theories propounded by those now in power. But as a servant of Justice I am bound to admit that new solutions must be found, new methods tried, if we are to accept the challenge thrown down by you and your kind.

'I have no hesitation therefore in applying the provisions of Decree One to your case, by which I sentence you to a period of exhibition in a public place, such period not to exceed three days. You will then be removed to a labour camp for a minimum period of five years. Particulars of your crime will be posted at the place of exhibition.'

The court shimmered with barely suppressed excitement. So one judge at least was with Wyatt. Justice was to be done but differently – shades of Solomon, how differently! Heads turned, necks craned to catch Simpson's reaction.

The little man had turned pale with the effort of understanding – grasped the rail before him as the warders edged forward. You could never tell what they'd do after sentence. Most took it quietly . . .

The killer opened his mouth, started to speak, faltered then swung round to face the crowded court.

'Exhibition! He's off his bleedin' head!' he screamed. 'He can't do that to me! I'm a human being not a bleedin' animal! I demand justice!' He fought the warders with the despair of a man fending off insanity. 'I'll appeal – you bastards – not an animal . . . human being . . . they can't . . .'

Long after he was hustled from the dock those in court heard his cries outraging like black bile from the cells below. They sat in stunned silence, realizing that they listened to more than a protest. The sentence was already taking effect. A man can accept loss of liberty, even the fact of his death to come; but to strip him of his dignity, to strike at his self-esteem is a terrible kind of execution, even though no blood is shed and no vertebra snaps.

11

French the Gypsy, silent and watchful; Baynard, eager as a buccaneer; Morrison, fiery as an overflowing lamp; Dowson, Professor, forgotten economist, a white-haired venerable; Sinclair, austere, scholarly and no stranger to the Foreign Office; Lorimer, lawyer and firestorming republican; thus the Council of Six.

They met as Simpson struggled and fought in the dock for the old order, deliberated while unemployed politicians, place-seekers and assorted delegations cooled their heels in the cheerless, powerless corridors outside.

And listened as Wyatt reviewed the situation. No serious opposition. Chief Constables throughout the country following the Police Commissioner's lead. The Commissioner! Wyatt explains with a spectral smile, 'I doubled his salary – immediate pay increases for all ranks – a promise of more civilians employed in routine duties.'

'Even so,' Dowson wonders, 'can we depend on them?'

'They recognize they've nothing to lose, something already gained, they can go all the way with us and not a single scruple stopping them – why? Because if I fall, no restored government would dare purge their ranks – bad for morale and whoever heard of lions being thrown to the Christians?'

'But will they co-operate?' Sinclair persists.

'They'll wait – and that's a form of cooperation. They'll keep an eye on us as an each-way bet – just to prove they're doing something in the way of opposition.'

He swept through their questions with storm force eloquence, then soared to the heights of monologue – analysed the grounds on which they could hope for UN recognition, predicted accurately official Commonwealth reaction based on the forthcoming Ottawa Conference. Then, nearer home, outlined plans to help the short end of the affluent society, railwaymen and the rest of the underpaid brigade – new wage agreements – not later but now. Can the nation afford it? 'Afford it! God in heaven, when the Singapore base costs us a hundred millions a year? Enough flesh on that white elephant alone to feed the old-age pensioners, to hell with what they do East of Suez!'

But even Wyatt has to pause for breath. Sinclair voices his doubts about the Simpson plan.

'We couldn't have started on a better note,' Wyatt assures him. 'Forget the higher purpose if it helps, and remember we needed a strong point of reference. Simpson is our statement of policy come to life; action – swift, dramatic and effective –'

Morrison has time to mention Russia. 'It seems they don't trust our revolution.'

'Why should they? they didn't foster it.'

And so on ... but in the corridors outside many tire of waiting and go home.

No serious opposition – a few whitewashed slogans, sporadic protest meetings and letters to *The Times*. Tennis clubs buzzed with counter-revolutionary talk; smart sets in Suburbia mislaid obsessions with 'Jags' and Hondas and argued instead a multitude of plans for rescuing queens – 'and that sort of thing'. Mild and bitter rugger talk, half-hearted nonsense that did no one any great harm ...

The week-end was a yoke of working days. Wyatt and his people laboured on, conferring with senior officials of various Ministries, discussing details of future decrees, arguing the need for new trends in economic policy, creating machinery or adapting what there was for swift initiation of Wyatt's priority calls. The Council of Six toiled round most of the clock; its collective energy left the bureaucrats gasping, and Wyatt himself worked, as one Permanent Secretary later recalled, 'like a man possessed of seven devils.' They were even more astonished, perhaps, by their own increased capacity for work. Faced with brand-new concepts, daring ideas, refreshing – even dangerous – they responded to the urgency of the moment, the thrilling sense of crisis inevitably demanding the best in men

who had too often been regarded as efficient cogs in an antiquated machine driven by a doubtful dynamo fed by a series of
worn-out batteries.

Events were still keeping pace. And the new dynamo sped a
few revolutions faster that morning when Wyatt's own trusted
messengers delivered top secret notes to the representatives of
certain African states . . .

The judge had gone crazy; they couldn't persuade Simpson
otherwise. Why else was he brought back to the 'Scrubs'?
The cage wasn't ready – cage? what cage? Warder's idea of
a kinky giggle . . . he'd appeal – what d'you mean no appeal
– decree? Get stuffed! Something wrong somewhere – see the
Governor – tell that lousy lawyer to demand a retrial – no call
to go treating a man like this just because he killed a bleedin'
copper.

So when they came for him he still refused to believe it, and
fought for his right to gaol pure and simple, with TV for being
a good boy and all the other privileges dished out to dangerous lads like himself.

They got him into the van and he was driven away. The
warders, sensitive to an atmosphere of pent-up emotions, recognized a strangely muted tension imprisoning the 'Scrubs'
for the rest of the day. Like the night before execution, the old
hands said.

Simpson rubbed a bruised arm as best he could with handcuffed wrists, passed his tongue tentatively over a swollen lip,
mumbled thickly at the uniformed guards.

'Where you taking me?'

'Where you belong,' was the short answer.

'I always said you mugs belong in the nut hatch,' another
mused. 'Even I didn't know I meant a monkey house.'

The little killer blinked and creased his forehead into long
lines of disbelief. He was trying hard to understand what they
were doing to him – nothing squared with the book. He gave
up long before the prison van swung through the gates of
Regent's Park.

*

Letter to the Editor of *The Times*, Saturday 27th. Signed by a distinguished philosopher, a distinguished lady novelist, a distinguished ex-convict and a rather amusing Bishop:

Sir – It is not for us to comment on the October Takeover, nor do we feel it necessary to state the obvious fact that some such demonstration of discontent was inevitable. We may perhaps express surprise at the means by which Wyatt seized power; but if revolutions were precise escalations of discontent they could hardly occur at all.

Your columns have been freely available to the many correspondents arguing the validity of Wyatt's 'non-representative two-thirds' theory. We beg leave to protest against a larger evil than the mere overthrow of a patchwork Constitution.

Our concern is with the infamous mode of punishment alluded to in the Criminal Penalties decree. Surely, if Wyatt believes Draconian methods will stem the current crime wave and command public support, he must not only lack political sagacity, but – and what is more ominous for the country's future – he must certainly be devoid of humanitarian principles.

To cage a man is to put back the clock to the darkest hours of our history. Such a punishment is a barbarous relic, pandering to the worst instincts of the people. Above all, it must destroy much of the good work undertaken by men and women of goodwill in the sacred cause of rescuing the socially sick.

We wholeheartedly deplore these vicious sentences in the sure and certain belief that we are not alone in our condemnation. Yours etc.

Extract from a Gallup Opinion Poll concerning the Wyatt takeover, published by the *Daily Compress* October 27th.

	YES	NO	DON'T KNOW
Do you consider Wyatt's assumption of power could benefit the country?	27%	32%	41%
Do you agree that the monarchy is a 'redundant institution'?	34%	29%	37%
Do you consider Wyatt and his followers to be traitors?	26%	35%	39%

Daily Compress leader for the same date:

The findings of the Opinion Poll published on our front page prove overwhelmingly that the people are unsympathetic to the misbegotten ideals of Wyatt and his henchmen. There is only one fact in dispute: what should be done with these men when justice finally overtakes them? This paper is in no doubt. On the day of judgement the voices of eight million readers will thunder: Put them behind bars. In a zoo!

A few minutes to eleven. Barely time to swallow black coffee and none at all to study his notes before Wyatt hurried down to face a second press gathering now packed into every available inch of space the House could offer. Baynard went with him.

'It's a funny thing, Skipper, the House was already full half an hour ago – all those journalists and God knows what sitting there as if it was the most natural thing in the world.'

Wyatt said nothing; he was studying the lists of press-men and the papers and journals represented. He looked up with a slight frown.

'Something wrong?'

'I was just wondering who Mr Lister of the *Northern Mail* might be.'

'A reporter, of course.'

'Possibly – but there's no such paper – now that's what I call a really funny thing, Harry.'

At eleven o'clock precisely Wyatt took his seat and surveyed the crowded benches until silence fell. The first question came unexpectedly as he was about to speak.

'Isn't this a damned funny time to call a presss conference?'

'It is – but these are damned funny times we're living in.'

Thanks to the *Telegraph* Wyatt launched his statement on a wave of good humour.

'First – Simpson. My latest information is that with the Chief Justice's concurrence and Judge Bourne's valuable lead the judiciary almost without exception is prepared to give effect to the provisions of Decree One. Simpson is now serving the first part of his sentence. Reaction has been divided. I quote one rather stupid comment made by a paper that should know better but never will: "Public exposure alone is not enough." Of course it isn't! Who suggested that it was?

'Two ships are taking on stores and materials. In a few days' time they will sail to an uninhabited island north-west of Scotland carrying an advance party of serious offenders. A volunteer medical staff will accompany them – there will also be two qualified doctors no less qualified because they were struck off the register. Most of the men will have experience in building and ancillary trades. They will lay the foundations for a labour camp. More offenders will be drafted at intervals to create a community built, administered and supported entirely by themselves. They will work for everything they need. They will build their own recreation centres, places of worship, factories, workshops.'

An approving rustle gave a wordless benediction to Wyatt's plan.

'Are there any questions on this?'

The Morning Star: 'No supervision?'

'None.'

'Isn't that inviting anarchy?'

'Necessity is the mother of responsibility. A community without law and order soon discovers the need for both.'

The Daily Mail: 'How many prisoners will this colony accommodate?'

'We're planning accommodation for five thousand long-term offenders over the first year.'

'How far will this answer the need for rehabilitation?'

'Conscious attempts to rehabilitate are impossible. Present-day society cannot maintain a holier-than-thou attitude towards the criminal and he knows it. If there is to be reform it can only come from within.'

The Daily Mirror: 'How can so many be self-supporting?'

'I thought I'd made that clear. The men themselves will construct small factories and machine shops under initial supervision. There will be quantity production of goods with no output restrictions. Wages will be paid at union rates. Offenders must be given the means and opportunity to work – there's no other road to self-respect. Part of the money earned will be deducted towards the cost of their support.'

'The unions won't stand for it!'

'I imagine the taxpayer will approve whatever the shop stewards think.'

The Sun: 'Is this an indication of your attitude to the Trade Union movement?'

'Trade unions as well as criminals must learn to take their proper place in society.'

As the laughter died away he continued almost casually, 'Our troops are to be withdrawn from Germany.'

They were suddenly in danger of drowning in a sea of wild excitement. Truly, this man was breathtaking in his audacity. Two minutes later Wyatt continued, 'Our decision has full Defence Ministry and Treasury approval and was subject to consultation with Army and Air Chiefs of Staff. The West German Government has been informed. We are convinced this decision will command the whole-hearted support of the British people.'

The Daily Telegraph: 'Don't you believe it!'

'I'll tell you what we don't believe! We don't believe in the artificially stimulated threat of Russian aggression. We don't believe these men cannot be more usefully employed elsewhere. We don't believe our economic position justifies the continued wastage of money and manpower. We do believe the Germans are right. If our presence in Europe isn't worth our keep why should they pay – and why should we?'

Only the thought of being crushed to death in an attempt to reach a telephone kept them in their places. No one seemed able to question – the thunderbolt had stunned them into silence. There was also a forlorn hope that they would hear more astounding revelations.

'Some of BAOR will be disbanded. Most of them are highly-trained technicians desperately needed on the industrial front. Others will be retained on the home strength.'

The Daily Mirror: 'And the rest?'

There came a long interval of silence.

'The rest of the British Army of the Rhine is to be assigned to the United Nations as a peace-keeping force. It will be freely available for action anywhere in the world at the request of the Security Council and in accordance with the terms of the Charter. All expenses for the upkeep of this force will be met by Britain as its share in the economy of the UN and as a gesture of faith in the fundamental soundness of an organization committed to the cause of international peace and good will.'

With the sure instinct of a great actor Wyatt built each sentence on the next with an upsurging volume that gave new grandeur to words many believed worn out with misuse. There was no doubting the mood of the majority now. Wyatt had thoughtfully informed the television authorities that a filmed version of the proceedings would be permitted.

That evening Britain saw a House crowded with journalists rising to cheer a man who dared to bestride mountains as though they were mere wormcasts.

Wyatt had no illusions; he listened to the ovation knowing it owed something to gratitude for worldshaking copy. He offered them a banquet of sensational information; they were bound to say grace sooner or later. What mattered was the public. The people's acceptance depended on just such a reaction . . .

If it had felt its cup was overflowing, or that Wyatt had emptied his cornucopia of intentions, then the sated concourse of journalists was gratifyingly mistaken. As they exchanged impressions or put finishing touches to sketchy reports or prepared, heads down, to storm lines of communication, Wyatt stood abruptly and waited for a patch of silence to add almost as an afterthought:

'A note is being delivered to Washington with Foreign Office approval, in which we make it clear that we dissociate ourselves entirely from the policy decisions of previous administrations with regard to the situation in Vietnam . . . the craven attitude of the late government in face of transatlantic pressures is not the people's attitude. They will never again be content with a revolting hash of bad expediency disguised and served up as an honest policy! I tell you and I tell the world: we will not be pressurized into nodding support for a conflict which owes everything to distorted ideology – *nothing* to genuine regard for the future of a small nation forcibly bound to an operating table and bloodily wrenched apart in order to inject and infect it with a germ of that self-same democrapulous ideology!'

Out of the stunned silence came a single fervent response ... 'At last!'

The tumult that followed was something to be remembered long after the event. The ancient modern Chamber shook with an explosion of frenzied enthusiasm never seen before or since. 'The Spirit of Dunkirk,' they would write. 'We're independent at last. No longer a tributary nation.' 'Come hell or high water we'll follow Wyatt.' Such were the headlines that greeted millions of readers next day. They read like defiant obituaries on those dead years ...

Simpson shivered in the cold autumn air, peered through the bars of a cage – a cage! not even a bloody cell! What gods could rule now, that he should be treated like this! Stripped of his clothes and thrust in like an animal just because he'd shot a bleedin' copper! He could see nothing beyond the bars except a high partition leaving a gap wide enough for – for what? People? Public exposure, they could pass from one end – he could just see a kind of gap – to the other. He looked round at the straw-covered floor, stared up at the band of grey-coloured sky joining the upper edge of his – cell – with the blank partition, and listened to the distant cries of animals – animals ... and the familiar hum of human voices somewhere beyond ... they couldn't do this to him – not to him! What did they say? Fed three times a day – he was to clean and sweep out his – his cage – each day. But a bed? no bed – I gotta have a privy – Jesus Christ you can't! No privy – nothing. What had he done to ... The spasms of raging self-pity were interrupted by a sudden shuffle of feet, and the first casual sightseers, tourists, genuinely censorious or plainly curious began to stream through. At first he stared with a desperate, brazen defiance at the never-ending panorama of silent witnesses ...

In accordance with Wyatt's instructions he was under constant observation. A film unit recorded his every movement.

Minutes after the press conference an SB man, having shed the flimsy disguise of a journalist, was informing the five men at Bookers of all that he'd heard and seen. The Cabal was left in no doubt of Wyatt's success.

Deep silence followed his departure. Wynlose ransacked his considerable intellect for some grain of comfort. Minter tried not to think in terms of stock market advantages; Compton-Douglas reviewed imaginary battalions before settling the usurper's hash in an autumn blaze of glory; and Rigg, his peevish anger growing with every phrase of the undercover man's report, now waited, with a self-righteous 'I told you so' expression, for Langley to make the first comment.

The ancient peer had a lot to think about, it seemed. He was in no hurry to speak. For the first time in a long life he had to acknowledge miscalculation, of a man, a situation, even the mood of the people. Difficult to exchange the tailored cloak of infallibility for a drip-dry shirt of Nessus at his age. He stirred at last and made little effort to avoid Rigg's coldly virtuous eye. It was time to attack in his own defence.

'Obvious what you're all thinking. As for you Rigg, no point in sniffing like a Puritan because you smell a cavalier.'

Rigg resented the role of Aunt Sally. 'That's just about it! A cavalier – laughing – doubled up with laughter – at us! A nonentity six days ago and now look at him – firmly in the saddle.'

The others murmured agreement. Langley realized the unthinkable was happening; his supreme and seemingly eternal authority was being called in question. The Langleys were accustomed to assaults on their judgement – but their authority ... he cut like a claymore across Minter's deceptively gentle criticism. 'I think we've made things difficult for ourselves –'

'Very well! Allow yourselves to be fogged by the smokescreen of his good intentions! You know the game as well as I do. He's doing his damnedest to win the people's confidence. What else did you expect?'

'And you still say wait?'

Almost impudent and a trifle inelegant of Minter to pose the question direct.

'Yes!' Langley was now committed to an attacking policy, so he could afford to pause and fish for a reason certain to be swimming around somewhere in a vast reservoir of experience. He allowed the affirmative long enough to sink in before leaning forward to make his point.

'Wyatt's doing what both the major parties have been wanting to do for years. We were scared, scared of the electorate, world opinion, opinion polls and too damned inhibited by our past mistakes. Do you realize no major policy decision's been taken since 'fifty-six? Along comes Wyatt, unbinds Prometheus, takes naïve actions that cut right across the sophisticated eunuch-ridden politics of the day – and it works. But he'll make a mistake – they always do. When that happens we'll get the Queen out of cold storage, make advantageous terms with a highly relieved Washington – and put the electorate back where it belongs.'

Only Rigg was sufficiently critical to ask: 'And where do you suppose it belongs?'

Langley cackled, sensing that he could afford a display of good humour.

'Like a nut my dear Rigg, caught between the Right and Left of the democratic nutcracker.'

12

At 2 p.m. our time Washington announced that the President would broadcast to the American people that evening.

At 3 p.m. a messenger from the French Embassy handed a note to Wyatt. It bore a word and a name: 'Congratulations. de Gaulle.'

A telephone call from 'Millionaires' Row' informed him Minister-Counsellor Serov would be pleased to call on Captain Wyatt 'when convenient'.

An emergency meeting of the NATO Defence Council was called to discuss 'Operation Crash Crisis'.

Not since the Cuba affair had diplomatic activity been so intense. Ambassadors, first, second and third secretaries, counsellors, press and military attachés, found themselves cruelly overworked, overwhelmed with demands from insatiable governments for detailed reports on every possible aspect of the situation as it developed from hour to hour.

At UN Headquarters corridors and committee rooms buzzed with rumour and speculation. And all this because of Britain – or Wyatt – which was which.

It was a tribunal in the best Fouquier-Tinville sense of the word, hurriedly created by Order in Council, masterminded by Hartfish, unwillingly presided over by a nominal Lord Chief Justice. Yet it still managed to convey the time-honoured illusion of British justice: most grave, most potent, most theatrical.

Hartfish, the periwigged producer with a Reinhardt touch, stood like a fragment of the black mass in the brightly lit Hall and stared through the young man in the witness box. He was about to pull the delectable plum from a pudding. It was pleasant to savour the moment . . . then suddenly:

'What rank did you hold!'

'Rank? Lieutenant, as you know.'

'As I know.'

Hartfish paused and appeared to be shaking with suppressed laughter: 'Lieutenant Slingsby,' he murmured to himself as though it was too good to be true. The throng of spectators craned forward and wondered dutifully.

'As you know – Lieutenant – the Enabling Act gives me powers to call the accused purely in connection with such matters as evidence of identity and so forth. A necessary formality in view of the complexity of the case and the great numbers involved. You're here today in order that we may establish the part you literally played in the events of October last. You are here so that we may strip away the mask behind which you and many of your confederates acted.'

Hartfish allowed the stage directions to sink in while he sipped from a glass of water and turned briefly to assure himself that Langley and Rigg were in their usual places.

'Now, Lieutenant Slingsby, you and your troops were given the task of occupying the headquarters of the BBC?'

'Yes.'

'You entered the premises with weapons concealed in instrument cases, rather in the manner of Chicago gangsters?'

'Really Mr Hartfish, these surely are facts to be determined at the trial proper!' The Lord Chief Justice's voice trembled with anger – the rules of evidence –

'With respect my Lord, we should accept those facts that speak for themselves. Well, Lieutenant?'

'Gangsters ... the description does credit to a vicious imagination.'

Hartfish afforded a smile while grudging the expense. 'Weapons concealed in instrument cases seems to me a strange perversion of innocent functions in Chicago or anywhere else. More to the point, had you or your "troops" any training in the use of these weapons?'

'None.'

The Attorney-General waited for silence.

'None ... had you any military training at all?'

'Søme of the men –'

'I'm asking if you had any military training!'

'No.'

'Have you ever served in the Army at all – Lieutenant?'

'... no – never.'

Hartfish sat abruptly, prim and complacent, as he listened to the ushers grumbling for silence from a reactivated audience.

Entry from the private diary (to be published) of J. G. Jarman, former United States Ambassador.

Saturday 27th October

Four days of bad dreams adding up to a nightmare. This is bad for America – bad for Britain. If we allow Wyatt to act out these insane policies it could mean the end of our authority in Europe. This man threatens to extinguish the torch of Democracy, a torch we did so much to rekindle, threatens to plunge a continent back into the Dark Ages.

I hardly know how to record my impressions of the day's news. His press conference was a triumph for the Reds. Even if Wyatt can be eliminated fast, a great blow has been struck at our prestige in the West and I don't see how it can end there. Even if this damned régime topples tomorrow NATO is finished and Germany's out on a limb. The Russians must be laughing. As for Vietnam – it's terrible to think our boys are shedding their American blood for Democracy while this cheapskate stabs them in the back.

We'll have to lean on the British a little – withdrawal of investments, suspension of WMF facilities, maybe total embargo on imports. Or they can get rid of Wyatt.

Milly Lavery sat huddled over the TV thinking about those two men she'd found at the front door – raincoats, hands in pockets and a thin look about the mouth: 'Mrs Lavery?'

'Yes,' she'd whispered above the pulsating spasms from 'Five o'clock Pop.'

'... a few words with your husband.' She'd thought of tally-men, Gas Board inspectors and everything else except the obvious as she told them he wasn't at home. 'Any idea when he's likely to be?' She hadn't. The two men hesitated, glanced at each other, and left without another word. She gazed bleakly at the announcer with his dentrifical smile. '... and the question everyone is asking tonight is how the Forces in Germany will react to Wyatt's proposals – official comment from Bonn itself: "most unfortunate". The verdict from Washington: "tragic". The feeling is that there are bound to be serious repercussions ...'

She didn't dare think about the sudden ten pounds Fred'd given her for the housekeeping.

Tommy Mostyn, the after-shave lotion fresh boy of TV satire, was about to give one of his celebrated Top Pop Dinner parties in the 'I did the décor myself' pent-house high above Sloane Square; keeping it up, as he so sparklingly put it, with the Peter Jones's. Tommy's meteoric rise from sewer to gutter had a lot to do with his genius for making the noble art of mud-slinging *fun*. With tremendous reserves of spittle as his main stock in trade he had publicly and liberally spat in the eye of every and any body or institution or ideal or cause that happened to catch his attention. His brand of nastiness appealed to the latent nastiness in most human beings, so the people loved Tommy – not for his nastiness, but because he was so *clever*. But even he couldn't keep it up for ever. One day the spittle-wells would run dry and he was busy even now seeking insurance against the future. The image needed plastic surgery; but slowly – an inch at a time. He began to drive over delicate sensibilities thoughtfully with a 'this hurts me more' expression angled at the viewers. They thought he was going soft, but he was simply going up, climbing rungs, shedding the past. How else could he become a Man of Consequence?

So he won friends, and collected influential people, and discreetly spread the word that he was ready for transfer, willing to play centre forward for Wolves in the power game. Party politics bored him, but with his boy scout mentality he could delight in tying people, like bits of string, into complicated knots. What else was power for?

Then Wyatt happened. Mostyn read every available report, saw a number of people, made phone calls, then retired to bed for forty-eight hours to take thought on the advantages to be gained from an altered situation.

On the Thursday he leaped from his highly sprung mattress, safely delivered of an idea; a gimmick with a sure-fire touch at a time when parties of any kind were far from the minds of men shaken out of office.

Why not get Wrigley and Meaker together? An exchange of views on neutral territory provided by Tommy; just a small gathering, discreet, select – and well publicized. Let the people know the Party leaders were united by Wyatt's tyranny, *and* still able to relax with a stiff upper lip. A boost to the country's morale ... he found a host of reasons why it could be in their interests to appear, began to feel like the saviour of his country. At the very least, providing a field of cloth of gold would create obligations.

Wrigley had been there before, and as he was doing nothing

and the idea appeared to have merits he graciously accepted the invitation. It was nice to feel wanted once again. Meaker was more difficult, having suffered the spit in the eye direct on more than one of Tommy's programmes; but he wasn't doing anything either and there might be something in it. The other guests were unimportant: Herbert Snooper, a Tory back-bencher; Margaret Fishtree, ambitious to be the first woman Prime Minister; a Bishop who knew he was on God's side but who was God? Psycho-analysts were still working on him. And for light relief a queer peer who was the 'in' thing if one's tastes ran to crashing wits. He positively *throbbed* at the thought of dining with all those politicans: 'Is Wyatt invited? Oh, what a pity! And what *about* that man – isn't he a riot? Oh, very well I won't mention his name unless they do ...'

Dinner was ordered, the wines chosen, flowers arranged and Fleet Street briefed. The scene was set for no useful purpose whatsoever; but they remembered the gesture long after – remembered the host who symbolically joined Left and Right for the public good. One more rung up the ladder at a cost of thirty-two pounds ten, including booze. Cheap as rungs go, the future Sir Thomas Mostyn might feel.

He gazed round the garnished table, now a disorder of post-prandial debris, assumed a solemn air. 'Miss Fishtree – gentlemen, I consider it my humble duty to propose the only possible toast on this sad occasion – the Queen ...'

He noted with downunder amusement the rheumy eye of a much affected Prime Minister. For a moment, as they responded, nearly all hearts were in some sort of communion ... it was a first rate claret.

'I wonder,' said Snooper, after a decent pause following the press photographers' departure, 'I wonder what we're waiting for?'

All eyes were turned on Wrigley who knew damned well everyone was waiting for him. He made a show of considering Snooper's wonderment.

'It's obvious what everyone's thinking. As Prime Minister I should give a lead. Suppose I did give orders: storm the Tower – rescue the Queen; suppose by some horrible mischance they disposed of the Royal Family first? It'd never be forgotten that we'd set Wyatt on a regicidal course.'

'Very true,' Meaker agreed, 'but has it escaped everybody's notice Wyatt hasn't said a word about regicide? In my opinion it's a little too freely assumed.'

Mostyn doubted with suitable deference. 'Isn't it a valid assumption? I mean he can hardly make the implied threat explicit and still hope to keep public opinion on his side.'

'What,' Meaker drily inquired, 'does a man like Wyatt care about public opinion? He's said as much. I'm willing to admit he has the instincts of a good actor – knows how to keep an audience in suspense – but I question his ultimate intention.'

Fishtree boomed a trifle indelicately, 'You're saying Wyatt has no more intention of doing in the Queen than a stage Othello has of killing Desdemona?'

'Well, as the Cardinal said, if you can't read the *Tablet* take the beastly pill,' the peculiar peer observed. Mostyn hurriedly offered him port but the Bishop intervened.

'A Cromwellian dilemma,' he purred, carefully disentangling the words from the wine.

'Cromwellian?' the peer seemed puzzled.

'Nothing Cromwellian about it,' Meaker abrupted. 'He's simply created a situation in which we're supposed to supply the dilemma, and we have.'

Later the gathering adjourned to another part of the penthouse, leaving the two Party leaders alone for a few moments' consultation. Meaker's brief from above was to the point. Delay Wrigley's reaction by confusing the issue.

'It's a great blow for you, Kenneth,' Meaker sympathized comfortably.

'It's a great blow for all of us,' the PM amended. 'It'll take years to recover from this – especially after today.'

'I shouldn't take it too seriously. After all – we're discovering a few of our enemies, and he might have done us a favour in other respects.'

'You're not serious!'

'We might as well face it – he's doing things we'd all like to have done but for outside pressures, public opinion and so on.'

'I can perfectly well run the country without Wyatt's queering my pitch!'

Meaker made a hasty amendment. 'Of course you can – no one doubts your abilities – but let's be honest. The country's in a mess. Not you or anyone else could pull it out of the doldrums in five minutes. Either people are old enough to be scared of the past or they're too young to think prosperity's anything but a bottomless well; so we can't take enough unpopular measures to stop us sinking. Only one lifeboat and everybody's convinced they've got a seat. What can we do? You introduce a policy of restraint – I have to oppose it. If things get too bad the people panic – you're out and I'm in – and off we go again.'

'True up to a point, but what else is there?'

'There's Wyatt. Call it fate or what you like but it's not a bad moment for someone to appear on the scene and take the problem out of our hands – for the time being.'

'What about the German business?'

'He's saving us forty millions a year.'

Wrigley barely hid his surprise: 'I suppose you can afford these comforting thoughts in Opposition. But I can't find much excuse for his treatment of –'

'I agree, only it might be better not to overplay the monarchy question . . .'

Again Wrigley caught himself wondering. Mindful of his reputation for shrewdness he refrained from asking Meaker exactly what he meant.

People not only bought armfuls of Sunday papers – they even read them. Quality newspapers offered analyses in depths unfathomable; girlie rags execrated the violator of the Queen whose portrait shared front pages with Annies and Fannies dangerously verging on stardom and heavily attired in nothing very much.

Two of the more significant news items are quoted, one of which was to earn for its author a six month prison sentence; the other, in question form, was to be answered in full at a later date.

The Clarion:
High treason is one of the very few crimes still punishable by death. Why did the former Labour Government, ideologically opposed to capital punishment, see fit to destroy all the paraphernalia of hanging except in one instance? Wandsworth gaol alone retains the necessary apparatus.

Might it have been pointed out to those in office that something of this kind could conceivably happen? If Wyatt had failed, or if he does fail, what connection would exist between the crime of high treason and a death cell waiting in Wandsworth?

Thomas an Williams in the *Sunday Examiner:*
I see nothing very remarkable about Her Majesty's dispossession. What about the old lady thrown out of her flat after forty years – by the Queen's own son? It's true the nominal landlord was the Duchy of Cornwall Estate, it's true the Prince of Wales never visited his south London estates; it's even true he never personally received her rent with his own hands. But he gets it eventually and the fact remains she was chucked out. Now if the Crown is under no obligation to prove the old lady was a nuisance – if she has no right of appeal to the Rent Tribunal – why should Wyatt show her landlord's mother more consideration? If the Crown is above the Rent Acts, then QED it's above the law. So it might as well go. So my thought for today is this. When you're seventy an eight-roomed flat in the Tower is better than nothing . . .

John Citizen cheerfully accepted the division of informed opinion, experienced a delicious sense of satisfaction at 'their' dilemma. 'They' had been outsmarted by a simple ruse, not a single life lost and not a penny spent – a bloodless revolution for free. In the afternoon he took his family to the Tower, pointed out to bored infants where the Queen lay in custody.

In Regent's Park long queues shuffled past the barrier to see a man in the death-throes of shame.

The best of the rest took injured pride to St Paul's, where the Archbishop fed hopes of retribution on a sermon distorted by Revelations and gave a sharp warning to God that this sort of thing must stop. His flock included those members of the Royal Family who felt left out of things – and the Cabal at full strength.

Madame Tussaud's remained open for two extra hours to

cope with crowds anxious to see Wyatt in effigy – and the Lord's Day Observance Society issued a statement deploring the fact that he had obviously been running the country on a Sunday.

At the end of the day Scotland Yard reported a decrease in the number of weekend crimes of violence. Road casualties appeared to be down – and the AA commented on the overall improvement in driving standards.

John Citizen retired to bed that night wondering what the morrow would bring apart from Monday; but on the whole he decided he was feeling better for the change.

Baynard came sprinting in with a fresh morning look and the day's agenda. He found Wyatt at the desk, eyes closed, the desk lamp still burning, and Jennings just drawing back the curtains.

'Asleep?' he yelled at the Sergeant in a loud whisper.

'No but he ought to be. You can't tell him anything.'

'Go away Sergeant and don't come back without a couple of pints of coffee.'

'Yessir.' As he walked out he said loudly. 'Overdoes it – that's his trouble – he overdoes it.'

'Tired?'

'It's been a long weekend.'

'We got through it – thanks to Horlicks.'

Wyatt smiled at Baynard's good humour, and wished he too could see nothing but success. It was worth a lot to be young enough to radiate high noon and not a shadow in sight. Not old enough to know or care that the hands move on to a minute past twelve. And yet it seemed to Wyatt he'd spent a lifetime looking ahead ... he listened casually through a veil of tiredness as Baynard rambled on – his thoughts were far away ... Rosetta Street – a part of the dream become reality ...

There's a funereal sadness about Rosetta Street. So much died so suddenly. Only the echoes remain: streetsellers' cries, barrel organ melodies, mingle with the coalman's roar, the long ago laughter of children skipping to salt-mustard-vinegar-pepper in patched clothes and worn boots, the Saturday bawling of pubs and the Sunday wailing of chapels, the sing-song of Jenkins the Milk and the Cockney German of Mama Schmidt with the smiling face who sold Coburgs and Cottages in the little front room shop of the house in Rosetta Street.

Nothing left of the past except the house on the corner and the bakehouse filling the garden space. Old Schmidt's ovens are still there, rusted with time, just as the Republicans saw them behind the speaker at their meetings. The older locals still call it the Bakehouse.

And back across the river they talk of the Bakehouse Plot.

The entrance is tucked away round the corner, in Campion Street. The sign on the door still exists: 'Campion Street Fifth day Conventicle. Services held Monday, Wednesday and Friday at 7. Sunday 6.30.' Interviewed by the police, local residents would later swear they had no idea what went on in the bakehouse. Why should they? What concern was it of theirs if a lot of kinky religious maniacs wanted to get together for Gawd's sake? As their spokesman put it: 'Wild 'orses on their bended knees wouldn't've got me in there!' Which was Wyatt's obvious intention.

He purchased the future HQ through the Morrisons, who occupied the house. From 88 Rosetta Street they kept a strict account of the organization, extended it, co-ordinated the groups, edited and printed his pamphlets and forwarded his instructions to the area leaders. They ran the meetings and generally acted for a leader necessarily absent for much of the time. All this they managed without arousing the least suspicion. The Morrisons? Oh nice people, quiet – we thought they was caretakers for the Church ... nice people ... Paul – the best of the men, the nearest thing to a friend he'd known since the day that damned flying-bomb ... and Mary ... he forced himself not to think of her – and Rosetta Street –

'You asleep?' Wyatt opened his eyes to find Baynard studying him like a doctor looking for life signs in a patient.

'No – I was thinking.'

'About Rosetta Street?' Wyatt looked vaguely surprised. 'You mumbled it just now.'

'Rosetta Street ... yes I was remembering the night I announced the crux of the plan to the area people.'

'My God, that was a cloak and dagger affair if you like – and a bombshell thrown in for good measure.'

Wyatt smiled. 'The Police Constable?'

'Well it's the last thing you expect at a seditious meeting – coppers putting their heads round the door to ask if anyone owns a car, licence number GBC 3811.'

'Fortunately no one did,' Wyatt said.

'The case of the curious Constable,' Baynard chuckled. 'Remember your answer when he asked what sort of religion it was? "It's a sort of silent religion – our beloved Founder believes that people talk too much." I dunno how we kept straight faces.'

'He was difficult to get rid of,' Wyatt admitted.

'Until you invited him to join in singing the sixty-fourth Psalm.'

'A difficult evening.'

'Old Turner didn't make it any easier.'

'Impossible!' Turner was the first to speak.

'Very well then it's impossible!' Wyatt paced with an almost feverish urgency. His head ached with the enormity of the idea, but he could think of nothing except the need to win over Turner and the handful of waverers showing signs of doubt – even distaste. 'If you know another way, if you think the Government will tamely hand over power on demand, if you think we can break the two-party stranglehold on power by legitimate actions – then take my place.'

'We could make a legitimate attempt.'

'Ask the Liberals how far they got with legitimate methods! A pack of romantic virgins dying for love of constitutional government. They didn't dare live in sin – they couldn't help ending up as barren spinsters!'

He found time to wonder how he could have been such a fool as to trust Turner. In fact the area representative, an engineer in his fifties, was one of Wyatt's staunchest supporters; but he had a contentious manner and more than his share of caution. Now, it seemed, he was arguing for the monarchy, the very pinnacle of Establishment which they were pledged to destroy.

A child could have seen the tremendous logic of his idea, could have seen that there was no hope of success without it. Now he was faced with indecision. If even a few backed out now – the whole movement was lost; someone was bound to talk; an anonymous phone call to the authorities – and finish!

'I'm quite prepared to do everything in my power to throw out the old system – but the Queen ...' Turner paused. 'I tell you honestly Wyatt – it just isn't on.'

'We'd lose sympathy,' Canning, the parchmenty schoolmaster observed.

'We're not seeking sympathy. We're enforcing recognition of our existence! Our aim is power! And if we can't find it legitimately then we grasp it dramatically. We *have* to decapitate the body politic to prove the corpse can be resurrected – can live and breathe without a Royal pardon for living.'

'Of course monarchy has to go – no one denies that – but I thought once we seized power ...'

'Good God, can't you see she's the only person alive who could guarantee our power to act!'

'Even so ...'

'Even so, Turner, the cause has no place for sentimental hangers-on! It isn't the Queen we're attacking, it's all she stands for – the pomp and circumstance obstructing progress, mental attitudes, slavish sticking to principles that went out with Novello's Ruritania! You *cannot* have it both ways; either you're for her or you're for the Republican ideal!'

Wyatt was no longer speaking to Turner or anyone else. He paced like a caged tiger, unaware of their astonishment – unaware of anything but the need to convince.

'Those of you who wish to withdraw will do so now. There can be no compromise on this, no dualistic attitudes. I can count on two hundred or more to follow where I lead and I shall lead. As long as one man knows his own mind there will be others. You, Turner – do as you please and be damned, but remember it was given to you to serve fifty million people, not one of whom is a jot less important than your Queen!'

He continued pacing in the silence, a long silence through which he trod a dangerous path armed only with a slender thread of ideas, in search of an impersonal minotaur. If he dropped the thread ... the failure of a dream seemed to be in sight in the bizarre setting of a disused bakehouse. At that moment Wyatt could have murdered his own soul in the bitterness of a looming defeat. The great tempest abated, he looked up, aware at last of the silence created by his forty chosen followers ...

'What I'll always remember,' Baynard mused, 'is the fact nothing was said – Turner and the others – not a word. One just knew they were with you, whatever you did, but nothing said ... very impressive.'

What Wyatt was remembering had nothing to do with Turner. He'd never thought of Mary as anything but an efficient cog in the machine – Paul's wife, that was important too ... but as he turned, he caught the transitory spark of God knows what emotion in her eyes ...

'Yes, Harry,' he smiled briefly. 'I remember very well – nothing was said.'

The reminiscences were pushed aside like last week's newspapers and Wyatt thankfully got down to work.

13

Extract from the Housing Decree:

The Administration is determined to put housing high on its list of priorities.

Consideration is already being given to the problem in consultation with the Ministries concerned. We are taking immediate steps on short term proposals.

It is a national scandal that a country boasting of its capacity to maintain a 'world role' – whatever that may mean – is still one of the most poorly housed nations in the Western world. It is no less than criminal therefore that a government committed by Socialist doctrine to the people's welfare should so consistently have put national prestige before national needs.

Their insistence, for example, on ordering a hunter-killer submarine – people cannot live in submarines.

We have cancelled the order.

The money – £20,000,000 – is being immediately allocated to those Councils faced with the greatest housing problem. The loan will be at nominal interest, and will ensure decent homes for five thousand families.

More will be done in this direction as and when economies can be made. For the rest we have the support of the Treasury in our conviction that we can double the percentage of the gross national product allocated to housing. We will then be spending as much on providing accommodation for the inadequately housed as does Italy. Furthermore, we will take steps to provide cheaper money for loans to corporations. This again is a matter of effecting economies elsewhere.

We further decree that the former Buckingham Palace shall be declared forfeit to the State. All movable property shall be returned to the former residents, officials, servants and employees generally.

The property will be transferred to and administered by the Greater London Council for the purpose of providing temporary accommodation for the most urgent cases drawn from the seven thousand homeless citizens of London.

Sandringham Castle is to be given into the trusteeship of the Health Ministry to be converted as a convalescent home for the people.

Windsor Castle to be expropriated by the State and administered by the local authorities for the people's benefit as a place of recreation and for general activities tending to the welfare of the community.

All rents and other profits from the Duchy of Cornwall Estates shall accrue directly to the State and be appropriated by the Ministry of Housing.

The deputation from the Trades Unions Consortium was in its place punctually at 10 o'clock to question Wyatt and present a resolution that 'This Council is gravely disturbed by the situation created by Captain Wyatt's assumption of power and it seeks an assurance that all matters relating to Union policy will be respected during such period as the present Administration may be in effective control of the country's affairs.'

Wyatt, after a five minute nap and black coffee, was no less punctual. The House was filled with his followers, CBI members, civil servants, industrial correspondents and other reasonably interested parties. Union men crowded the public gallery and others waited in a lengthy queue with no hope of getting in.

The BBC had permission to film the proceedings for an evening telecast. It was that important. Almost crucial, some thought. In a sense Wyatt would be on trial before the Consortium. His attitude to a pillar of strength must have some effect on the workers' readiness to accept his authority.

Baynard watched Wyatt take the former Speaker's chair. He looked damned tired, he thought. How could he hope to stand up to these toughs on catnaps and coffee?

Mr Tom Tully rose confidently to his feet, angled himself a hair's breadth for the cameras' benefit and opened his mouth. He held himself something like a brass band cornet player and bellowed in the manner of a Boanerges addressing an audience of mental defectives.

'... and what is more my colleagues and I seek from you an assurance, a public assurance, that your assumption of power has no parallel with that other momentous occasion when Hitler shocked the world by his ruthless persecution of the Unions, a persecution which led to the extinction of the German Trades Union movement, the workers' sacred right to strike and the cardinal principle of collective bargaining!'

Tully sat down to a scattering of applause. Only the whirring of cameras bridged the gap of silence that followed. Then Wyatt stood with a smear of thunder etching his brow, and stared for a long minute at Tully's well-fed air of complacency.

'I need no one to give me lessons in history. But if we're being asked to dip the long spoon into memory I'm ready to debate at length the betrayal of the workers by the Union leadership in 1926!'

Tully and company sat up sharply, realized for the first time they faced a man of power. Non-unionists were plainly delighted. Unemployed car workers in the gallery above grinned.

'As for persecuting you,' Wyatt continued, 'persecution is as much a question of the martyr's misconception of his importance as it is of the persecutor's fears. If Wrigley himself didn't consider you important enough to fear, then I'm damned if I do!'

The members of the public gallery were dancing with delight. Baynard relaxed a little as Wyatt waited for the chuckles to subside.

'The truth is, you're dying to be persecuted as a sex-starved spinster unconsciously craves to be raped. If only I would shoot one of your colleagues – not you personally, that would be unfair rape – or did something on my part that'd give you a martyr's crown, give your antiquated institution the shot in the arm you so badly need!'

Lorimer glanced at the Captain – then at Baynard, raised his eyebrows questioningly. Is he going too far? But Wyatt rode on roughshod over the muttered protests.

'The Unions over which you have lost control have made this country a laughing stock – their irresponsible actions over the years, actions which you failed to curb, have a large share in bringing the nation into disrepute.'

Tully almost flinched, stared open-mouthed at Wyatt's outstretched finger. No one pointed a finger at Tully.

'I accuse you and your hierarchy of allowing a state of affairs to develop which can only end in completely discrediting a movement of which you are the guardians!'

Several members of the Consortium started to their feet with 'I protest' and 'This is an attack on the workers!'

'Sit down.' Again the razor sharp edge of a voice hardly raised but charged with megatonic intensity. They sat down.

'Who accuses me of attacking the workers? An ex-machine minder risen from the factory floor to Union leadership. I remember very well the ex-machine minder posing at the door of his Bentley for the press photographers. The caption? "Union leader Percy Moggs on his way by invitation to dine with Her Majesty." What the hell did you or any of you have to do with Her Majesty outside of grovelling for knighthoods!

153

Whose eye do you suppose you're spitting in when you seek to enter the Establishment on terms that can only militate against the workers? You proved your stupidity over and over again by allowing them to coerce you, manipulate you, knight you, possess you body and soul as a means of keeping the workers under control!'

Wyatt paused, but no one seemed anxious to speak.

'Do I have to provide you with voting figures from any union you care to name – returns for any issue involving any particular class of workers? Do I have to tell you why ninety per cent of members of almost any union fail to exercise their voting rights? Not apathy, not an attitude of couldn't care less – but a profound and correct realization that their leaders are useless time-servers!'

The men in the gallery cheered openly. There were no ushers to prevent them. Wyatt's raised hand was enough.

'The Union movement is a history of fine men fighting not for the paltry trappings of power but simply for the good of others. Their principles have been eroded by ambition, subverted by the scramble for power at any price, and distorted in order to resist change in a changing world. Today, worst of all, the movement by its sins of omission has allowed the workers to incur the wrath and contempt of those who would like to see them put in their place. It follows that you have betrayed the workers and it is for you to defend yourselves.'

The Chamber was in an uproar. Baynard and the others smiled, knowing Wyatt had done it again.

Tully conferred hurriedly with his colleagues. Should they answer, or withdraw with what dignity they could muster? Enough damage had been done, in fact the nation would see and hear too much. Better to walk out in silent protest. But Tom Tully was not one to resist a challenge, or, as one of his colleagues bitterly remarked, he just didn't know when to keep his mouth shut.

'I've heard some vindictive speeches in my time – but this beats all. If this is an indication of your future attitude to the unions then God help them. You've made a damaging attack on a legally constituted movement and I hope to see the day you stand trial for illegally promoting the nearest thing to a fascist régime this country's ever known. You ask me to defend myself. I'm not bound to defend myself or the movement to you or anyone else!'

'What about us?' the galleryites shouted.

Tully went so far as to forget himself by reverting to street corner oratory.

'What about you!' he bawled. 'You wouldn't be where you are now if it wasn't for us!'

'We're unemployed so that's true enough,' came the short answer. Tully decided to stick to the line of injured innocence.

'We came here today to invoke your protection in our cause. Instead we leave borne down with insults, flouted by a two-penny-ha'penny usurper. We know what conclusions to draw. We shall warn our members to guard against a tool of the capitalist class masquerading as a friend of the people.'

Wyatt leaned forward in his seat. 'Before you accuse others of being capitalist lackeys I suggest you give up your subscription to the Conform Club, one of the most capitalist-ridden hot-beds in London.'

Even Tully's own colleagues began to feel he was asking for it. The mood of the House was hardly in his favour. And Wyatt gave no quarter.

'You might also take a cut in your over-inflated salary as a gesture to the two million workless now enjoying the doubtful blessings of unemployment benefit.'

He stood with startling suddenness, brandished a single sheet of paper.

'And I advise you to reflect on the folly of addressing this kind of letter to Prime Ministers who might also reflect on the folly of leaving such stuff lying about where any twopenny-ha'penny usurper might happen to find it.'

Tully, white faced, roared at the Captain. 'You don't bloody dare!' but Wyatt did dare, and he read in a loud, clear voice.

'"Dear Ken, I'm afraid I'll have to make a show of resistance to your proposals. If the figure of 2 per cent unemployment suggested by your advisers is a conservative estimate – then I have to speak out on the assumption that it will be worse. Privately of course we accept a higher figure with due reservation but I can hardly say so in public. So while I settle for 2 per cent, I shall thunder against 3 or more for old times' sake. I hear you've caught a cold again – there's a lot of it about." '

There was indeed. Tully and company could only retire. Wyatt had made a few more implacable enemies. Even Tully would have admitted brotherhood has nothing to do with being found out.

Report on James Simpson.

On Wyatt's orders observations of Simpson's behaviour were made covering a period of forty-eight hours. The following extract concerns the first seven hours.

Saturday, 9 a.m. Simpson fought like a man possessed. Have never seen anything quite like it. It took four men ten minutes or more to shut him in. Violent now, abusive and self-assertive; clings to the bars as though trying to project himself beyond obstacles ... periods of pacing back and forth – more violent abuse – screams, shouts ... failing to attract attention he begins to pay minute attention to his cell much as an animal examines its cage. Finding nothing of interest he again grows violent, kicking the straw through the bars, then throws it out in handfuls. His nakedness doesn't seem to worry him. Curiously, at one point he stood quite still in the centre of the cage and laughed.

10 a.m. The first members of the public begin to pass through. Their reaction is interesting in itself. Curiosity almost without exception, but no signs of pity or aversion that I could see, more the detached curiosity over the waxwork model staring back at its audience ...

Simpson attempts to brazen it out – significantly, from the centre. Incapable I think of standing close to the bars, what I would call an inner shrinking from public attention already operating – certainly a marked contrast to his arrogant bearing in custody and during his trial.

10.30. A return to arrogance briefly. For five minutes perhaps he shouted at the crowd – then dawning realization that he is an object, a thing to be studied by all and sundry as one might observe an organism under the microscope. Such remarks as

'What's the matter – frightened of me, are you? Scared of a killer?' followed by 'Say something! Why don't you say something?' These bore a hint of desperation. It may be that the collective wisdom of the crowd is sometimes in doubt – but it operated splendidly on this occasion. Nothing was said, not one person made an attempt to reply. They simply passed through in absolute silence from the entrance to the exit.

11.15. Simpson stands literally with his back to the wall. At one point he made a compulsive move to cover his genitals – a belated recognition of utter defencelessness. He no longer looks at the people – stares at his hands, examines finger nails in an attempt at indifference or gazes at a spot above their heads. Difficult to interpret his expression – something I imagine like this: 'Now I know I'm here – now you know I'm here – so what?' Hard to say at the moment.

12.20 p.m. Over a period of twenty minutes he has edged towards a corner – the unconscious seeking of a refuge . . .

1.00. A bowl of food was passed through a trapdoor on to the floor. He looked startled, glanced at the queue as though to see if anyone had noticed. He put out a hand to reach it, by now he was sitting on the floor, hands clasped round knees tightly drawn up. He took the bowl and looked for a spoon or some kind of cutlery automatically – then realized he was to eat with his fingers and put the bowl down violently – but carefully . . .

2.00. The crowds continue to file through. But Simpson is concerned only with his hunger; he drank from a mug of water, but plainly he's fighting the need for food, determined to preserve the last shreds of self-respect, unwilling to surrender the elementary habits of a civilized man. He rests his head on his knees . . . for all of ten minutes.

3.15. Signs of restiveness. For some time, a period of twenty-five minutes, he watches the moving line of spectators with concentrated attention. This appears to be unmotivated behaviour but is in fact dictated by the need to relieve himself – the battle with hunger has become secondary, once again the terrible realization that he faces the greatest indignity of all – performing a basic function in full view of others . . .

4.00. Five minutes ago Simpson urinated in a corner of his cell; he noticed gaps in the queue, no more than a few seconds. He had waited, hoping to get it over before they passed through, but they were there – long before he'd finished. For a further ten minutes he stood facing the back wall of the cage, no movement

157

at all. Then he turned slowly and walked to the food, sat down and began to eat; there were tears in his eyes. He has not looked at the crowd again.

Wyatt found the report on his desk when he returned from skirmishing with the TUC. He read it carefully and sat staring into a distance ... Baynard waited.

'Harry, I want a car standing by for me at twelve.'

'You're due to see Saunders at 11.30.'

'Saunders won't take up more than half an hour. Read this.'

Baynard read slowly through the report then considered Wyatt. 'What d'you want me to say?'

'Anything or nothing – more important, I want copies of this sent to everyone on this – let's see, where is it? – this list.'

The lieutenant took the list and read the first name: 'Bourne J. Yes all right – I'll see to it right away.'

'What's wrong, Harry?'

'Nothing – I feel sorry for Simpson that's all.'

'Well?'

'I hope you're damned sure of what you're doing!'

'Because –?'

'Because it's too much otherwise!'

'Paul's words exactly – even Lorimer was against it.'

'Don't you have any pity?'

'He killed a man – get that into your head! If he loved life he'd go down on his knees and thank God for being alive enough to suffer! What I do feel is satisfaction.'

Baynard began to wonder: could anyone really know this man, strange in the ways of his thinking, ruthless in the pursuit of paradox – was degradation any better than death? – he brushed cobwebs of worry from his mind and queried Wyatt's satisfaction.

'Yes – satisfaction that a man can die and be born again. You think I'm ruthless, Harry – glory in the power to reduce a man to nothing – but I've done no more to this man than a good gardener would do to a sickly rose bush – cut it back to the very stock. Pity – yes I feel pity; not for Simpson the thug – but Simpson the product of society.'

'You've said yourself, a man has free will.'

'Of course! And the labour camp is Simpson's punishment for choosing to kill. But it's what we do to him afterwards that counts, don't you see? It's making the wrongdoer an important individual in his own eyes that ruins him, irretrievably, no matter what the psychearchs do or say. He's become the darling of smart social authors who sit in on sensational murder trials visibly concocting Freudian phrases to explain away the thin-lipped killer – he's become the subject of slob stories about thugs who aren't violent, only misunderstood.'

'Where does that leave Simpson?'

'It leaves him and others like him with a chance. He's being denied the unnatural right of his kind to a place in the sun. Above all Harry, he's living at this moment to regret what he's done.'

Baynard looked at the report in his hand.

'No cutlery . . . is there any detail you haven't forgotten?'

'Simpson?'

'I meant in running the country.'

'I can think of several. By the way, see the press gets this report and while you're about it ask Lorimer to drum up everything he can lay hands on about Don Dexter. I'd like a full briefing before six – what about the arrangements for this evening?'

'It's all laid on – Morrison's handling it.'

'Good. If you find Saunders hanging around, send him in.'

There was time to read a note from Marsh just delivered. By hand.

Dear Wyatt. Do you know your phone conversations are getting through to the wrong people? I thought soldiers never give away ammunition – but that's your business. I've been putting the finger on a few pulses – the going is good in most quarters but watch out for the Cabal – my inspired guess is that it's gunning for you with a silencer . . .

Timon Marsh

He knew nothing about the Cabal – behind-the-scenes men obviously. But if they were enemies sooner or later they'd have to make an appearance. Time enough to worry then – meanwhile what could he expect? A queue of well-wishers dying to shake him by the hand? Wyatt smiled at the thought. It was a quirk of Wyatt's bequeathed to him by his father – 'never stop laughing at yourself, Dick'. No one else knew about it. He turned his attention to the abstract of Decree Four, moments before Lord Inkley, Britain's UN representative, was announced.

Suave and elegant from his thoughts to his boots, Inkley flowed rather than strode into the room, the glissando movement of a man whose life is one high-powered conference after another. Wyatt, deep in the abstract, noticed nothing of this.

'Sit down, Mr Saunders.'

Inkley did not sit down; his professional expression of noncommittal suffered a sea-change as he bridled – visibly.

'Perhaps I ought to remind you . . .'

'You needn't.' Wyatt sounded as casual as a weather expert. He glanced up at the dumbfounded peer, studied him briefly – then smiled disarmingly. 'As a matter of fact I was just putting my signature to Decree Four.'

'Decree Four?' The lordly brow buckled with the effort to comprehend.

'Yes, four already – Crime, Housing, Arms agreements – cancellation of, and this . . . and we've only been here six days or so – not bad eh Mr Saunders?'

'That depends on many factors and I might remind you . . .'

'In a sense you're witnessing a moment of history – instant history you could call it. This decree abolishes all styles and titles as from now, you understand.'

'I don't.'

'No . . . well it means that lords and ladies, dukes and duchesses, kings, queens, princes and princesses now belong to the past and children's story books. You are now an English gentleman in a nation composed entirely of ladies and gentlemen – allow me to congratulate you on being the very first to be obscurely aware of the fact Mr Saunders. Now where are we?'

'Wait a moment – do you honestly think you can do away with a thousand years of tradition, just like that?'

'Regard it as done, Mr Saunders. Shall we consider . . .?'

But the erstwhile lord refused to consider anything but the fact of his life peerage. Some people said he was in love with it. Certainly he was reconciled to his title going to the grave with him – but that it should go before him was unbearable.

'You won't – you won't get far with that one, Wyatt. I don't care how many devils you have on your side – monkeying with the peerage will do for you.'

'I quite understand, Mr Saunders, and I can even sympathize with you in your sudden bereavement, but you'll come to realize the Honours system is the jar of sweets kept on the top shelf doled out from time to time for good children – if it's wrong for children to be rewarded for doing what they should . . . now what shall we discuss first?'

Saunders saw he was getting nowhere; his state of mind made argument difficult. He had a curious feeling that he'd been quite suddenly sawn in two – Saunders and Inkley – a desperate matter of amalgamation.

'You realize I've been waiting to see you for some days?' he accused.

'No slight was intended. Apart from anything else I needed to gauge UN reaction to the new situation.'

'I hope you're satisfied.'

'Extremely.'

'Personally I consider our position at the UN quite untenable while you're in power.'

Wyatt took some time to reply: 'You did say at the UN?'

'What the devil do you mean?'

'My information is that you paid a flying visit to Johnson – at his request of course – before returning to England.'

'How . . .?'

'The point is, I know. Now Mr Saunders, why is our position at the UN untenable?'

'Oh very well . . . it was made crystal clear to me that the United States would do everything in her power to reduce our standing as long as you held the reins of government.'

'And your reply?'

'I could only assure the President I would put his views to whatever happened to be the government on my return.'

'Views ... Tell me Mr Saunders, were you annoyed at being asked to convey a message baldly hinting at blackmail?'

'Oh come now . . .'

'As a diplomat I expect you to define a spade as an implement used possibly for digging – I'm talking about bloody shovels.'

'Perhaps,' Saunders conceded, 'I was a little resentful – our people in Washington are under pressure you know.'

'I know. Well – let's consider your brief. Do you have any plausible arguments against China's admission to the UN?'

'Well – not exactly – it has to come sooner or later.'

'Then press for it – sooner. You might also tell the Americans to get out of Vietnam.'

'What!'

'Well they're doing no good there are they? If they're not bombing themselves they're wiping out South Vietnamese villages – I mean if they go on like that they'll all end up dead anyway –'

'But . . .'

'Don't be afraid to speak up – just tell them to go home.'

'You must be joking.' The diplomat was horrified. 'You simply can't be . . .'

Wyatt cut through his objections like a bacon slicer. 'I was never more serious in my life! Listen Saunders, three years ago they contemplated bombing the North – it happened – now the Pentagon's pushing for the use of nerve gas – it'll come. Unless someone – you – stands up before the world and says we – England – will have no part in the whole filthy business!'

'The repercussions . . .'

Wyatt pushed a bulky file across the desk as he spoke: 'Thirty-three pages of cogent arguments for our attitude couched in language you can understand. Take it or leave it and make way for a man of more spirit. I can name a dozen FO types who'd go to New York tomorrow – today – at half your salary for the privilege of telling the world we will now do our thinking for ourselves. Well?'

'You don't understand, Wyatt – the checks and balances creating any given framework of international policy are – it's the result of years of give and take ... you can't switch about without a great deal of preliminary ...'

'I can and so will you. Remember this, Saunders – when you speak at the UN you're not the mouthpiece for checks, balances, factions, parties or any other sectarian interest, you speak for Britain's belief in the greatest good for the greatest number – you debate as the representative of Britain and no one else.'

Saunders glared sulkily at his polished shoes. In five minutes flat he had lost his peerage, his *savoir faire* and his entrée into a dozen of the best family mansions on Long Island.

'Why not Great Britain?'

A long silence forced him to glance up, he found himself at the receiving end of an incredibly penetrating gaze.

'Where is our greatness?'

The diplomat made no attempt to look for an answer. In any case Wyatt was switching to another mood.

'Come now, Saunders, I've read most of your speeches in the General Assembly. No one could do your job better – but you always had to cut your coat from other people's cloth. Forget the Western equilibrium mentality and speak on the side of natural justice. And while we're on the subject take this file too and give it your best attention. You'll do credit to it.'

Saunders listened carefully, searching for a hint of expedient flattery in Wyatt's words. It wasn't there. Suddenly, he had the feeling of a man being shown the world at a great height by a benevolent devil. Whatever Wyatt was, he sensed he would have to follow him right or wrong – the scoundrel was a born leader. A little sadly, he put the peerage behind him and took the file from Wyatt's outstretched hand.

He looked up from a brief study of the preamble.

'For God's sake! Is this agreed policy?'

'Discussed and agreed by all heads of departments concerned. It's top secret of course.'

'What about the Defence Ministry?'

'Notified – but it isn't strictly their concern.'

'And they agree?' Saunders was incredulous. 'But this could lead to a continental explosion!'

'My feeling is this will prevent one.'

'Suppose they fight?'

A gleam of amusement high-lighted the Captain's eyes. 'And suppose they don't? Give your best attention to it Saunders. And good luck.'

Saunders left London Airport that night bound for the United States. He allowed no one, not even his trusted secretary to carry a brief-case which he handled as gingerly as an explosives expert suddenly stricken by an attack of hiccoughs. He assured the reporters he was happy to serve under Wyatt's administration and that he would defend it vigorously at the extraordinary session due to be held on Wednesday.

14

Soon after he got the message, Don Dexter of Dallas had publicly gone on record with the news that Wyatt could be none other than anti-Christ. In a nationally hooked up, souped up telecast the crusading evangelist bowed his beautiful head in shame and admitted the failure of his punk peddling trips to England. Perfidious Albion, my friends, is gotten out of the fold, and before my God in heaven and sweet Jesus Christ right there with him I hold myself responsible for this Great Relapse. Now, can the British afford, he cried, accompanied by a long drawn out basso profundo chord from the TV company Wurlitzer, can they afford to lose a Queen and gain a one-way ticket to Perdition? Incredibly, Don went on to challenge Wyatt to an immediate and open debate, to answer 'in the court of world opinion the charge that he, Wyatt, was anti-Christ and Public Enemy Number One.'

'Make it for Monday – Westminster Hall. TV coverage and public invitation.'

Baynard and Morrison stared at Wyatt as though he'd taken leave of his senses. His acceptance surprised them as much as it surprised – and worried – Dexter.

He paused on the point of considering further business. 'Well?'

Morrison played the spokesman: 'What possible importance can you attach to a nasty little moralizing muckraker?'

'We've got enough problems without inviting them,' Baynard said.

'You're forgetting our policy. We take on all comers – we don't gain anything by ignoring Dexter. He's exactly what you say he is, Paul, and a lot more. He's backed by big business interests Napoleonic enough to agree religion is opium to the people. He's organization Man at its lowest – stands for everything we're against. See the arrangements are made, Harry. I shall enjoy putting one of America's plastic idols on the mantelpiece.'

'Easier said than done.' Morrison sounded gloomy. 'I don't doubt you can handle most of them – but a Fifth Avenue witch doctor . . .'

'Let's see how it looks on the night,' was all Wyatt would add to the subject.

The following letter was received by Commander Perrins, officer in charge of Special Branch investigations, code name Operation Shadow:

Concerning your query of the 26th I have made inquiries in my capacity as GOC Southern Area, and have learned that no more than a dozen men are AWOL including Wyatt, Baynard and Jennings. This makes nonsense of your assertion that two hundred men in my command must be missing. Any further information you require will have to be a matter of agreement between you and the Defence Ministry. I am forwarding a copy of this correspondence to Army Chief of Staff.

Lumley

Perrins sat back and thought for a bit, re-read the letter then passed it to Curly Lingfield. 'Read that.'

Lingfield did so, pursed his lips and muttered, 'Well, if that doesn't beat the lot.'

'Quite so. We've covered every Command in the country – and it's Southern – only twelve professional soldiers involved.'

'Then we're not up against the Army?'

'We were meant to think so. A clever man this Wyatt – twelve soldiers and a couple of hundred civilians. It'll be interesting to know how he managed it.'

'We'll find out sir.'

'Yes – I suppose we will.'

'Very cautious of Lumley, informing the C – o – S.'

'They all did. Buttering their bread on both sides. That's what we're up against – everyone being so damned careful in case Wyatt lasts.'

'D'you think he will?'

The Commander caught himself wondering – then decided to play safe. He trusted no one, least of all Lingfield.

'Hard to say – in any case it doesn't depend on us.'

'The Commissioner seems happy enough.'

'He's no choice – could be kicked out at one o'clock and somebody'd be warming his seat by half past.'

'We might as well be back on the beat,' Lingfield grumbled.

'That reminds me. You and your lads may soon be seconded to the Drug Squad.'

'The Reefer Gang!' Curly looked disturbed. 'Since when?'

'I had a report this morning – orders from Wyatt. He thinks Special Branch might be more usefully employed in tracking down one of the country's greater evils.'

'You're not taking orders from ...?'

'Confirmed by the Commissioner.'

While the Sergeant let this soak in Perrins went on thoughtfully: 'He's got a sense of humour this Wyatt – "Keep all the men you need for shadowing my people." '

'The sooner that bastard comes a cropper the better it'll be for everyone,' said a sorrowful Curly. 'I reckon we ought to start working out a plan of rescue for the Queen.'

'Excellent idea, you do that Curly – while I wrestle with *The Times* crossword ... we'll see who finishes first.'

At about the same time Wyatt was being shown to the temporary detention room fronting the cage. A purely functional affair containing a small table and chair.

He waited while the duty warder fetched the prisoner who entered dressed now in greyish regulation stuff. He stood looking down at the floor. The warder withdrew. A long silence.

'Do you know who I am?'

'Captain Wyatt – they said.' He spoke to the floor.

'Look at me.' Simpson raised a reluctant head. His gaze wavered before a steady scrutiny – but there was no escaping it . . . like a surgeon's probe . . .

'Do you understand now?' Wyatt asked.

'Yessir.'

'Do you know why I didn't enjoy doing this to you?'

'I – I don't think so.'

'It's unpleasant – having to prove that however civilized we think we may be, we're nearer to the animal nature than we care or dare to admit   does that make sense?'

'Yessir.'

'Only we're worse than most animals – they don't go in much for viciousness, malice, envy, spite. Man has the exclusive rights to these thought processes – that means you, me, the man next door – police, Popes, any and every one. What we are depends how far we curb them. If we don't or can't, if we kill or hurt our fellow men, we're no better than the worst of beasts, human jackals, thinking vultures . . .'

Wyatt studied the man with an almost frightening deliberation. Simpson couldn't know how desperately the Captain strove to stand in his place.

'They tell me you were a bricklayer.'

'I – yessir – at first.'

'I'm sending you with an advance party of men like yourself to a labour camp on an island. You'll be building your own quarters to start with. Eventually you'll be earning a wage comparable with outside rates. Two thirds will be deducted and paid into a compensation fund for victims and dependants. One half of the remaining third will be deducted towards the cost of your support, the rest saved against your eventual release. By the time you've finished your sentence we'll have established a training school. You'll have time to think about what you want to do – it's a question of starting again. That's all.'

The warder removed Simpson to a police guard waiting to take him back to gaol. They treated him gently, like a man, almost like one of themselves.

Wyatt sat in the barely furnished silence, deep in thought. When the warder returned he found the Captain still sitting at the table, hands covering his eyes, oblivious to all the world it seemed. 'Just as though he was praying,' he told a colleague later.

'You have a full house,' Baynard informed him. 'Queueing in all parts.'

'We can thank the BBC. I believe they interviewed Mr Dexter last night.'

'They did. I've got a transcript here if you want to . . .'

'No thank you, Harry.'

'For someone who doesn't believe in the limelight you're getting your share tonight. They're showing the TUC wrangle in five minutes – incidentally Transport House moved heaven and hell to get it banned – and then the viewers'll be treated to your ugly face again at eight . . . are you all right?'

There was genuine concern in Baynard's voice. He'd been checking through a sheaf of papers needing Wyatt's signature and only eventually noticed the silence, the pallor, the closed eyes of a man almost slumped over his desk.

'Come on – there's time for a rest.'

'Those papers –'

'Damn the papers – two hours' sleep in seventy-two, how the hell do you expect to – you need a break – Jennings is rustling up a meal. Ten minutes on a couch won't do you or the country any harm.'

Wyatt allowed himself to be shunted towards the couch, but still mouthing protests . . .

'Maybe, but you don't always know best – you've got a gruelling half-hour ahead of you and why you have to waste time on Dexter I –'

But Wyatt was already asleep.

She'd expected it, hadn't been altogether surprised when they came for Fred, not if half he'd said was true. They searched the flat, found the box of cartridges and off they'd gone with Fred in between. Shot a nightwatchman, they said. She was sure he hadn't meant to. If only the old fool hadn't got in the way Fred'd be sitting there now, grumbling as usual – instead of which . . .

Westminster Hall is an impressive setting for any occasion. The large audience gathered there must have thought so too. It would be a unique experience, sitting in the hall of Kings listening to Wyatt and Dexter – the one setting words on fire – the other dotting his i's with haloes and crossing his t's with crosses.

Dexter was already in his place when Wyatt entered the hall flanked by Baynard and Morrison. The audience cheered and for the first time that his friends could remember the Captain looked surprised – even embarrassed. Next day the *Compress* would be quick to point out that most of those present were teenagers.

Wyatt dominated in a chair set above the flight of stone steps descending to the body of the hall. Below him sat Dexter, who was forced necessarily to look up most of the time, an unusual experience for the evangelist. Soldiers casually guarded the entrances.

A large group of girls in white sat behind Dexter. These appeared to puzzle Wyatt who was seen to question Baynard before he stood and briefly gave his reasons for accepting Dexter's challenge. He then invited the man from Dallas to make his point.

The camera zoomed in to give millions a close-up view of a golden-haired Fauntleroy, a kind of man-child they swear can do no wrong, and if he does then it must be right. His light-of-the-world expression glistened like a wet Holman Hunt canvas, a frank 'let's be brothers but not comrades' kind of expression. In short, if the Daughters of the American Revolution could have managed one immaculate conception between them – Dexter would have been the blessed jackpot.

At the moment it was Don, the shrewd, sharp-dressing religio-politician, who prepared to speak. 'Captain Wyatt,' he drawled, 'Ladies 'n' gen'lmen – it has pleased Almighty God to call on me to offer a few words of spiritual advice that may, with all respect, Captain, bring you to a true understanding of the terrible tragedy you have unleashed on to the heads of millions, "for they are in perils in the city and in perils among false brethren". I hope before this meeting is through to bring you to a true repentance in the name of Christ our saviour, for I believe your soul has much to answer for . . . before I begin I shall ask the Sweet Singers of Jesus to lead us in a hymn of hope . . .'

The Sweet Singers of Jesus were only half out of their seats when Wyatt spoke. 'I'll gladly listen to your arguments for your sake, but for Christ's sake spare us your virgins, Mr Dexter.'

The red-faced songstresses subsided into their seats and the audience somehow managed to keep straight faces as befitted the occasion.

Mr Dexter gazed up at the shadowy wooden angels seeking badly needed inspiration. He could just manage without Mac at the Wurlitzer, but the girls were a great emotional booster with their singing, guaranteed to get 'em into orbit, make 'em receptive, responsive; now he'd have to start cold. Maybe he could make something of it.

'I assure you, Captain,' he intoned sadly, 'you have nothing to fear from songs in praise of God.'

'We're not here to praise God, Mr Dexter. We're here to be told why you challenge my authority and by what right you presume to call me to account.'

'By God's right!' Don Dexter thundered, throwing his arms wide like a crucified tailor's dummy. 'In my prayers, I have sought his divine guidance, and in the hour of need he did not fail me. Go forth Don, he commanded, go forth across the seas, seek out the enemy that never sleeps, go forth and do battle with the anti-Christ who has risen in your midst!'

The audience almost visibly wilted. Not the words alone, but cadence, intonation, the whole bag of oratorical tricks with an indefinable plus. All this Don could handle with the dexterity of a card sharper. Baynard looked angry enough to make a retort. Wyatt restrained him and stared long and hard at the evangelist.

'You seem to be on remarkably good terms with your God, Mr Dexter.'

'He is my judge, my creator, and my Father.'

'I see . . . go on.' Wyatt seemed as mild as milk. Something or it may have been God, told Dexter he was not evoking the correct response. Mention of anti-Christ, and in public, should've had him on his feet, emotionally disturbed, protesting at the greatest of all charges; then he, Dexter, would simply wade in with the old one two.

'Before God and your conscience do you understand the gravity of the accusation?'

'Oh quite. I am it seems the anti-Christ. Well then Mr Dexter?'

Don began to sweat a little: he couldn't figure this guy's line one little bit. Why didn't he attack for Chrissake . . . for Jesus Christ's sake? He's Goliath and I'm poor li'l David – hell, how can I play it forward while he's playing it backward?

'Sir . . . I have made an accusation which it is your duty to refute. No Christian community worthy of the name can tolerate a man who does the devil's work on its behalf. It is for you to satisfy, not me – I know where I stand in allegiance to Jesus Christ and my country. It is for you to deny the charge that I make in the name of fifty million people who are in jeopardy of their souls.'

'Very well then, Mr Dexter. You now appear to require a denial. I willingly give it you. I am not, to my knowledge, anti-Christ.'

Baynard and Morrison eyed their chief with some anxiety. Had he ordered them to arrange so much, so quickly for so little? A mere denial having no force, no conviction and no hope of victory for anyone but the evangelist? Dexter was also worried. If that was all Wyatt had to say, they'd have to pack up and go back to the Hilton. He'd have to deliver the punch line right now and hope for the best. The audience was restive, plainly disappointed with Wyatt and Dexter's performance.

'Then, sir,' the evangelist searched frantically for the right words, 'I ask you in the name of Jesus Christ and Christian democracy to abandon your hell-bent course, restore the Queen to her throne, her Parliament to the people. In the name of Jesus Christ –'

'You are too free with the name of Jesus Christ!'

The words rang through the Hall, needing no microphone; the audience sat up and stared and Dexter stared comically as the cameras offered his close-up to the delighted crowd of millions.

'I've been patient with you for the people's sake. I've listened to your arrogant stupidities so that they could see for themselves what you are . . .'

'I am a man of God!'

'You are a creature of the Washington Administration!'

The crowd gave an offbeat rendering of the 'Halleluja' chorus.

Wyatt pressed hard: 'You took a trip to Washington, saw the President, sought his divine guidance in this matter – and he did not fail you. Get over there, Don, he said, get over there and do what you all can to stop that damned rubberneck from fouling up the situation America-wise!'

'Captain Wyatt –'

'Do you deny you saw the President?'

'That's hardly . . . what I'm trying . . .'

'I've no doubt what you're trying to do – but I'm trying to tell you we're sick and tired, Mr Dexter, of your untimely, unwanted visits to this country; we're not even superficially impressed by your executive suite religion and we don't believe your brand of Jesus Christ superwhite soap powder washes whiter than any other. We resent being bombasted for our sins when we see enough happening in your country in one day to keep a *battalion* of Dexters busy for all eternity. Look to your own national dirty linen Mr Dexter – go back and convert the poor white trash; go home and sing hymns of praise to God and the Ku Klux Klan and the Brights and the Gold-waters; blast your countrymen's conscience with Vietnam; tell those teenagers who pour petrol over sleeping Bowery tramps before setting fire to them about sweet Jesus; when you've made the Pentagon safe for humanity – when you've excom-municated corruption from Congress to California, called your Christ to witness against an Administration befouled by an overkill-escalation-death-to-the-Reds mentality – then come back and we'll talk about anti-Christ. Meantime, Mr Dexter, take your virgins and your business managers, your sermon ghost-writers and your sickening hypocrisy back where it all belongs.'

Then Wyatt turned abruptly and walked out followed by Baynard and Morrison. There was nothing to stay for, no reason to acknowledge the audience's cheers. It had all been said at last and Dexter knew he had no answer. He flew home with his entourage next day, like a discredited prophet retreat-ing to the wilderness.

Baynard and Morrison returned to Wyatt's room. Wyatt seemed calm enough, but they were like members of an audi-ence trying to recapture the highlights of a superb performance.

'I didn't see it coming,' Baynard admitted.

'How could you have lost?' Morrison wanted to know.

'By arguing with him. I could only win by making a greater emotional splash than he could manage.'

'Maybe – but it was to the point,' Baynard muttered. 'By the way, how did you know Dexter saw the President?'

'I didn't.'

His friends stared at him.

'Well, how the devil –?' Baynard began.

Wyatt rarely laughed aloud. 'Perhaps it was divine guidance,' he said.

French called later that evening to make his report. The two men discussed security arrangements and agreed that more pro-fessional troops were needed to garrison the Tower. Volunteers could be drawn from Colchester. No problem there. There seemed nothing more to keep French; he wasted few words.

'Is that all?' Wyatt asked.

'No – the former Queen wants to see you.'

'Interesting.' He thought for a moment. 'What visitors did she have today?'

'Wrigley – the former Lord Chamberlain – the Archbishop –'

'Ah! Anyone else?'

'The Armstrong Joneses, Hendricks, a biographer, and the Australian High Commissioner. That's the lot.'

'We'll make it tomorrow – tell her I'll see her at ten.'

'Right.'

'What's your opinion, French?'

'An enemy reconnaissance – in strength.'

Wyatt smiled. 'You're probably right. We'll know in the morning.'

15

Wyatt seldom moved from the Palace precincts. He took what exercise he could on the terrace overlooking the river. Sometimes the guards might jerk into watchfulness then relax as they recognized the lone figure pacing innumerable corridors – a man following a thread of dreams through a labyrinth . . .

Moments of leisure were hard to come by, and it seemed like an outing – a breath of fresh air'd do him good, Jennings reckoned – when he set off, by appointment, to see the former Queen. There were no outriders, he travelled alone except for Jennings his driver. The car passed through busy streets and interminable traffic jams; no one recognized the man who presumed to run a country without a shred of authority. Special Branch officers followed of course, and an unobtrusive car carrying three watchful occupants followed the SB.

Within half an hour Wyatt was in the presence of the Queen. She was quite alone; but her quarters were cramped enough for children's laughter to be heard not far away, mocking the antique silence. She stood by the window, finger-tips barely touching a polished oak table on which a mass of chrysanthemums erupted like star-shells. The day's newspapers lay neatly folded on a sofa. He sensed they had been well read.

Inevitably the two incompatibles observed each other with concealed curiosity. Wyatt waited for her to speak . . .

VIP lounge. Kennedy Airport.

'Lord Inkley, you said a few days back you'd return to New York with everything in your country back to normal. How d'you feel about it now sir?'

'Lord Inkley' clutched his brief-case that much tighter and cleared his throat. Difficult enough at any time coping with the American press-gang; remembering Wyatt he could only smile with the doubtful assurance of an agnostic facing the Inquisition. 'First – you'd better refer to me I think as Mr Saunders, my er – maiden name before I married into the peerage!' Sound policy to kick off with a witticism.

No one laughed. The journalists were incredulous.

'Mr! You've renounced –?'

'It's been renounced for me – all styles and titles etcetera are now abolished in Britain, I thought you knew.'

'You mean you're going along with this guy?'

'I go along with my country.'

'With a republic?'

'If you're asking whether or not Britain is to become a republic all I can say is I don't know.'

'Why isn't something being done about Wyatt?'

'I've no idea.'

'What about the Government Mr Inkley?'

'Saunders! Which government?'

'The one Wyatt hi-jacked.'

'It wasn't there when I arrived in London. The country has to be run; if the people who usually run it aren't there, then it must be run by those who are.'

'How about Anglo-American relations? Is this Wyatt gonna do the right thing by us?'

He climbed on to his diplomatic dignity: 'I think Captain

175

Wyatt feels the United States is quite capable of taking care of itself.'

Acutely conscious of the brief-case and its contents he begged to be excused, fought his way out of the lounge and into his car.

News travels fast in New York, supersonically in Washington. Within an hour of Saunders's brief airport interview the first stones were being hurled at the British Embassy's windows.

Lorimer, Morrison and Sinclair were already assembled in Wyatt's room when he returned. A full meeting of the Council was rare, one or more would usually be occupied with committees or discussions with Ministry co-ordinators. The trio waited with some impatience. Something had gone wrong – why else his air of preoccupation?

'As you know I've just seen the former Queen – it appeared to be a question of minor matters – tutors for her children, an assurance that her eldest son would be permitted University entrance on the same terms as other children ... all this French could have handled.' He paused. 'Rather suddenly, she came to the point.'

In the last five minutes the Queen had made no move – the outstretched fingers still touched the table-top like those of a blind man tentatively seeking support.

'I want you to know that it is my intention to abdicate.'

Not the flicker of an eyelid disturbed his expression.

'I see. Your reasons?'

'I think it's enough to say that it's in my country's interests.'

'Your counsellors have given you advice no doubt?'

The Royal gaze wavered and came to rest on the nearby flowers.

'A personal decision.'

'May I ask if this is a threat or a statement of intent?'

'It is my will.'

Almost a flash of anger, but spoken like a queen. Wyatt could admire her even as he smiled to himself. They thought they were playing a brilliant game – take his Queen – checkmate – she would become a commoner. He could hardly keep Mrs Mountbatten locked up – public opinion would be against it and quite rightly. He felt he was being closely observed for signs of irresolution ... he showed nothing.

'Very well – an instrument of abdication will be drawn up for your signature. It's a simple matter but –'

'But it isn't a simple matter!' Lorimer objected. 'According to their reading of the Constitution there could be no abdication without an Act of Parliament.'

'I was about to say. I pointed that out to her.'

'Therefore I'm afraid it amounts to little more than an empty gesture.'

'I'm assured my declaration will be enough in the circumstances.'

'It's a trick,' Morrison exploded. 'If we're kicked out all they need do is pass a special Act of Reinstatement – she'd go through a form of recoronation and it starts all over again.'

'There's a precedent for it – the Normans,' Sinclair murmured.

'Did you put it to her?' Lorimer wanted to know.

'Something she already knows. But it isn't the point. It wasn't for me to seek assurances that her decision was irrevocable – and yet she gave them.'

'I hope you understand – it is not an empty gesture.'

'I imagine I'm intended to understand as much by your advisers.'

'My advisers are not responsible for my conviction that the country appears to manage very well without me.'

Wyatt permitted himself the suggestion of a smile.

'I really don't see what there is to smile about Wyatt – this places us in a very awkward position.' Lorimer looked angry and disturbed.

'As a lawyer you should be smiling more than anyone,' Wyatt said. 'Your reaction is exactly what they intended.'

'They've succeeded as far as I'm concerned,' Sinclair admitted. 'I agree with Lorimer, this creates a dangerous situation.'

'Let's think about it a little more, shall we? Look at it from their point of view. It's quite clear, they reason, the Queen is the only ace in the pack, the only guarantee Wyatt's got – therefore if she goes – he's left with no visible means of support.'

'Well it's true isn't it?' Morrison seemed exasperated by Wyatt's calm appraisal.

'Not as true as all that – as I pointed out.'

'If you wish to make a personal declaration after the accomplished fact I've no reason to prevent you. I hope you understand it makes no difference to my position.'

She regarded him impersonally – no trace of surprise that Wyatt could see.

'I don't think I do understand.'

'At the moment our opposition has no wish to end the Monarchy. It's prepared to sacrifice a queen; but it still considers itself bound by the constitution such as it is.'

'Which no longer exists.'

'For them it exists.'

'Well?'

'You may renounce the Throne – in your own name – but of course you can't renounce it in your children's name . . .'

She knew exactly what Wyatt was driving at – but her composure seemed impregnable.

'Go on.'

'Regretfully, they would remain in custody. Do I make myself clear?'

'Perfectly.'

'May I assume therefore that your abdication would be an empty gesture?'

The Queen made no reply.

From a BBC special report for television on London's homeless and the Palace:

The people you see here are waiting in what used to be the Ballroom of the former Buckingham Palace. They're some of the dozens of London's homeless about to be allocated two or three rooms to each family in this six hundred roomed building. The rooms have been stripped of all personal possessions, furniture, carpets, everything – the magnificent Durbar canopy above the thrones which themselves have gone into cold storage – and the bareness emphasizes the departed splendour, the enormous scale on which many of these rooms were designed. Over in one corner are some of Wyatt's officials directing Operation Move-in. I asked one of them what could possibly be done with some of the largest rooms . . .

'In a city starved of space that's really no problem.'

'But they're not suitable for housing families surely?'

'No of course not. That wasn't Captain Wyatt's intention. You must remember there's an acute students' accommodation problem. Three or four of these State Apartments will be converted into a kind of hostel for upwards of two, possibly three hundred. This room alone would seat two hundred for meals – the Green and Blue Drawing Rooms will provide an adequate area for study and recreation.'

I then asked some of the families themselves how they felt about it all. Mr and Mrs Stone for example:

'Mrs Stone, you've just been allocated three rooms I hear.'

'Yes – in the servants' quarters – we've three children.'

'How do you feel about living in a Palace?'

'It's like a dream.'

'An improvement on hostel life?'

'It means I can be with my husband again.'

'Had you been there long?'

'Several months. My husband fell ill, we got behind with rent and had to move – then there were complaints about the baby – they told us three was too many – so we had to go – somehow it went from bad to worse – we slept out a couple of nights . . .'

'Does it worry you – about the Queen?'

'I'll answer that. She's got an art collection here worth four million – she won't starve or go without. And I'll tell you this – most of us in our position aren't the lazy layabouts some of the papers make us out to be – you can still fall on hard times in this country, never mind what the politicians say.'

'So you think Wyatt's good for the country?'

'If that man declared war on Russia today I'd join up – he'd have a good enough reason for me – and I'll tell you something else – when we demonstrated outside the law courts – an army officer stopped and spoke to us – only one who did besides reporters. "It won't always be like this," he said and slipped a couple of quid in our hands to get sweets and that for the kids.'

'Really – d'you think it was Wyatt?'

'Your guess is as good as mine.'

The Times political correspondent reports for November 3rd:

There is considerable speculation in Whitehall and Fleet Street circles about Wyatt's plans for at least a part of the Rhine army now in process of withdrawing. As some battalions return home by air, many of those near the centre of things are asking, what next? A precipitate evacuation at such short notice suggests more than penny pinching concern to reduce overseas spending. We know that some of these men are to be offered to the UN as a peace-keeping force – this is commendable and has been generally applauded at home and abroad. But what about the rest? Why such urgency to get them home unless something is afoot? So far Captain Wyatt has been at considerable pains to keep the public informed of his intentions. It would be both regrettable and dangerous if he were to cloak his intentions at this stage.

The Times correspondent had cleverly conveyed to its readers a cause for apprehension in what appeared to be an innocent redeployment of the armed forces. Clearly there could be no purpose in a lightning withdrawal unless Wyatt was about to embark on a military venture. But, *The Times* mused, where in the world was there scope for a spot of sabre rattling? Then its Man in Westminster had a thought. Wyatt is reported to have had talks with representatives of certain African states; he has made his position clear, by implication at least, on the Rhodesian question. Could it be ...?

On Thursday morning the London clubs were fermenting with excruciatingly restrained excitement. Top People were determined to read into a piece of intelligent guesswork revelations properly belonging to a scoop. Since Wyatt had summoned a Press conference for the next day, they felt justified in putting two and two together.

The Cabal went into conclave at ten o'clock. Langley was late as usual, but the others, incensed by the apparent march of events, discarded the rule of silence and fulminated to no very great purpose except to agree that Langley or no Langley, some kind of action was now urgent. Rigg alone kept silence. He was saving his self-righteous venom for the former earl. He launched his carefully worded assault almost before the old man entered.

'Well *Mister* Langley, do you still say do nothing?'

The ancient sprig of an Elizabethan oak paused in the act of lowering himself into his favourite chair. He stood upright, took a step or two towards Rigg and stared not at, but through him.

'You forget yourself Mister Rigg,' he spoke quietly, then turned away and took his time about sitting. He gazed at no one in particular as he queried, 'I take it we've all read this piece in *The Times*?'

They had. And the Field Marshal added there must be something in it since no other paper carried anything comparable.

'There is something in it,' Langley's voice trembled with the effort of keeping anger under control. 'I have it on the highest authority. Wyatt intends to deliver an ultimatum to Rhodesia – he'll probably announce it at the Press conference tomorrow.'

The faint sounds of traffic in the twentieth-century world outside hardly skimmed the silence as the four Cabaliers absorbed the news too starkly uttered.

'We could have prevented this!' was all Rigg dared to permit himself at that moment.

'Surely we still can.' Minter tried hard to sound confident.

'We have a duty . . .' Campbell began.

'You all talk as though we're up against a fool!' the old man hawked to clear his throat of emotion. 'They tried the abdication ploy – I told them Wyatt would see clear through it and he did. I've said all along – wait till he runs aground – well he has – sooner than I expected . . .'

'A question of rousing public opinion,' Wynlose said.

'The Press will do so – but it isn't enough – the BBC's pro-Wyatt and a damned sight more powerful. And that's another little nest of intellectual anarchists to be fumigated when the time comes.'

'Meanwhile?' Minter queried.

'Meanwhile, I paid a brief visit to the Commissioner before I came here – measures will be taken. It's time for a war of nerves – time to create a *cordon sanitaire*.'

'What does he have in mind?' Wynlose wanted to know.

The ancient chuckled as he contemplated a clawed hand made for dabbling in the excremental depths of statecraft.

'He has my suggestions in mind. We should be seeing results soon I imagine.'

16

Wyatt's third press meeting was something of a progress report. For all of his brief reign he never lost sight of the fact that people should be well informed.

He gave figures to prove that crimes of violence already showed a significant drop. Only twenty-five offenders were on view throughout the country. Road accidents had plummeted. People were driving carefully – the thought of being permanently deprived of a passport to heaven was as nothing compared with losing a driving licence. Confidence abroad was climbing – there had been no flight of Sterling – the pound continued to gain strength. America's threat to withdraw investments had not materialized. How could it when two – as Wyatt pointed out – could play at that game? Trade missions were to be exchanged with China following a full resumption of diplomatic recognition. He revealed the full text of a protest note from Ottawa and announced the resignation of two Service Chiefs.

The newsmen rustled. Could this have a bearing on the

Rhodesian question? None of them guessed the explanation could be as sensational.

'They resigned,' Wyatt continued, 'because they were incensed with my decision to cut Defence spending by one half. One thousand millions a year would now be available for schools, hospitals, houses and even the great "technological revolution" now lying embalmed like Lenin – a great idea but dead – in the Smith Square mausoleum.

'We mean what we say!' Wyatt thundered. 'We don't give a damn how many Service Chiefs resign – they're no more good to the country than Defence Ministers who whine in double-think terms about a greater defence policy or none at all.

'Defence!

'Our attitude reminds me of a wealthy widow living alone in a large house crammed with jewellery, *objets d'art*, Cézannes and God knows what else. She installs electronic burglar alarms, buys the most expensive safes, locks, catches and booby traps. She hires private detectives to patrol the grounds – barbed wire everywhere – Alsatians – but it's not enough: obsessed with defending her precious possessions she hires private detectives to watch the private detectives.

'When a sex maniac actually managed to break into her bedroom she cried thank God, gave him her blessing – herself and five pounds for being an honest man.

'That's what defence has become – a neurotic pastime for those who don't know how else to spend money they never even earned! Well I refuse to believe we can't use a thousand millions to better advantage – providing a decent standard of living for the millions in this country still bordering the poverty line!'

It went down well with the gathering but Wyatt gave them no time to catch breath.

'The motorways programme is to be slashed. The late Minister of Transport wanted it both ways; massive expenditure – eight hundred millions – to attract more and more people to the dubious pleasures of driving on the roads, equally massive expenditure to promote public and even private transport concerns as a social service. False economic practice consistent with the previous administration's imbalance of possibilities – or – you can't have it both ways.

'The transport Decree will be advertised next week. Railway services will be restored and railwaymen will be given the square deal they deserve. You'll find we intend to make more efficient use of the road network already existing. It will be maintained and improved by an enlarged labour force. We're a small country – it follows the road network must be correspondingly small. We cannot afford to ape America by providing a communications system based on their continental scale.'

Almost as an afterthought he added: 'I have been assured by Counsellor Serov that the Soviet Union will be glad to broaden trade relations as an earnest of that country's good-will and faith in our future. Indications are that the Soviet Union is ready to place orders in those areas of industry most in need.'

Which information was meant to reinforce in the audience's mind the essential fact. The régime had been accepted. Questions followed.

The Glasgow Herald: 'There seems to be some doubt about the future of Holy Loch and US air bases in England. Could Captain Wyatt throw any light on this?'

'There is no doubt about these bases. They are to be evacuated within the next few weeks. Meanwhile they cease to be operational at midnight tonight.'

The Sun wanted to know what Wyatt was doing about unemployment.

'Our aim is full employment. I tell you, if for nothing else the Wrigleys of this world deserved to be kicked out for their cynicism, for daring to suggest that "a maximum of two per cent unemployment is permissible or possible or acceptable in the circumstances". Is this socialism or ostracism? No figure above zero can be "acceptable" unless we're creating a new class of economically indigestibles!'

'But if work doesn't exist . . .' *The Daily Mirror* began.

'Then it must be created! What kind of a state is it that

taxes a man out of the labour market! In that respect the Selective Employment Tax is to go. We cannot progress as long as employers are saddled with stultifying stupidities having no validity beyond the small world of the LSE.'

The Telegraph: 'Have you any plans to meet the heads of other states – France for example?'

'I haven't been asked. The world is still dealing with a new boy; generally speaking contacts with other countries can only be made at ambassadorial levels.'

'Isn't this disadvantageous?'

'Why should it be? If you can name one solid advantage gained by past Prime Ministers gadding about the world at the nation's expense I shall be glad to hear of it.'

The Daily Compress: 'Captain Wyatt, there's some concern about a report in yesterday's *Times* which seems to imply a sinister motive behind your action in withdrawing the BAOR. As you appear to be the kind of gambler who lays all his cards on the table – can you comment on this report?'

Baynard glared at the speaker; Dowson did his best not to look worried. At this moment plans were being worked out at high pressure. He wondered how Wyatt could possibly reconcile candour with the need for secrecy . . .

'As I said before – one third of the force will be run down – more than a third will be retained on the home strength – the rest will be allocated to the UN subject to that organization's acceptance.'

In fact, Wyatt knew the UN had gladly accepted the offer only that morning – but the news would keep.

'Can we,' the *Compress* man persisted, 'have your assurance that those troops to be placed on the home strength will not be used against Rhodesia?'

Even Wyatt breathed a disguised sigh of relief.

'You have my solemn assurance.'

Wyatt sat back, suddenly tired maybe of the mass of documents, reports and abstracts avalanching over the great desk. He watched Jennings pour coffee and felt grateful for the sergeant's stolid presence.

'It's incredible Jennings – we've been here less than a fort-night.'

'Well sir?'

'I was thinking – the only places I've been to – Regent's Park and the Tower of London.'

'Dunno what you're complaining about,' he took his time stirring sugar into the coffee. 'You didn't have to pay did you?'

There was nothing else for it – Wyatt returned to work.

The Commissioner had little to thank Special Branch for. If they hadn't made a mess of escorting certain important persons Wyatt wouldn't be where he was now, holding Sir John – as he almost retorted to Lady Grace in a moment of exasperation – by the very short hairs.

They needed to be taken down a peg or two – the country's security was all very well, but pulling in a few spies when it was too late gave them no cause for acting like a lot of little Jimmy Bonds. Now, thanks to Langley, he could tell them what to do for a change. Nasty work: the fastidious Commander wasn't going to relish it overmuch. He waited for the knock at his door with a pleasing sense of anticipation. When it came his 'Come in' sounded positively good humoured.

Perrins entered cautiously, half wondering if it was about his last report – it was sketchy – bound to be – as for the SB's negligence in the first place – his responsibility ... He looked forward to a touchy half hour: yet the Chief seemed genial enough, even offered him a drink ... then he remembered – old 'Razor Blades' could be genial to the purpose which – more often than not – was not nice. Perrins poured himself a large gin and tonic to keep out the cold. Sir John smilingly waited for him to settle into a chair.

'Nasty business, Perrins.'

The Commander sniffed suspiciously at the summary and decided it was harmless – 'it is indeed, sir' – he watched the Chief assume an air of utter mystification.

'Must've been going on for months – years even – and no one any the wiser.'

The Commander of Britain's Own Watchdogs shifted un-comfortably as Sir John innocently inserted a very dead needle.

'And in the Army too – sort of part-time cover I suppose. Incidentally the Defence Ministry's furious about your investigations – seems to think it's Military Intelligence's pigeon.'

'I'd have thought it was anybody's pigeon, sir.'

'Nobody seems to want it.'

'Playing safe –'

'Yes – well I suppose we're all doing that. But you didn't really think it was an Army game did you?'

'There was the occasion when a number of soldiers put themselves forward as Parliamentary candidates. I thought it worth checking for a connection.'

The Commissioner admitted there was something in that. 'So,' he added inconsequentially. 'Here we are.'

'Yessir – here we are.' Perrins waited for it.

'Pity we can't rescue the Queen.'

'Too risky, sir – I don't think they'd stop at –'

'Quite. So it's the old game – string along till we can string 'em up. Pity in a way – he's making a good shot at it – the Crimes and Penalties decree – it works ... I thought he was a crackpot – didn't we all?' The Commissioner stared moodily at the studio portrait of Lady Grace standing on his desk. 'He's no crackpot!' Then with a chuckle. 'Abolishing the peerage'll do for him – he's made enemies from Garters to MBEs.'

'The country's taking it very well.' Perrins wondered how Mr Blades felt about not being Sir John.

'More than I can say for the Missus. Don't mind for myself – but if she's anything to go by Wyatt should've dropped dead long ago.'

Perrins could believe it: 'She's obviously not in favour, sir?'

'You must be joking – she's damned near out of her mind in case the neighbours say "Good morning, Mrs Blades." Refuses to go to her club because she's certain they'll all think it even if they don't actually say it. Humiliating she says.' He sighed heavily. 'She certainly didn't marry me for my title but by God she'd rather be widowed than be without it.'

Perrins murmured vague commiserations and assumed he was being led to the point.

'So you see, Perrins, we've got to do something if only to restore Mrs Blades's peace of mind.'

Perrins finished his drink before he spoke, then asked the silliest question he could think of. 'Do you have anything in mind, sir?'

'Had a visitor recently – one of the Cabal.'

Perrins almost dropped his empty glass – worse than he'd expected – much worse – he put down the glass steadily, deliberately. 'Oh yes?'

'Not an ultimatum exactly – they're too smooth for that. Just a discreet indication that heads will be rolling if we don't get the ball rolling.'

'I see.'

'I assured my distinguished visitor you would.'

The ball had rolled well and truly to Perrins' feet.

'Wyatt?'

'No – funnily enough. Not French or Baynard either.'

'The others seldom move out of the Palace – except Morrison of course.'

'That's right. Get rid of him.' The Commissioner might have been offering Perrins another drink, which in fact he did. The Commander refused, felt unsure of his direction – even wondered if he'd heard aright.

'They – must have a good reason sir.'

'We've got to soften them up – make 'em jumpy – dammit they're succeeding because they feel secure. We've got to start somewhere.'

Then Perrins realized the Chief was avoiding his eyes, glanced out of the window, inspected the bookshelves, the great wall map of the Metropolis, even stared at the ghastly photograph of Grace, anywhere but at Perrins. Blades no more cared for the job than he did.

'Killing Morrison,' he spoke deliberately, 'killing him won't do Wyatt any harm with the public.'

'For heaven's sake, is he an enemy of the State or isn't he?

You're talking like an Aldermaston marcher! What do you suppose the public cares about Morrison – or Wyatt for that matter? They'll sit watching as though its another thrilling episode of "Danger Man". Bread and televised circuses, Perrins – that's about the limit of public concern.'

But Perrins, listening to the troubled conscience of a man trying to keep his job, could only hear the coldly uncompromising voice of the Cabal.

Security – what the devil did that word mean any more? And why should he concern himself about Morrison? An enemy of the State – orders from above – eliminate. That was his job – how to make a man disappear – find him first, then kill him – security ... he was sure of one thing. This would be an outside job – it was too dirty even for his lads.

With that much settled he sent Lingfield searching for information, then sat back to forget the whole sordid business, surveyed the old and familiar trappings of his office – and suddenly realized how drab it all looked. Counted pins stuck into wall-papering maps – he knew where they all were – knew where to find them – wasn't that power? The carpet was threadbare in places – why hadn't he noticed before? Of course – security – too busy chasing the Enemy ... but who was the real enemy – the Russians, Blades – Morrison – Wyatt or Langley? No – that wasn't power – from Blades down to the lowest nark – they were slaves and servitors of the System ... and the System was stirring again – demanding the Fe-fi-fo-fum blood of an Englishman – Morrison – an enemy of the System ... Lingfield returned as Perrins slowly surfaced from contemplating the frayed carpet, knowing he was nothing more than an instrument of revenge.

'Well?'

'There's only one "recent" sir. Villains are a bit shy on gun-slinging since Wyatt's decree – this one's got a CRO as long as your arm though. Are we back in business then?'

Perrins ignored the question and a gleam of hope pin-pricking Lingfield's tiny eyes. He'd often thought of Curly as an ideal concentration camp adjutant – if such a thing could be imagined in England ... Curly liked messing about with people the way some people enjoy messing about with boats and things.

'Is that his file?'

'Yessir.' He handed it to the Commander who read rapidly through, paused thoughtfully for a moment then murmured – 'Gun happy.'

'Top marksman in the army this one – he's never forgotten it.'

Perrins reconsidered the file. 'Three years for armed assault – how very euphemistic.'

'Very what sir?'

'Sawn-off shotgun. He shot a man's legs to smithereens in a spot of gang warfare; armed assault sounds better.'

'Will he do?'

'Oh yes ... I see he has political convictions too – yes Curly – he'll do. Make the necessary arrangements, will you?'

'Spring him?'

'And quickly.'

The next few days saw no startling developments. It was as though the country had suffered a severe earth tremor, settling into a more comfortable topography after the first shock. Someone was governing, that was the main thing – never mind who or how – doing as well as the last lot if not better. Food prices remained stable, investments were improving, he was tackling unemployment – and there were only forty-odd shopping days to Xmas.

But the poor purblind public never sees the danger till it's poking out the collective eye. Domesday for Wyatt was nothing to what the powers-that-would-be had in mind for an ungrateful mob which had so obviously allowed democracy – 'their' kind of democracy – to go by default.

A controlled society – Rigg had no doubts about that – with cheerful viciousness he summed up the need for a tighter grip on the hoi-polloi to an after dinner assembly of weekend guests at his country house.

'It happened because we pandered to these jumped-up peasants too much and too long – time they were taught a lesson.'

'Martin loves the people.' His wife, Helen, smiled dazzlingly as a Cartier shop window, mockingly as Woolworth's.

'People! World Cup Willies! I'll tell you what they are, your people – gutter sweepings – left overs twice removed from a breed of domestic servants – workhouse candidates promoted by the Welfare State and overtime earnings until they think they're as good as or better than their betters!'

'That's us,' she informed their guests. They smiled knowing it was true.

Rigg was indulgent. 'Very well – smile – but you know damned well I'm right.'

They did. They all said as much. Everyone that is, except Rigg's dark little protégé, the man he had chosen to take his place in the Cabal when he was no more.

As he listened to the familiar diatribe, the man behind yellow tinted spectacles let his mind wander into the future. He was the chosen one, the man born to make the cabalistic dream of a 'controlled society' come true. Merely a question of time and spidery patience . . .

No one was more surprised than Milly when he came home all unexpected that day. Just when she'd got used to the idea he might be away indefinitely. The excuses were all ready for Mum. He'd got a job up North – on a building site – very good money . . . but she wouldn't need them now. He was home again – and he hadn't done it. She felt ashamed for thinking he ever could do such a thing – the nightwatchman and all that.

Only . . . he sat there staring at the Leaping Horse print her uncle gave them for a wedding present. She knew he didn't like it . . . then he looked at her, and it chilled her a little. He didn't look like Fred somehow even when he spoke.

'They knew – Alf told 'em where it was – but shove off they said – we'll let you know. And then . . . and then they gave it back . . .'

'Gave what back Fred?' she faltered.

She might have been walking round the supermarket for all the answer she got.

17

The West Germans watched the Rhine Army pulling out with some misgivings. There, quite suddenly was the reality. Part of their bastion against the Communist world crumbling before their very eyes. The first units were going home.

Only the Officers' Corps Association cheered and sneered. If enough of these damned toy soldiers cleared out of the Fatherland, it could breathe again – expand and grow to its rightful stature . . . there was always the Wehrmacht – and the Americans were prepared to reconsider their atomic weapons policy in view of the rapidly changing situation . . .

TV interviewers were at the airfield ready to welcome the first contingent.

'Sergeant?'

'Stewart.'

'Sergeant Stewart, you're glad to be home of course?'

'Aye.'

'Do you feel Wyatt has gone too far in withdrawing from the North Atlantic Treaty Organization before renegotiation of the Warsaw Pact?'

'Do I what?'

'. . . feel that Wyatt has withdrawn precipitately from NATO?'

'Oh aye – he's withdrawing right enough – we're the first laddies out of Germany – you can see that for yesel.'

'What – what do you feel about Wyatt personally?'

'Couldn'a tell you – I've never met him.'

Eighteen days on and the country had all but taken the régime for granted. Not that people had lost interest. They

192

read the decrees, digested and discussed them as Wyatt intended. Instructions were issued to all state schools, 'eleven plus children are considered old enough to discuss the nation's affairs – Captain Wyatt requests that all decrees and national directives should be incorporated into those periods devoted to Current Affairs'. The Ministry of Education reported an encouraging degree of co-operation.

He never ceased to make it clear that every move he made was in the public interest, for the public benefit, that they, the public, had a right to know what was being done on their behalf – had a right moreover to comment on and criticize his measures.

As a result so many thousand letters were received at 'Wyatt's HQ, Houses of Parliament, Westminster' that an already formidable secretariat had to be expanded to deal with the correspondential flood. In less than three weeks Wyatt could claim that the country was more politically conscious than it had ever been. This, he always insisted was not only beneficial but necessary as a prelude to the eventual introduction of a truly representative constitution.

Plans were almost complete for the expedition. At the earliest opportunity Wyatt would announce that a small compact fighting force had been created through round-the-clock efforts by the Council, Ministry officials and senior members of the Services. In a few days the first air-lifts would fly Service personnel to bases in Zambia. Meanwhile top secrecy was the order of the day – speculation ran riot until it congealed into certainty – Wyatt was up to something. It could only be Rhodesia. . .

The next witness was Major-General Sir William Odgson – veteran of World War Two, unofficially billed as Army scapegoat number one. The Army too had to be taught a lesson it would never forget. Socialists, Tories and Hartfish were in complete agreement on that point.

Hardly a trial in the accepted sense of course, they daren't go so far as to antagonize the Forces, and create another Wyatt

193

... Hartfish's solution was admirable – the public pillory – nail the man to his military cross with words hard as nails. Force him into the box as a 'background' witness, drive him into a corner with the rest of the miserable crew. The Pro-Go had provided Hartfish with a remarkable driving licence.

'Sir William, you were closely concerned with the military operation in question were you not?'

'I was.'

'How did you first come to hear about it?'

'I received a communication in common with other Service Chiefs and M of D officials. It requested my attendance at a meeting of the full Council.'

'Having regard to your prior allegiance did you ignore the request?'

'No.'

'I see – so you went to this meeting over which Wyatt presided?'

'I did.'

'Had you ever met the man before?'

'No – never.'

'What opinion if any did you form concerning Wyatt?'

'I was impressed – first by his obvious sincerity – secondly by his grasp of the –'

'Very well – you were impressed. Tell me, Sir William, do you ever watch TV? Drama for example?'

'Quite often – when I have the time – yes.'

'Do you consider yourself to be a good judge of an actor's performance?'

'I – know a good from a bad performance I suppose.'

'I'm sure you do. At all events you were sufficiently impressed to accept a degree of responsibility for his military adventure?'

'I don't think your definition does justice to what Wyatt had in mind.'

'Would you accept that by any definition you as a professional soldier welcomed a little escapist expedition to ameliorate the boredom of peace-time inaction?'

'If you believe men who've been through a war and know its

194

consequences are anxious to go through it again as a mere alternative to boredom – then I can only say you're grossly mistaken.'

'Were you familiar with the complexities of the Rhodesian problem?'

'There were no complexities – as Wyatt made clear.'

This isn't a matter of white minorities or black majorities – the problem is about human beings denied certain basic rights by other human beings. I've just given you facts enough to prove Rhodesia is determined to create an apartheid mentality as obnoxious as anything to be found in South Africa.

This situation has drifted too far for too long. If like Wrigley we continue to shirk the issue, we prove to the so-called Third World that we consider white skin more sacred than natural justice.

We've heard all the arguments, listening to interminable discussions, teach-ins, news and views of everybody concerned – everybody? Where was the voice of two million Africans who have most to lose!

More coloured Rhodesians fought for this country in the last war than did whites – what colour blood do these miserable racialists think flows through an African's veins? Was it red enough to shed for the white man's cause!

If integrity means anything at all, we have more to lose in Africa than the doubtful love of the White Rhodesians ... if we do what's right why should we fear the censure of ultrawhite nations? Why should we even bow to the applause of ultrablack states?

But it will be written in the next chapter of history that we acted for the best, and in obedience to a trinity of principles greater than the Ten Commandments – Respect, Dignity and Justice for Everyman ...

'You recognize these quotations from his opening statement Sir William?'

'I do.'

'Are you prepared to say that this somewhat emotional rationale was persuasive enough to command your unhesitating co-operation?'

'Yes.'

'Tell me, Sir William, what would have resulted from a refusal on your part to sanction the use of force in Rhodesia?'

'I suppose someone else would have sanctioned it in my place.'

'So you agreed to the expedition because you knew if you didn't someone else would?'

'No – that is I –'

'Had you no moral scruples about white men spilling the blood of white men?'

'The question didn't arise!'

'It might have done. I say again you were unmindful of the fact that you assisted in promoting a civil war in which a brother might very well have shed a brother's blood?'

'You're making too much of a questionable emotional theme!'

'Emotional theme: that's how you see it?'

'Well, for God's sake, you might as well talk of the First World War as a "civil war" because the Kaiser and King George fought on opposite sides!'

'We're not concerned with the First World War. We're simply trying to establish where the Army stood in the Rhodesian affair.'

'It stood to attention and did its duty according to orders received – orders I should remind you not strictly given by anyone in this country.'

'I think we've disposed of that rather dismal piece of deception – the question of ultimate responsibility –'

'If you're attempting to fix responsibility on the Army command then I for one am prepared to accept it!'

'Imposed on you by an unknown captain, a couple of callow lieutenants and a few other odds and ends.'

'Captain Wyatt was a man of integrity and honour. He combined in himself a wisdom and understanding not to be found in six hundred of your self-interested parliamentarians!'

'Are you now setting yourself up as some kind of witness for the defence, Sir William?'

'I was led to understand I would be asked a few questions on the Army's role in Rhodesia. I was not prepared to be subjected to veiled calumny —'

'What else did you expect? The Order of the Bath for covering the good name of this country in mud? For failing with your colleagues to take action which could have crushed the coup in a couple of hours! For sitting quietly at home while the Queen, whose father himself created you a knight, was being humiliated and shamed in the eyes of the whole world! What did you expect — Sir William! I have no further questions to ask of this — witness . . .'

Perrins studied the man before him, wondering how to begin. Thirty-seven — looked ten years older — that was prison — a self-confident yahoo giving ground to a detestable anxious-to-please parcel of human trash, uncertain of himself but knowing for some reason he was off the hook. The half-smile sullying his coarsened features did nothing to relieve the Commander's feeling of nausea. He spoke sharply to cover a growing distaste for the job, for Lavery — for himself.

'So you like shooting nightwatchmen!'

Lavery licked a dry lip, glanced behind him for no very good reason.

'Three days public exhibition in a cage — does that appeal to you? That's what it's worth these days. Then ten years in a labour camp.'

'He's got no right — it's a bloody inhuman thing in a civilized society!'

Lavery was feeling doubtful in many directions but he felt sure enough about that.

'You savages are too free with the word "civilized". You're like bloody parrots with your cant phrases! Whatever else I think about Wyatt —'

He stopped, realizing he'd got on to the wrong track.

'You seem to be handy with a gun.'

'Er – yessir – that is – I did all right in the Army. Could've been a Queen's Medal man they said.'

'Enjoy handling firearms?'

'Well I liked shooting.'

'People?'

Lavery looked scared, thought it safer to keep silence.

'Politics?'

'Er – Liberal, sir.'

Perrins leaned forward. Another inch and those piercing eyes must surely have drawn blood. 'Don't try to be funny with me Lavery. If you make me loathe you more than I already do on two minutes' acquaintance I can make you disappear so thoroughly even your hardwearing wife wouldn't miss you – do you understand?'

Perrins made no pretence of waiting for an answer. 'Member of Grahame Windsor's Social Selective Party for two years, specialist in immigrant terrorization. Too vicious even for the SSP so you were thrown out. Two sentences ago you worked for a man called Rachman – now what could you possibly have been doing for our former Minister of Housing? Well!'

Lavery looked slightly desperate: 'You know bloody well what I was doing!'

Perrins appeared not to have heard. He might have been studying the file before him. 'So you have strongarm views about immigrants?'

'I don' like spades.'

'Why not?'

'Because I don't!'

'Your reasoning powers do you credit. You know of course Captain Wyatt and his people would hardly agree with you?'

Wyatt again. Lavery's mind was just cunning enough to recognize a tie-up. 'Well?'

'There are rumours circulating that Wyatt intends to invade Rhodesia – force the whites to submit to majority rule – the blacks, you know.'

Perrins watched Lavery's eyes fill with mucky-coloured anger.

'The dirty nigger-loving bastard! He wouldn't dare! There's not a man –'

'There are plenty of men who will. Unless we can stop them . . .'

Stop them! In Lavery's philosophy one could stop a night-watchman – dead if necessary. But a government? While he tried to think about it Perrins cut in, elaborately casual.

'It's worth five thousand.'

Lavery's mouth hung open – so that was it! Mention of money made the whole thing broad as daylight. But he had to ask, had to have it in so many words. He sensed too the Commander's reluctance to spell out the sentence.

'For the moment we want just one of them out of the way. The only one we can get at without too much difficulty –'

'You mean – you mean you want me to work for the SB?'

Perrins winced visibly: 'As far as we're concerned you don't exist – let that be understood.'

'Suppose I refuse?'

'Try it Lavery.'

Lavery gratefully refused the invitation. 'What do I have to do?'

'My subordinate will give you all the information you require.'

Lavery's brain began to race in all directions at once. 'Five . . . and I'll be doing the country a favour.'

'It might help to steady your aim if the fact happens to cross your mind,' Perrins observed drily.

'Nothing interferes with that, don't worry. Five thousand! wait till I tell the wife . . .'

'If your wife – or anyone else – hears about one word that's passed between us – we'll know – and you'll be dead before you can say "funeral expenses".'

Lavery stared disbelievingly: 'I believe you would too.'

The Commander's contempt, for himself as much as for Lavery, killed the amusement he might have felt at the man's naïvety. In five minutes the fool would be chatting to a genial Curly who in other circumstances would shoot him as soon as look at him. The interview was over. Perrins had hired himself an assassin.

*

On the nineteenth day Wyatt addressed a slightly frigid meeting of the CBI at the Commons. The bunch of hard-headed business men were less interested in his plans for constitutional reform, more concerned with remedies for economic ills. But wasn't it obvious, he demanded, that their problems were connected to the root cause?

'Your dilemma is the nation's dilemma whether you like it or not. We can continue to keep up ludicrous appearances, insist on our right to play a so-called world role, put ourselves in pawn to the continental bankers – is International Assistance better than National Assistance? Or we can face up to our internal responsibilities, make a strategic withdrawal, concentrate our forces and resources on the task of shaping our society as a worthwhile entity.

'Take your choice – strong reserves, a favourable balance of trade, the strengthening of our currency, or a succession of monetary crises, credit squeezes, panic budgeting and consequent economic stagnation.

'Your production difficulties, labour relations, problems of expansion arise from the stupid, unrealistic policies of past administrations who preferred guns to economic growth and stability. These policies became criminal in the hands of Socialists who were convinced they could have guns, butter and jam.

'There is only one answer – throw these policies overboard and with them the imported economists, paid to prove they could work if only two and two made five! In less than three weeks I strengthened our internal position simply by halving defence expediture. They howled for my blood – so perhaps did some of you. Well now I'm going to tell you something.

'Out of that one thousand million pounds we are allocating a hundred millions *immediately* for the purpose of assisting our ship-building industry to compete on equal terms with the rest of the world.

'Why shouldn't we build three hundred thousand ton tankers? The short answer is – we can – and will. If there are shipbuilders among you take the news back to the workers up North – tell them when I talk of industrial development I *mean* industrial development not the piddling tinkerings of Socialist Micawbers waiting for God knows what to turn up.

'Economic viability or international swaggering – but you can't have it both ways.'

Wyatt went on to give news of newly formed Trade delegations to be sent on roving commissions abroad, removal of import surcharges on manufacturing materials, relaxation of credit restrictions, and he stressed the need for greater diversification in industry. It was essential, he said, to break away from a dangerously obsessional dependence on, for example, car exports as an economic mainstay.

It was a fighting speech all the way. Wyatt knew he had to attack, to force the pace if he was to break down overt suspicions, latent hostility. By tone as much as by content he won them over – encouraged and inspired, set them alight with his own inflammable sense of purpose. They breathed in the very spirit of the man who said – it can be done – and we can do it. One member commented later: 'This chap's dynamic and his proposals are constructive – I don't know what more we could have wanted.'

18

At eight minutes to ten on the evening of the twenty-third day Paul Morrison left the Palace of Westminster. He was tired and irritable, having spent a day fighting up-hill with the Reform Committee on the franchise question – slow! men of vision with leaden feet! he'd hurled at them in a moment's frustration – if only they could see with his eyes Wyatt's panoramic concept of a new society – it was all there in front of them – eighty pages – logical as blue-prints – creating a framework to build next door but one to Utopia. To be fair to them, they tried, sometimes even caught a glimpse of the future by the light of the fire in their eyes – but they were civil servants after all, inhibited by qualifications and reservations ... leaden feet!

'It's raining pretty heavily Mr Morrison.'

'Let it come down,' he quoted bitterly – exchanged his epitaph for an old raincoat with one of the guards at the entrance and set off to cross the Square, walking briskly up Parliament Street towards his Downing Street quarters. Excepting French, the rest of the Council members preferred to live 'on the premises'. It was safer – and convenient. But Downing Street means something to the people – one of us should live there – better not to leave a vacuum. He refused absolutely to consider a bodyguard; never knew that Wyatt had detailed a man to shadow him as closely as possible – only a sixth sense operated, as he once told Mary, to convince him he was being followed.

A Cortina was parked, illegally, a few yards from the corner. The engine revved on a high frantic note as he approached, it covered the sharp crack of revolver shots. Morrison fell, his escort, too far away, fired after the car as it swerved to gain cover from a northbound bus. He ran to the crumpled figure, blood-stained and rainsoaked, on the pavement – it was crawling inch by inch forward – the last futile gesture of a man who knew there was so much to be done.

Morrison died on the way to hospital ... and the rain still came down.

Wyatt was immediately informed. He sent a message to French at the Tower, issued orders for the guards to be alerted and summoned the remaining members of the Council. He showed no trace of emotion, simply gave them the facts and waited for the shadow of silence to pass.

'Terrorist tactics,' Baynard was first to speak.

'A prelude presumably.' Sinclair tried hard to match Wyatt's calm.

'We must take counter measures,' Lorimer insisted.

'What do you suggest?'

Lorimer glanced uneasily at the others – what do you suggest? – a thin gruel of words from a man like Wyatt.

'Well – the police . . .'

'The police! We didn't buy them – we only borrowed them! Give them the benefit of the doubt if you like but don't imagine they're our friends.' He turned away to stare out at the lights flecking the surface of the Thames, hands clasped tightly behind his back. 'You deceive yourselves if you think they'll clear up our mess for us ... and there's Special Branch – they don't exactly worship us.'

'Do you think they're responsible?' Baynard asked.

Were they? Wyatt considered the possibility – then remembered Marsh's Cabalistic warning – gunning with a silencer – but now the silencer was off.

'Responsible? No – not ultimately – they take orders – execute – by appointment ... the opposition firing the first shots –' He turned suddenly: 'They want us to panic – lose our heads – even to retaliate by shooting a member of the Royal Family – perhaps after all, they think we're capable.'

'If we don't,' Baynard murmured, 'they might think it worth a rescue attempt.'

'They might.'

'What do we do?' Sinclair was plainly worried.

'We carry on – make our point while we can.'

'And let ourselves be shot down one by one!'

Wyatt's eyes were all fire as he rounded on Sinclair. 'Above all we don't panic. D'you think endeavours like this are nothing but items in an account book – debit one – two – three lives – credit seven decrees – carry forward a little international goodwill! If any or all of you has a book-keeping mentality then for God's sake go!'

No one stirred. They watched as he paced, knowing the room – the Palace – London – even the world was too small for a man composed of warring elements. He grew calm by degrees and only added in a voice strangely unlike his own: 'If we believe in what we're doing – we have to believe in the death that may go with it – as Morrison did.'

They left soon after – but no one backed out.

Rigg got the news on the teleprinter at Bookers. He ordered champagne before searching out Lord Wynlose in the library.

'I hear the Council of Six has had a spot of trouble,' he informed his Lordship.

'Splendid! Has something happened at last?'

'It has – and then there were five,' he murmured. 'Care for a drink?'

Milly Lavery went to the window for the fiftieth time. Far away and below in the street she could see the matchbox shape of the new Cortina, maroon red and shining in the green wastes of the Council landscaping. Her heart fluttered at the thought, first that it was theirs, last, that it must have cost a fortune. And there was Fred sitting in the next room as calm as you like. 'Working,' he explained and for once her miniature mind had rebelled, more for the baby's sake than her own. 'You're not doing anything wrong, Fred. You promised –' And he'd danced her round the table like a kid out of school and she'd tried to keep up with him for all her clumsy bigness ... It wasn't often she saw him in that mood – in fact she couldn't ever remember Fred laughing so much. He was the nearest thing to being – happy.

'It's legal I tell you – it's the most legal thing I ever did in all my natural only I can't talk about it see? Well I wouldn't get a car like that and expenses would I? Twenty quid a day – and that's just expenses. You wouldn't even believe me if I told you how much it's worth.'

'When – when d'you start Fred?'

He stopped laughing then, looked at her like he was searching for a speck of dust in her eye.

'Yesterday,' he said.

She felt cold suddenly and wished he would laugh some more.

An armoured car and a lorryload of heavily armed men screeched to a halt outside the Commons entrance. On French's orders they kept a tight grip on triggers – the Gypsy himself leaped from the car before it stopped, brushed past the guards and marched straight as a black line of menace to Wyatt's quarters.

The Captain was alone, working by the concentrated light of a desk lamp; hardly looked up as the door burst open and

French, ignoring the guard's protest, advanced on a last great wave of fury.

'You should be at the Tower,' Wyatt observed mildly but continued writing.

'Am I a member of the Council or not?'

'You're also in charge of security.'

'While decisions are made a mile away.'

'If you've a specific complaint to make then make it.'

'I waited an hour for orders – an hour!'

'Orders?'

'Those bastards shot Morrison didn't they?'

'Someone shot him.'

'Then it's time for reprisals.' Pure venom in every syllable – the overflow of a pent-up hatred that threatened to swamp reason itself.

'What are you here for?'

'Your authority to take an eye for an eye – what else?'

'You have someone in mind?'

'Anyone of them – her husband! It should've been done at once.'

Wyatt saw how near things had skidded to disaster. If French had taken immediate action ... 'And what would it mean to you personally – liquidating Mountbatten?'

'It means making the score even. How else do we assert our authority?'

'Don't even begin to imagine you can deceive yourself or me – it'd be nothing of the kind. Your sort of hatred doesn't feed off one man or twenty – but if all the bullets were one bullet and all guns one gun and all men were one man then by God you might just be satisfied with shooting him dead – I promise you, French, there isn't enough blood in the world to cover your shoes ...'

'Perhaps we're both disillusioned. I thought you were a leader of men – not some kind of Jesus Christ wearing steel gauntlets over velvety hands – you know as much about people as he did and that was damn all!'

'Tell me then!'

'Either Caesar or nothing! for you – there's no middle way

205

– we took power by force good! Therefore we have to hold it by force, *that* they understand – but just try turning the other cheek and see if they don't smash your face in!'

'We accept the risk – meantime there'll be no reprisals.'

'Then don't be surprised at what comes next! Wyatt's a man of straw – no intention of touching a hair of their heads – what's to stop us going in to the rescue? they don't dare fire a shot . . . well Captain – what then?'

'Then we do what has to be done.'

'I'll tell you what I'll bloody do – if they try anything I'll shoot every bastard I can lay hands on.'

'French . . .'

'I don't want us to fail!'

'Fail! Us!' The words came like two shots from ambush – French stood his ground as Wyatt rounded the desk to face him like a firestorm gone berserk. He realized his anger was a puff of wind compared with –

'Who do you think you are – or any of us! What do you suppose failure or success means to an idea! We're nothing – unimportant – rubbish to be thrown away when we've served the purpose. Win or lose we fight to make a point, show the way, prove there's a workable alternative to the democratic dung-heap we've only this minute *started* to shift – be damned to death or glory! It's the idea that counts – it'll be there long after we're dead – it'll be passed on like a smouldering firebrand – waiting to be rekindled – but the price has to be paid – and that means you, me, all of us, get that into your head. Now go back to the Tower – guard those people with your life . . . and wait.'

The Gypsy stared unblinking at Wyatt, ashes of rebellion glowed dimly – but Wyatt had drawn the fire. The line of his mouth curled into a tortured arabesque that might have been a smile. 'Wait – for the end . . .' He turned abruptly and reached the door before Wyatt's voice checked him.

'All the power we have is in your hands . . . I trust you because I chose you.'

French paused, eyes fixed on the door facing him – then opened it violently and was gone. He never saw Wyatt again.

Press communiqué released from Wyatt's HQ, Westminster 11 p.m.:

At approximately ten o'clock this evening, Paul Morrison, member of the Provisional Council, was shot dead a few yards from Downing Street.

The circumstances surrounding this attack make it clear beyond any doubt that opposition to the régime has chosen assassination – the most despicable of all weapons – as its principal argument. It must now convince the people that it can succeed with bullets where slogans have failed.

Exactly twenty-four hours later Wyatt received the following:

The Rhodesian Government takes note of your intentions in relation to this country. Since we regard your authority as spurious, based on force, Communist inspired and above all, alien to the constitutional ideal, your actions can be of no possible consequence to the Rhodesian people. If you see fit to appeal to the United Nations we can hardly prevent you; our case is clear and stated, and as such, has the sympathy of world opinion. As for your specific demands, I regret, we are not empowered to treat with an impostor.

Smith

Marsh was at the Commons by six of the clock. He found Wyatt shaving in his room, accepted the Captain's gesture towards the coffee pot and poured himself a strong black syrupy mixture, waited for the hum of the electric razor to unblock the silence . . .

'An ill wind, Mr Marsh?'

Marsh looked severe for him, the avuncular expression lay hidden under creases of anxiety.

'You're in trouble laddie.'

'Morrison?'

'That was predictable.'

'Well?'

'I got it on the grapevine about Smith.'

'Change your grapevine Mr Marsh. I released the text of my message –'

'I mean his reply.'

Wyatt seemed perfunctorily surprised. 'I only saw it myself six hours ago.'

'Be your age man – if I didn't know what was going on –'

'Are you printing it?'

'I'm playing fair with you Captain –'

'But?'

'If I know its contents – you can bet the last train to Ealing they know it too.'

'The opposition – yes?'

'Your message – Smith's reply– what then?'

'There are rumours – on the other hand there are counter-rumours.'

'Look this is no time for double-talk – not with the very few people on the outside you can trust it isn't!'

Wyatt carefully knotted his tie before anything more was said. Marsh had time to realize this was an office, dining-room, bedroom and old-fashioned parlour ... government from a bed-sitter.

'Saunders will support the emergency resolution this afternoon. He got things moving very nicely.'

Marsh drew a sharp breath. It was worse than he feared.

'Intervention?'

'Yes.'

'Stop him!'

'I'm sorry – it's all part of the plan.'

'Let me give you another bit of advice. Keep flexible – in politics nothing is forever.'

'In politics the right thing comes before expediency.'

'Tell that to the Brighton Brigade or the Blackpool Barkers! Listen Captain – you're on to something, you look like making it stick, the change is doing everybody good, including my newspapers – Goddammit some people even like you – trust you – they actually read your decrees – but you go into Rhodesia and you're finished.'

'If the people –'

'The people nothing! I told you already – the Cabal is your

bogeyman – they've been waiting for something to turn up and boy you've handed it to 'em on a plate.'

'The Cabal isn't the people.'

'You can say that again.' Marsh looked genuinely concerned. 'Not Socialists – not Tories – not even wise men step in where angels don't – I like your nerve from A to the cemetery Captain . . .'

'You're thinking of Morrison?'

'To them he's just the *hors d'œuvre*. Look you can do what you like with this country because in the long run they don't stand to lose a thing – everything's grist to their mill – but Rhodesia! It's black and white, Captain – like an article of faith more binding than dogma, and by the way they even got Rome gunning for you.'

Wyatt poured coffee as he listened, then paced the room deep in thought, continued pacing as he asked: 'If you were in my place – what would you do?'

'Hell, how should I know? With my kind of money I can buy anything except prejudice.'

'I'll tell you what you'd do Marsh – you'd go ahead.'

'Flattery isn't going to change my mind.'

'Because you'd know it was the right thing to do.'

'Who says it's the wrong thing? I'm not saying don't do it – just delay it.'

'It's been delayed too long.'

'By people who thought they had all the time in the world, only you haven't. You need every second to consolidate – what the hell, you think people change overnight? Mould public opinion and they'll go anywhere you say – only it takes time.'

'Whose time? What we intend doing is first for the Africans, second for Africa – then for us and the rest of the world.'

'OK Captain and I see your point. But while you're sitting at home the world looks a lousy place when the house starts falling around your ears.'

'You think we'll fail?'

'I don't think – I know – they'll make sure you fail.'

Wyatt knew the press magnate was right, saw clearly that his venture, guided by inescapable and personal logic, followed a collision course that must end in destruction. But he could only follow – there was no other way.

They talked a while longer; Marsh pledged his support without saying as much. Then they took leave of each other knowing it was for the last time.

The debate on Zambia's resolution was in its second day. African and Asian representatives had already stressed the need for action before Smith 'implanted a white cancer in the heart of black Africa'.

The Hall of the General Assembly was capacity crowded when Mr Saunders, our man at the UN, rose to speak.

He began by outlining Britain's past efforts to achieve a genuine settlement with the Smith régime based on the Six Point Declaration, touched on the history of UDI and the matter of sanctions.

'But,' he continued, 'we now see these piecemeal efforts as nothing more than a calculated policy of procrastination; past administrations were all too clearly prepared to sacrifice majority rights to minority interests in Rhodesia and in Britain.

'The member for Zambia has warned that unless positive measures are taken immediately, provocation and counter-provocation by mutually incompatible states may well touch off a train of events leading to bloodshed on a scale only to be compared with standards of slaughter set – and I quote – "by yesterday's so-called civilized Europeans". Britain therefore it seems to me, more than any other nation of "civilized Europeans", is on trial today as accessory before the unpalatable and not improbable fact . . .'

Saunders paused at the cross-roads, barely glancing from left to right before he marched straight on.

'In view of these and other considerations, I am instructed by my Government to support Zambia's resolution that action be taken in Rhodesia at the earliest possible opportunity. We pledge our support for all measures considered necessary by a majority decision of the Assembly, in accordance with the principles of the Charter.'

Saunders sat down to the greatest ovation of his career. Even Russia beat its stubby palms in a brief tattoo. A demonstration in favour of Wyatt, Saunders guessed, but at least he had handled it all rather well.

The United States was on its feet at once. 'I never thought I would live to see the day of the kettle calling out the pot for being black. Here we have two illegal régimes reaching for each other's throats in the name of justice.

'What in the name of sanity is Britain doing here? If we are a gathering of accredited representatives of legally constituted states how can we possibly accept a statement inspired by an illegal régime which *ab initio* must lack binding force concerning any state against which that statement is directed?

'The United States, and I believe all right-thinking sovereign states, are bound to declare themselves against a device emanating from nowhere but the mind of one man – the resolution is a stratagem engineered by a home-made government having no higher purpose than its own entrenchment . . .'

The United States sat to complete silence. Britain took the floor once again.

'First, I would remind the United States, we are not responsible for the resolution. As for the validity of the government which I represent, I would remind you it is recognized not only by this organization and so by most of the world, but surprisingly by the United States itself. It still trades with us, still invests with us, because it knows that a country does not cease to exist by reason of a radical change of executive government – except China of course.

'Presumably that is another matter; but I would also say this. If an ageing warlord in Formosa is acceptable to the United States as President of the Chinese People's Republic and is thoughtfully permitted a seat in the Security Council for good measure . . . then surely Captain Wyatt . . .'

The rest of Saunders' sentence was swamped by a wave of laughter. He realized vaguely that he might possibly be enjoying himself.

'We have stated our position. Britain supports the resolution unreservedly. The United States uses the opportunity to

211

call our authority in this place in question. Perhaps it is now prepared to clarify its own position regarding Rhodesia.'

United States: 'The United States cannot concern itself with furthering the aims of a military adventurer.'

Great Britain: 'Our aim is a positive settlement within the framework of the United Nations. It is a matter for international co-operation – the legality of our government cannot affect the overall question – either you are for the resolution or you're against it.'

United States: 'I'm waiting to hear why an illegal régime refuses to accept the existence of a prior régime also based on illegal seizure of power.'

Great Britain: 'The two cases are totally different! Our country experimented with the elements of political science long before the United States came to independence. It is experimenting once again, breaking free of outworn formulas, of clogging tradition, in an attempt to re-examine democratic principles in the context of entirely new imperatives. The British people are politically conscious enough to understand and acquiesce in what the régime in its caretaker capacity is attempting to do.

'In Rhodesia a few hundred thousand white settlers have taken over a country which is theirs only by right of a former conquest. These first, second, or third generation immigrants are denying to many times their number of Africans certain rights which the United States itself is unable or unwilling to secure for its own coloured population.

'I therefore challenge the United States to say why it looks askance at our country for temporarily assuming minority rule while it supports Chiang-Kai-Shek as the Ruler of all China; why it insists on shedding blood to gain minimum rights for the peoples of Vietnam when too obviously it is not prepared to do as much for the majority population of Rhodesia!'

United States: 'Immaterial and irrelevant!'

Great Britain: 'It is also prejudicial to the high purpose of these proceedings that you question our good faith in seeking to avert a catastrophe capable of setting fire to Africa from end to end!'

According to a precedent originally agreed by the United States in 1950 whereby endorsement by the Security Council could be by-passed, Zambia's resolution calling on the General Assembly to sanction military action against Rhodesia was approved by a large majority, Portugal and South Africa dissenting; the United States and West Germany abstained.

It was Saunders' greatest triumph as a diplomat, but he would never again speak for Britain. Following his trial and a suspended sentence of five years 'for collaboration', he lived on for some time in ill health and obscurity; wrote his memoirs of course. They have still to be published. He died unrepentant of his part in the events of those days.

Rigg and Company had to push their way through groups of excited members discussing the latest news from the UN as it stuttered out of the teleprinter. Herbert the hall porter gave up tearing off the sheets which he usually pinned to the enormous green-baized board alongside his cubby-hole.

Upstairs, away from the hum of speculation, were gathered the Five – even Langley was on time. The last to arrive of course, but punctual. He studied their brooding silence with frosted amusement before stepping into the charmed circle.

Compton-Douglas spoke first, which was unusual. 'We've acted too late – they're off tomorrow or the day after – five thousand of our best men – it's a national disgrace!'

Minter spoke quietly or anger smothered his voice. 'Should've taken steps before.'

'Morrison's dead,' Langley reminded him.

Rigg erupted violently. 'Morrison! What the hell does that mean! One nonentity – we need a clean sweep of the whole damned crew – and Wyatt first!'

'It's unbelievable what's been said at the UN in our name.' Lord Wynlose sounded less detached than usual.

'Bloody nigger-loving extremists!' Rigg bellowed.

'It isn't going to help matters if we allow ourselves to get worked up,' Langley admonished cheerfully. 'Everything's going nicely – very nicely indeed.'

They stared like visitors on a first trip to Bedlam.

'Nicely?' was all Rigg could manage.

'He's made the move we needed – didn't think he'd do anything quite so stupid – Wyatt's committed himself – cardinal sin in politics – should've known better.'

Rigg threatened outright rebellion: 'We can't let him get away with it!'

'Of course we can't.' The old man was sweet reason itself. 'But we have to let the situation ferment – to our advantage ...'

'And then?' Minter wanted to know in a hurry.

'Well then – we do the right thing – can't jump our fences if we rush 'em. We arrange a little meeting – Meaker, Wrigley and ourselves ...'

He then gave the Cabaliers an idea of what the discussion should be about. Within ten minutes they had reached perfect agreement.

19

Mass media coverage of the UN resolution and news that a British contingent was to spearhead 'police action' released a widespread explosion of Smethwickian protest going far beyond words and phrases. Illogical anger spilled over wherever there were sizeable concentrations of immigrants; Birmingham, Slough, Nottingham and London caught much of the blast. That night and all next day these trouble spots were the scenes of isolated, sometimes organized attacks on coloured people, their cars – even their homes. Men beaten up, their families terrorized, providing the first casualties in the Rhodesian conflict; petrol bombs flung through windows and passage-ways were the first tokens of destruction to come ... slogans mushroomed on walls everywhere 'Niggers go home'. One day the agitators would gain their point, but not while Wyatt was there. He ordered stringent measures to be taken – directed the police to clean up 'the white trash that litters every community'. But reports trickled through – nothing was being done ... this too appeared to be a kind of writing on the wall.

From an early hour next morning crowds began to collect in Parliament Square. Small knots of figures coagulating into outraged lumps of humanity. The guards sent word to Wyatt. Baynard made a swift tour of inspection – ordered the great gates surrounding the Palace forecourt to be closed. Guards at all entrances were reinforced by a few regulars, volunteers from Colchester. Having satisfied himself that nothing more could be done for the moment, he lingered to watch the crowds, before hurrying to Wyatt's room.

'Our first demonstration,' he announced, almost too lightly. Wyatt seemed unworried.

'A safety-valve.'

'All the same it might be wise not to take it at its face value – there're thousands of 'em, jumping up and down like dervishes with their little placards "Hands off Rhodesia" and "Hang Wyatt".'

Wyatt smiled and wandered over to the window, appeared to be deeply interested in the grey blanket of cloud hanging over the south bank; a powered barge slipped beneath Westminster Bridge, hooted derisively like Nemesis blowing a raspberry. He turned back to Baynard, thinking of other things.

'How many men do we have?'

'Two hundred and thirty odd.'

'Yes.'

Baynard frowned – yes – what was that supposed to mean in a moment of crisis? 'Suppose they rush us?'

'You know your orders – warning shots – in the air.'

'And if that doesn't stop them . . .?'

'This is a demonstration Harry – not a counter-attack!'

The Lieutenant kept a civil tongue, replied evenly: 'You'd better have a look for yourself,' and withdrew.

The green spaces were blacked out, orderly beds of shrubs and late autumn flowers trampled; the protestants spilled into the roadway muddying streams of traffic in the full spate of an early morning rush hour. The more daring spirits were already crowding the St Stephen's entrance, openly taunting the guards who patiently played the waiting game. Wyatt ordered the door to be closed and sandbagged before 'incidents' developed, noticed the police were conspicuous by their absence.

From the communications centre he got through to French at the Tower. The Gypsy was terse and battle-hungry – yes there were demonstrators – a couple of thousand perhaps – but quiet – reasonably orderly. All defensive positions were manned. No cause for alarm.

In three hours' time the first troop-transport planes should be taking off, armed with staging and overflight facilities all the way to Lusaka.

And while crowds clamoured in Westminster, Smith broadcast to the country – and to the world. In slightly shaken tones he announced that mobilization was complete, the frontier posts strengthened and that Rhodesia would fight to the last man against 'black extremist inspired aggression'.

'We want the British people to know,' he declared, 'that we are not as afraid of Wyatt as they themselves appear to be. In the long run we may be fighting for their liberty as well as our own.'

A fighting speech from Rhodesia's number one prevaricator; surprisingly no plea for discussions about talks about fighting. It may have heartened those whites who consider themselves Europe's finest Africans – but foreign observers noted that the only cheerful looking Rhodesians in Salisbury were the African Africans. No one was asking them to fight for anything.

But still nothing happened – not in London – at the centre of things. The crowds remained remarkably well disciplined. The most dramatic event was provided by a deputation of Young Conservatives from Wimbledon Central. These idealists called at the Ministry of Defence to urge it to abandon its policy of aggression 'in the name of sanity'. They were handed a brief memorandum making it clear that the Ministry was no longer involved. Protests should be addressed to the UN, NY, USA.

At Wyatt's headquarters business continued in an atmosphere of siege. After instructing Baynard to strengthen the riverside positions he attended the daily session of the Council. Details referred back by the Draft Constitution Committee to be discussed and settled, a measure to reduce the number of Assize Courts – the fate of Prices and Incomes policy – immediate investigation of backroom insurance companies – no mention of Rhodesia. But at midday their eyes strayed to the clock. It was a question of orders: either the Air Force would obey or it would refuse. Either the Army accepted the directions of the UN military purposes committee or it would obey the injunction of the *Daily Compress* to refuse 'to carry the weight of the Wyatt man's burden on its shoulders'.

Wyatt argued the items on the agenda as though nothing else existed. At six minutes past twelve he received information they had all been waiting for; the troops were on their way. No disturbances. Eyes burning with the inflammable stuff of triumph, he listened from a thousand miles away to the delighted reaction of his colleagues and Ministry officials.

'Now,' he said evenly, 'let them do as they please.'

At one o'clock he learned from Baynard the crowds had melted away under attack from the weather; rain squalls cooled by a knife-edged north-easterly drove all demonstrative thoughts from their heads – and besides, it was lunch-time.

Baynard reminded him of his appointment with the recording technicians. While he made last-minute alterations to the text of his speech they chatted with Jennings, described the crowds outside and how they'd got through. 'Easy really,' they admitted. 'Just tell 'em BBC and you're through like a dose of salts.'

Extracts of Wyatt's speech, broadcast by all services of the BBC the same evening:

Rhodesia's history is one of uninterrupted exploitation of its people, of its resources, and now of its potential as another proving ground for the gutterbred ideal of white supremacy. Today it is in the hands of a filthy-minded racialist minority imbued with a paranoiac belief in the importance of a lily-coloured epidermis. Their prejudice is one of the true crimes against humanity.

... once for all we are faced with an eleventh-hour choice. Either we identify ourselves by inaction with those who cannot live without social scapegoats to justify their existence – or we demonstrate that our concept of civilized behaviour is more than a mere façade of refrigerators, hi-fi equipment and central heating ...

The basic and over-riding issue is respect for others. It is an issue none of us – none! can afford to shirk or ignore. How else can we begin to live together in peace and good fellowship? The world is too small, too interlocked for us to be divided by the criminal stupidity of race or class or religious prejudice. We are no longer five continents but one world, and what touches one man to the detriment of his mind, body or soul must sooner or later touch us all.

Every report passed through Wyatt's hands. Detailed progress on the island labour camp: two hundred and fifty men were already moving into well-built quarters – the plan was working – no trouble or outbreaks of violence, they had a purpose, a reason for living. Prison conditions were improving as another five hundred prepared to join the community. Details of the new housing drive; details of crime statistics and road casualties – both sharply down – six thousand licences withdrawn in the first week, ninety-four in the week ending yesterday. Details of industrial production: a slight upward curve, exports were improving; detailed plans for health centres to beat the shortage of GPs – these he was pleased to see were in an advanced stage, the Health Ministry was working all out to get things moving. He turned to education – new subjects to be introduced: philosophy, comparative religion, the elements of logic; subjects to make children think – think for themselves – question – and above all, think. All this and more, a mass of material studied in detail. It was typical of Wyatt – the need to sift every matter to its finest particle; he missed very little, never ceased to urge everyone around him to do the same. The broadest based policy must fail he insisted where the smallest items were ignored or overlooked.

For over four hours Wyatt remained lost to the world, absorbing facts and figures, making notes, amendments, suggestions, secluded as a monk spinning dogmas in his cell.

Wyatt perhaps, the rest of the world certainly, waited for Smith's response to the challenge. Either he resisted the UN's authority or he surrendered. No amount of double-talking could save him from decision. True the militants were unslinging their rifles and marching by automobile to the frontiers along which most of the Rhodesian forces were already strung out; but it was an ersatz conception of frontiersmen prepared to fight for their country – unrealistic as Disneyland. Reports that South Africa had offered a volunteer brigade proved to be unfounded. The Rhodesian Air Force had sufficient fuel reserves to remain fully operational for ten days . . .

Troop transport planes touched down in Lusaka on the long flight from England. The men were greeted as liberators by a deliriously happy population. Next day they would be convoying south to set up advanced operational bases just inside the Rhodesian border. They learned that martial law was the order of the day 'over there'. Already countless Africans were under sentence of death for jubilating their country's liberation too soon . . .

Text of the President's speech to the American people. November –th.

It is now just over a month since the world saw an act of history committed in the United Kingdom that has overshadowed all other events from that day to this. We in the United States have always believed that a nation is free to work out its own destiny, but I for one fail to comprehend how a country old in time, rich in political wisdom and dedicated unshakeably to the glorious democratic ideal, can allow its destiny to be brought to a full stop, unmindful of protests from those of us who have her interests at heart.

If it was simply a matter of readjustment in the internal workings of a nation's governmental machinery we would have no cause to comment – no reason to criticize. But the radical technique of a power-hungry consortium headed by a fanatic is in danger of touching us all – and I mean the whole world.

America has been reviled; the hand of friendship Uncle Sam extends to all has been spat upon, the justice of our cause in Vietnam derided, and our pleas for peace in that sad land of Rhodesia have been spurned by a malcontented majority in the UN.

In one short month this man has destroyed years of labour

devoted to creating a bond of strength in Western Europe. The NATO organization of which we had some cause to be proud now lies in ruins.

Having defied every conceivable type of Communist stratagem, having protected the world from its incursions into the sacred groves of Liberty, we are now asked to open our hearts to Red China and by someone never heard of till now.

But whoever rules the roost in England or anywhere – we say this: our cause is the same now as then. We fear no man, no nation, no ideology and no change of world opinion. We shall go forward undeterred by calumny, discharge our obligations as we understand them, and we will continue to fight for the rights of those who invoke our aid and protection. Without asking by-your-leave of men like Wyatt.

This much we concede: if it appears the United States stands no higher in the world's estimation than the head on Wyatt's shoulders, then we may be obligated seriously to reappraise the value of continuing in membership of the United Nations. To this end a Congressional committee is to examine the possibility that continued association with that body may, in the present circumstances, be prejudicial to the national interests ...

20

Lingfield's entrance was almost unceremonious. 'Have you seen the papers sir?'

'Just looking through them Curly. Something worrying you?'

'There's no doubt about it – they're all set to go – why don't we go in and clean 'em up?'

Perrins listened carefully to the insubordinate tones. 'Who, Curly?'

'Those nigger-loving sods down the road – I thought we were supposed to stop 'em!'

Perrins remained cautious – Curly sounded quite unlike his old genial self – the tiny eyes blazed with outraged indignation.

'You thought wrong. A warning shot ...'

'One man! What do they care?'

'I don't know what they care – our orders . . .'

'That's the point sir – whose orders? If Wyatt's nothing then who's giving orders?'

'The powers that will be . . .'

'I've never heard of 'em!'

'They had Morrison shot . . .'

'Why stop at Morrison?'

'Perhaps they feel public opinion will rise up and do our job for us – more refined – more effective.'

'Public opinion! There's nothing more effective than a few bullets in the guts.'

Perrins stared at the statement with the expression of a man about to swallow foul medicine. 'Then we must wait for public opinion to pull the trigger.'

Something in his voice told Curly he'd learn nothing more. He crossed to the door – turned.

'Do you think Smith'll fight sir?'

The Commander's caution fled to the four winds. 'How the devil should I know!'

'I've got a good mind to go out and join him if he does.'

Perrins sat staring at the account of Johnson's speech long after Lingfield's stormy going. But he read nothing of consequence.

And on the seventh day there were protest meetings throughout the country, which was to be expected. A mass rally in Hyde Park gave Morgan an opportunity to figure prominently . . . an artificial atmosphere of crisis hung over the country – an eleven o'clock the third of September and what-happens-next mood. 'If they mean business they'll try something today –' Lorimer suggested.

Wyatt conceded the possibility. 'They'll have to move fast – it means clearing us out of the way, and recalling the troops before morning. But I imagine they'll wait – hoping we make a mess of things.'

'I don't see what they can do – we've still got the Queen.' Baynard sounded confident.

Wyatt said nothing.

The weekend Press reacted predictably. 'Will Smith Fight?' typified rhetorical headlines. 'War in Africa' darkened the *Lewds of the World* front page. Editorial comment was equally divided between the qualified approval of the heavies and the outraged sensibilities of the *Choppers Gazette*. One paper, spending most of its time and advertising revenue in searching out sin (its casualty rate for journalists is phenomenal), looked at the UN action in Rhodesia from a typically horizontal viewpoint. 'The red light is being given for the greatest upsurge of rape the Dark Continent has ever seen. Through the criminal folly of one man, the holocaust of blood lust to come threatens to sully the name of British decency for all time. In Salisbury white women are trembling behind locked doors today, fearful of what tomorrow will bring. We can only hope that our team of on-the-spot reporters will have good news for readers in next Sunday's edition . . .'

But it all came to nothing – so much printer's ink down the drain – whatever happened in Africa there was the car to clean, the family clamouring for a car outing, the gardening: the papers were thrown aside with Smith, Rhodesia and the UN. Wyatt was there – the rank and file had no complaints. There were petitions of course – but a petition of the Right is still a petition, and when it's handed in an anti-climax is still an anti-climax. Even the mass rally in Hyde Park slithered down green slopes to become a large-scale picnic as the demonstrators' hard feelings melted in the unsuspected warmth of a late November sun. Few disturbances were reported from the rest of the country, and as darkness fell Wyatt could congratulate himself that not one drop of English blood had been shed for Rhodesia or racialism that day.

Eight o'clock found everyone in a state of wondering. Would Smith fight or back down? His words were belligerent enough – but then Smith's words were about as meaningful as an undischarged bankrupt's chequebook.

For Wyatt none of his followers' self-inflicted doubts and misgivings, no sign of anxiety, nor a scintilla of speculation about Smith's intentions. He knew the outcome – knew the plan would succeed – looked ahead to the immediate future with its promise of a fair start for a new Rhodesia. Never doubted he was nearing the end of his own road – never mentioned it.

At precisely eight hundred hours our time, while fingers toyed with triggers from Kanyemba to the Victoria Falls, a long range transport aircraft circled in from the north-east, flew deep into Rhodesian territory to unload forty men and a major of the 136th Parachute Regiment. It was a beautiful drop. They floated down tight onto a sports ground in the Salisbury suburbs. Assembling in less than ten minutes they hailed a passing bus crowded with Africans who looked up at the sky, looked down at them, then dismounted in helpless laughter. The paratroopers piled in, directed the bus driver to the broadcasting station which a detachment promptly occupied, while the rest were taken by an ecstatic driver to Mr Smith's residence. After a brief skirmish with his dumbfounded guards, Smith was found and placed under close arrest. Twenty minutes later the Rhodesian army, still waiting along the Zambesi for the UN invasion, listened in astonishment as their bemused Prime Minister announced that Salisbury had been occupied, that he was in the hands of the UN forces, and that all resistance was at an end. They watched open-mouthed as the advance units rolled across the frontier – and at twenty to nine – our time – it was all over before it began.

The world soon learned the brief story of Smith's mini-war and while bits of it screamed treachery! great chunks of it fell about laughing and between paroxysms took another look at the man who had played it coolly again – and won again. The classic pattern: a swift strike at the root cause with a force of unknown strength. United Nations or not the audacity of the plan pointed to Wyatt.

The Cabal thought so too. Like everyone else they'd been caught napping, so busy searching with a candle for the cause they were knocked sideways by the abruptly exploding effect. Reinforced fury and injured pride went hand in hand as they

gathered at Bookers soon after nine-thirty for a most extraordinary meeting. Never before had a Cabal deliberated in
that hallowed room overlooking St James's with an outsider
present. Moreover it transgressed Nature's laws that there
should be two visitors: Meaker and – a sure sign that God
was dead – Wrigley.

The damned fool had tucked himself away for the weekend
in his constituency. Frantic efforts had been made to find him
and not until late Sunday evening did they discover that he was
as Rigg put it: 'doing a spot of crafty advanced electioneer-
ing'. He refused to do more than catch the first train next
morning . . . while they waited Meaker wanted to know why
things couldn't proceed without him.

'Because he's still the Prime Minister, dammit!' Rigg
snapped. The man seemed to have aged ten years in as many
hours.

'Don't be so constitutional Martin.' Langley wagged a mocking finger. At his age he could afford to weather storms threatening the younger men; deploring the situation then enjoying
the search for solutions – it was all of a piece with his passion
for jig-saws. Martin merely scowled and wondered how the old
man could take it so lightly – he himself made a point of taking
everything seriously.

Rules were scattered to the winds; Minter and Wynlose sat
apart venting vitriolic opinions on the morning's developments
in well-bred undertones. Compton-Douglas quietly brooded
over the fact that forty men could bring a country to its knees
and not a shot fired. Inconceivable as the Light Brigade charging through the Valley of Death and landing up in Moscow!
Langley missed very little.

'Something rankling Douglas?'

The nation's hero surfaced from unmentionable depths mut-
tering incoherencies, then barked: 'I think I shall go stark
staring mad!' The others stared at him with mild surprise –
his gaze wandered with an idiot's fixity round the room.

'Our Queen stuck in the Tower – d'you realize I'm the
Deputy Bloody Constable! Wyatt – our troops turned into
medieval mercenaries – England a republic the year of our

224

Lord 196– and here I am, God forgive me, sitting on my arse doing nothing!'

Langley engraved his face with lines of sorrow but the silver point eyes twinkled ... 'Don't worry Douglas – soon have your fort and your soldiers back.'

The PM's arrival killed Compton-Douglas's retort if he'd had one. The Labour leader looked tired and harassed; his constituents were giving him hell, the TUC had sent him to Coventry, he was having trouble with his memoirs and the Ministry wanted to know why he hadn't signed on for unemployment benefit.

Naturally the meeting was chaired by Langley, who set the tone with refined cordiality edged with sympathy for Wrigley's 'unfortunate predicament'. While the rest sat loosely about the conference table, the vagrant PM sat rigidly perpendicular, his sensibilities on the *qui vive* for any slight, real or imagined. But they wanted something; they could only get it through him. What happened to him afterwards was no concern of theirs – in the eyes of the electorate he was already done for – but constitutionally ...

'. . . we could almost certainly have prevented this Rhodesian business some hours earlier. Unfortunately we had a little trouble getting hold of you. Stupid of us – might have guessed you'd prefer to be with your constituents in these troubled times.'

Wrigley nodded but said nothing. There was very little he could say – he wondered if he could smoke.

'No doubt,' the Earl continued, 'we've all been feeling as you did, that no positive action could be taken against Wyatt till he made a worthwhile mistake. I'm sure we're agreed a wait and see policy was the best if not our only course.'

Wrigley nodded again. He noticed there were ashtrays.

'This Rhodesian business for example – once he acted to prove he's prepared to defy public opinion, opinion which if I may say you so wisely incorporated into your dealings with Mr Smith, then I think we must all be agreed, the way is clear for a coup de grâce.'

Wrigley agreed. All the ashtrays were clean – perhaps they

had a no-smoking rule before twelve. His lordship seemed a nice old chap – sensible . . .

'I have to admit – and I'm sure I echo your own feelings, this morning's news is a complete surprise – I don't think any of us could've foreseen the speed with which our rattlesnake struck?'

The PM shook his head and half reached for the cigarette case in his left pocket.

'Can't make any bones about it – I for one have entirely misjudged Wyatt – had no idea he could be so wily – and so dangerous. By destroying a régime in ten minutes or so he may very likely have increased his prestige.' Langley felt Wrigley was giving his brief appraisal less attention than it deserved. Politely he inquired if Mr Wrigley agreed.

'Yes,' Mr Wrigley replied. Realizing it was hardly enough he added thoughtfully: 'I agree.'

'It comes to this then,' Langley continued with a flickering glance at Meaker: 'unless we stop this man dead – and quickly – the task will become progressively more difficult with every swing of the pendulum.'

'Yes – that's true enough, but what can we do so long as he has the Queen?'

The other five men tensed expectantly. They knew as though they shared one mind what was to follow. Wrigley forgot his need to smoke as he sensed the tightening atmosphere.

'Suppose,' Langley said, 'I told you that in an hour from now – the status quo ante could be restored, the whole thing finished in less time than it took to begin?' He pressed on regardless of Wrigley's incredulity. 'If Wyatt can move swiftly – why shouldn't we move like lightning?'

The Cabal watched the old Earl carefully and in complete silence. At that moment he was the indisputable leader. They knew he would gain his point, bring the matter to a satisfactory conclusion as he had done since Zinoviev's letter and the dark days of the Abdication. Minter found himself remembering how Langley had steered them clear through the embarrassing episode of Hess's flight to England . . .

'I wish I could agree with you.' And Wrigley at that moment

devoutly wished he could. It was humiliating to be left in the dark when one's political opponents appeared to be seeing the light . . .

'It all depends on you – Prime Minister.'

Good – very good – Lord Wynlose thought. The Old Man was excelling himself. Meaker looked solemn and dared not look at the others. Minter told himself it was no laughing matter and clenched his teeth.

Wrigley had the worried expression of a man who glances over his shoulder before he speaks. 'Me?'

'All you have to do is give an order to the Chief Commissioner requiring him to place Wyatt and the rest of his gang in the Palace of Westminster under immediate arrest.'

Wrigley stared dully at the Earl. There was no doubting his Lordship's earnestness as he leaned forward demanding in every bone of his skeletal being an assent. One of the old breed of Tories – a man who loved his country to the exclusion of . . . The PM glanced at Meaker who ostentatiously stared down at his reflection in the table's polished surface. Something he'd said at Mostyn's – don't make too much of that theme – even so . . .

'I'm sure Meaker – as Leader of Her Majesty's loyal Opposition – would admit that such a course of action – desirable in itself I don't deny – poses the gravest threat to Her Majesty – and other members of the Royal Family.'

Meaker remained silent. The five high Tories sat immovable, uncompromising as effigies. Needles of ice punctured Wrigley's spine. Were they really suggesting –?

Langley relaxed the pressure a little. 'I understand your feelings. Believe me, we've all suffered these agonies of conscience – but I think we'd bear ten times the suffering for our country which is greater than any single one of us . . .'

Wrigley searched the statesman's manual and pulled out an authoritative stop: 'I cannot countenance any measure which must inevitably place Her Majesty in jeopardy.'

Rigg almost gave the game away with a show of contempt, but Langley knew his man, knew Wrigley had reached the high tide of outraged refusal, ready to ebb into acquiescence.

'Her Majesty would value your sentiments – no one more. But she's been well educated in the hard school of duty – sacrifice ... besides,' he added casually, 'has it ever occurred to you Wyatt's bluffed his way in from the very start?'

Again Wrigley glanced at Meaker before eyeing the Earl warily. 'I don't follow.'

'Why should we assume Wyatt ever intended destroying Her Majesty? What could he hope to gain? A dead Queen would be far more dangerous to his cause than a live one. If he got rid of them all I can name you forty-seven next in line of succession from memory – and there are many more. As it is, all his actions seem to suggest an aversion to bloodshed ... might it be,' the old man mused, 'we simply ascribe to him a certain course of conduct simply because we ourselves would understand its necessity? but to understand is to forgive ...'

'... Does anyone mind if I smoke?'

Suddenly they were offering cigars and cigarettes. The Old Man had all but landed his fish, the fish could smoke itself to death, have everything it desired till time came for stuffing and the glass case. Wrigley excused himself from smoking any but his own brand and too late they remembered he smoked a foul herbal concoction in deference to a slight asthmatic condition. Nothing to do but put the best possible face on it. He lit his cigarette and immediately relaxed as the others tensed.

'I feel,' he temporized, 'we should discuss this with the Archbishop.'

Wynlose and Minter looked solemn to hide their exasperation. The General crossed ostentatiously to open the window. What the hell, demanded a silent consensus of opinion, did the ... Archbishop have to do with it? Langley managed to bend over backward an inch or two.

'I agree – yes – in other circumstances our old friend's presence would be not only comforting but necessary.'

'It's a question of time Wrigley,' Meaker observed as he gratefully breathed in the aroma of freshly laundered handkerchief.

'Exactly!' the General boomed from the furthest end of the room.

Fortunately Rigg could say nothing. He was feeling slightly sick. Wynlose and Minter stared at each other wondering how much more of it they could stand. Langley fanned himself with a copy of *The Times* as he continued: 'Believe me we understand your misgivings – we're all human – but if you delay action a moment longer – then I think it's safe to say that the political system as we knew it – is finished. In a few days' time Wyatt publishes the draft of a new constitution – the people are suggestible – they may come to prefer his cockeyed view of what government should be. Ask Meaker there – even in his constituency there's a feeling, not of satisfaction exactly, but disguised relief – the inner tension created by the two-party push and pull is slackening – if people find they can live without it – then we're finished – all of us . . .'

They waited while Wrigley smoked in thoughtful silence. 'I see all that of course but . . . I need to be convinced that Her Majesty –'

Langley rose angrily and stamped about the room, no longer concealing his impatience, which in any case he purposely exaggerated. 'That's impossible! Good God man, you're a politician – committed every day you're in office to gambling with people's lives – d'you think it makes the slightest difference one of 'em happens to be the Queen? Your political existence is at stake, yours! – why? because he holds the Queen – but you hold the ace of trumps – complete disregard for the Monarch in the people's interests. Very well then, he shoots the Queen – I've said already – there're others – and if he massacres the lot we could still create one if necessary! Was that Norman bastard born a king?'

'You say this?' Wrigley stared in open astonishment.

'Of course I say it! Perhaps because I don't believe in what appears to be the reality – but I do believe in Wyatt's bluff which gave him what he wanted. It needs the country's lawfully elected leader to call that bluff. Give the order now and I guarantee Meaker there will be slanging you across the Table of the House by Wednesday.'

It seemed an age before Wrigley spoke: 'Very well ... I'll do it.'

'Do it now – don't discuss the matter with your Cabinet, they'll bog you down in argument – the country counts on you to act with the same incisive authority as a Wyatt ...'

Five minutes later Wrigley was on his way to New Scotland Yard.

Langley was right about one thing – the old tensions were going. You could feel the new, finer sense of purpose in the air. The public face was losing its vacuous expression, aimlessness gave place to a confidence in what they were doing – where they were going – above all in Wyatt. If he promised the Rhodesians a constitution fair to all races then they'd get it – only his most prejudiced critics doubted that. And what about Rhodesia then – half an hour, eh? Forty men and a bus-driver! People were even beginning to feel proud of their man at Westminster. Said the man in the street to the roving interviewer: 'Well he gets things done doesn't he?'

Not one in a million knew that by nightfall it would all be over.

Eleven o'clock. As it happened the Chief Commissioner had never met Wrigley before, it also happened he was none too impressed with what he saw sitting at the other side of his desk in the large comfortable-looking office. He realized with mild surprise he was in duty bound to obey this chap's orders.

'I see.' The Commissioner omitted 'Sir' or 'Prime Minister' or any other form of respect because he felt none. 'There's just one snag. I can send a man along with a warrant, but what if Wyatt refuses to be arrested?'

'Then you can inform him steps will be taken to enforce the warrant.'

Sir John eyed Wrigley with some interest. Could a man of action be stirring after all beneath that ever so slightly seedy exterior? 'The Queen –' he began –

'The country's more important than the Queen!'

The Mikado of London's constabulary sat back satisfied. His

230

initial judgement still held; someone else had put the blighter up to it or he'd have had the Army out on the 23rd and to hell with the Monarch. The signs he decided were definitely cabalistic.

'Then there's no problem . . . if you can guarantee the Army.'

Wrigley looked annoyed, made a mental note against Sir John's future, unaware that his mental notes would soon hardly be worth the mind they were written on.

Eleven-thirty: Wrigley returned to the flat in Westminster where an anxious Cabinet sat in crowded discomfort awaiting his arrival. Their host, the PMG, cautiously opened the door and the PM dodged in just ahead of a badgering set of newshounds. He silenced a chorus of questions with an upraised hand, looked Chapel solemn as befitted the occasion, and studiously ignored the Foreign Secretary's smirk.

'Friends,' he began, 'let me say this – today we reach a moment of crisis – a moment of almost unendurable crisis. But we must all do our duty without flinching – without . . .' he was conscious of the electric kettle hissing in the kitchen – nodded briefly to the Minister of Fuel and Power who tiptoed away and pulled out the plug. Wrigley nodded his thanks and continued: 'I've decided the time has come to call Wyatt's bluff.'

'But you've been against it all along Kenneth,' the Home Office objected.

'It was a question of timing more than anything Horace,' the PM lied. 'Now I think we must strike before it's too late.'

'Rhodesia's decided you?' Dunne inquired.

'My own conscience decided!' Wrigley snapped. 'In the last resort I have to assume sole responsibility for what may happen – that responsibility is a heavy one. On my decision hangs the life of the Queen – perhaps of a whole dynasty – but –'

'Yes Kenneth, you've said all that before,' the Min of Def reminded him – 'the question is –'

'There are no questions. I want you to go up to the Ministry at once Alfred. Get them to order up a couple of armoured battalions – and I want helicopters with commando units standing by for an assault on the Tower.'

They stared dumbfounded at Wrigley. Even the Cabinet Secretary lost a couple of minutes.

'But Kenneth – the Queen!' the Min of Trans who shouldn't have been there at all almost swooned.

Wrigley opened both arms wide, threw his mangy leonine head back in a gesture of culminating, excruciated frustration and bellowed: 'To hell with the Queen! Do you or do you not realize that but for this woman who does nothing but open bridges, sign papers and possibly lends tone to some of our shabbier goings-on – but for her and her blasted family we'd still be running this country as is our right instead of sitting in 'ere like a lot of twerps in a goldfish bowl waiting for feeding time!'

The Derbyshire 'Twinge' grew thicker and thicker – hardly kept pace with the incensed leader's emotions. 'Now,' commanded Britain's Prime Minister of Wrath: 'Are you going to get things moving Alf – or do I have to do all the bloody grind meself!'

21

That morning Wyatt had talks with the Zambian High Commissioner and later saw a group of officials from the Board of Trade. Arrangements were made for an evening press conference. The known facts suggest a business as usual atmosphere, but convey nothing of a Damoclean darkness settling over the Palace of Westminster – for his followers, first feelings of triumph gave way to an intangible sense of defeat in course of preparation.

At the Defence Ministry the Minister was obliged to wait while they prised Sir Joseph away from an early Athenaeum lunch. The Chief alone could make decisions regarding Army movements, and then only in consultation with Chiefs of Staff. But they quickly sensed which way the wind blew and by two o'clock the necessary wheels were turning. By two-thirty, the nearest army units available were converging on Westminster . . .

Baynard watched the operation from beginning to end, waited for the two lone figures to cross the deserted road before reporting to Wyatt. He looked serious for once.

'They've cleared the square.'

'It was to be expected.'

'You can't just let it go like this!'

'I told you – we're not important – there'll be others.'

'Jepson and Fleming are outside.'

Wyatt stared at his lieutenant for some time. 'Send them in.'

'Want me to stay?'

'It might be a good idea.'

The four men stood in a room empty of formalities.

'We've met before.'

Jepson smiled without displacing his mouth: 'I thought we'd meet again – under other circumstances.' He took a document from his pocket, tossed in on to the desk.

Wyatt kept his eyes on Jepson. 'The former Queen's writ never did run here – I thought you knew that.'

'Times have changed.'

'That much?'

Jepson glanced at Fleming, hands thrust deep in his pockets . . .

'You realize the consequences of resisting arrest?'

'Do any of us?'

'They won't be pleasant for anyone – under this roof.'

Wyatt studied the sad, unblinking eyes of the man facing him. 'I can believe it,' he just had time to reply.

Accounts of what happened that afternoon are still confused – almost artificially so. Facts started to blur as the police cordoned off the entire area. All streets bordering the square were closed to pedestrians, traffic was diverted, civilians working in the area were evacuated. Even Westminster Underground station closed temporarily. The operation began at 2.30 and was completed by four; last stragglers passed through the barriers as Big Ben struck the hour over a sudden oasis of stone and silence.

The Protector's statue stood like an omen carved out of black thunder, stolidly defying the obscurantist gloom of a late November afternoon. Outside the Palace gates scrawled headlines announced from a deserted news-stand: 'Smith Surrenders'. A faint roar of distant traffic lapped at the edges of the desolate scene as mortar detachments moved into position ...

The official film version shows Jepson and Fleming crossing the thoroughfare roughly from St Margaret's. Shots were fired five minutes after they disappeared through the St Stephen's entrance. These were followed by the single crumping explosion of a mortar shell. At that moment, the camera cut to the clock face of Big Ben – then swung down dramatically to show a detachment of plain-clothes men rushing the entrance – there were several bursts of machine-gun fire: long afterwards the question was still being asked: who fired those bursts?

'Inspector Lingfield, the accused continue to deny they offered resistance to the forces of law and order. Is this true – to your knowledge?'

'Quite untrue sir.'

'You were one of those who stormed the St Stephen's entrance were you not?'

'I was sir.'

'What exactly were your orders?'

'We were told on no account to open fire except in self-defence. Five minutes after the senior officers entered the building we received several well directed bursts from the sandbagged emplacement protecting the entrance.'

'Was anyone injured?'

'Yessir ... I received a slight flesh wound.'

'They could not then be interpreted as warning shots?'

'Definitely not.'

'In the event it would have been suicidal to storm the position?'

'Our casualties would have been pretty heavy sir.'

'Only the Army could effectively breach the defence?'

234

'Oh yessir. Inspector Wilton then called up a mortar detachment. He asked for one shot to clear the entrance.'

'And as we know the one shot was enough.'

'Yessir – we had no trouble after that.'

'Having reached the entrance, what did you find?'

'There were six or seven of Wyatt's men scattered around – dead of course – the actual portico was badly damaged.'

'You yourself collected their weapons and marked them?'

'I did sir.'

'Will you hand Inspector Lingfield exhibit 93? Now, is this weapon one of those marked by you?'

'Yessir, it is.'

'Had it been discharged when you found it?'

'The clip was empty.'

'You're quite sure?'

'Oh yessir – no doubt about that.'

'Only one other question for the moment. What was your immediate impression when Wyatt's men first opened fire?'

'Well – we thought . . .'

'Your personal impression please.'

'I – assumed they meant to hold our men as hostages, that they intended to show fight.'

'Thank you Inspector. That will be all.'

Mr Harmer, a ballistics expert from Bristol, was later called to give evidence on the nature of bullet marks pockmarking St Margaret's and other buildings and vehicles. Corroborative evidence left no doubt; the marks were made by bullets fired from Thompsons . . .

Jepson's examination by Hartfish – an abstract:

'Chief Inspector, the accused, Baynard, states that no attempt was made to resist you in the execution of your duty. Further, he has made certain allegations tending to reflect on your integrity as a police officer. I need hardly remind you you are on oath. Now, will you tell the court exactly what happened?'

'I gave Wyatt the warrant and informed him it was my duty to place him under immediate arrest.'

'What was his reply?'

'He – suggested I might like to keep the warrant for toilet paper.'

'Were they his actual words?'

'No sir.'

'Very well – go on. '

'I asked him if he understood the consequences of resisting arrest. Just then we heard several bursts of gun-fire.'

'What did you assume – if anything?'

'I remembered thinking – they intend resisting – two more hostages to Wyatt.'

'What happened then?'

'I turned instinctively and Wyatt said: "Get him Baynard – the crafty sod's armed." '

Baynard shouted that it was a lie.

'You hear that Chief Inspector – is that or is that not what you heard?'

'It is – Chief Inspector Fleming will vouch . . .'

'I'm not interested in what Fleming will vouch for at the moment. Are you certain in your mind that that is what you heard?'

'I'm positive.'

'What followed?'

'Baynard drew his revolver and fired.'

'You were standing by the desk turning to face Baynard who stood with his back to the door?'

'That is so.'

'So a bullet fired in your direction could be expected to embed itself in the panelling behind you?'

'Exactly.'

'. . . now just take a look at this photograph. You will see quite plainly the panelling is splintered – top right hand of the picture. Is that to your recollection the impression of the shot fired by Baynard?'

'It is.'

'Could the shot have been fired by anyone else in the room?'

'Not possibly. In any case our ballistics report identified the bullet as coming from Baynard's revolver.'

'We'll leave that for the moment. Let's deal with Baynard's

accusation that he was shot in cold blood. Is there any possible basis for this allegation?'

'It's a complete fabrication. Baynard obeyed Wyatt's orders; we had to act in self-defence. As Baynard drew his gun and fired Chief Inspector Fleming also fired and fortunately disabled him – then the guard outside rushed in as Wyatt shouted "Get him!"'

Again Baynard shouted an agonized 'No!' that rang through the court. Again the interruption was ignored.

'And then?' Hartfish inquired in a quiet voice.

'I was forced in self-defence to shoot him.'

'You killed him?'

'I had no choice – one doesn't have time to argue with Thompsons.'

'That's quite all right Chief Inspector. We offer no criticism of your conduct. Far from it.'

Blood spattered the door, dripped over the green carpet. Baynard slumped against the wall, watched through a haze of sickness as it rivuleted down his sleeve. Jepson took his gun from its holster, prodding him savagely while Fleming covered Wyatt.

'Come on you bastard!'

Baynard, his arm shattered, half-fainting, made no move. Jepson gave the lieutenant a tremendous shove. He stumbled over the body of Wyatt's guard and fell heavily on broken bones. Wyatt took a step towards Jepson.

'The best police force in the world.'

'Everybody thinks we're wonderful.' No humour was intended.

'The best because it covers up its basic inhumanity better than any other,' Wyatt explained evenly.

Jepson stiffened, came near to smashing the revolver butt in the Captain's face. He was still living down an old charge – planting evidence.

'We'll talk about that later.' His sad, unblinking eyes never wavered.

'I'll remember this.'

Jepson threatened to smile: 'You day's over sonny – when we've done with you you'll be in no state to remember anything.'

Wyatt made no reply. Fleming's gun might have been a toy masquerading as the real thing as he brushed it aside, went to Baynard and helped him to his feet.

As they stumbled ahead of Fleming, Wyatt thought he heard a shot coming from the room he'd finished with; but it was one among many – a moment later Jepson rejoined them – raincoated men were everywhere, firing . . .

Just before five o'clock a call was put through to the Tower. Slingsby, second in command of the garrison, received the order from Wyatt himself. The fortress was to be surrendered at once. French would have nothing to do with the order. He sat in the comfortless Adjutant's office in the barracks across the way – and waited.

Slingsby went straight to the Queen, informed her she was now at liberty. She heard the news in silence and he withdrew to assemble his men. They abandoned their positions without a word. An order from Wyatt – well then, it was over. They knew what to expect.

Ravens strutted with funereal dignity as they marched in ragged formation across the square. Within ten minutes they were being packed into a fleet of police vans lined up at the approaches to the Middle Tower while a hearse-like limousine flying the Royal Standard glided past to receive the former captives. The nascent Republic was dead, long live the possibility.

Commander Perrins studied the frayed carpet with exaggerated attention. A message had just come through. It was all over. They were bringing the ring-leaders straight to his HQ, maximum security . . . the rest, four hundred or more, would be sorted out. A long job. Profoundly he wished himself well out of it – long and dirty. The mask of Janus – show a smooth, benign face to the public and the full treatment for treachery. Perrins' stomach was unequal to the measures that were sometimes necessary. But the area leaders had to be found. He

238

thought of men like Lingfield who carried out their duties willingly, so many levers for prising open people's minds . . .

Wyatt to be kept strictly incommunicado. This he found difficult to understand. He felt a professional curiosity about the man who was already a part of history. A meeting might be an interesting experience. Unlike his subordinates he harboured no resentment against Wyatt – it was a game like any other, he concluded. Wyatt had played high and lost – big men little fish, a penny or a million – they all lost sooner or later . . . and carpets fray . . .

Perrins' confused line of thought snapped with Lingfield's triumphant appearance.

'Well – what happened to you?'

'Flesh wound, sir.' Curly winked knowingly. His tiny eyes glittered and he was still panting with excitement like an animal in rut.

'Where are they?'

Curly looked disappointed; over and above his official report, he'd hoped to give Perrins a graphic account of Operation Break-in.'

'Outside, sir. Baynard got his arm smashed. We're letting him sweat a bit – may loosen his tongue.'

Perrins jerked out of his lethargic mood and flashed at the sergeant. 'On whose orders?'

Curly looked blank. 'Jepson's.' He could see nothing to make a fuss about.

'They're our responsibility – not Jepson's. Get him a doctor!'

'But . . .'

'Do as I say!'

Lingfield waited till he faced the door before he scowled: 'Right, Chief.'

'And send Wyatt in.'

'Alone?'

'Of course.'

The sergeant turned deliberately. 'Can't be done – our orders are . . .'

'I said send him in!' Finish. Easy enough to read the writing on the wall – all his own work in filthy great letters. Time to

239

start clearing out desk drawers – a small private detective agency on the South coast – they could do with a good one in Brighton . . . He stared reflectively at Lingfield who suddenly knew all about studied insolence . . . 'Send him in Curly.'

Lingfield smiled and shrugged, knowing this would get back where it belonged – just as well – Perrins'd gone soft on the job these last few weeks. He made an unhurried exit and Perrins had time to glance at himself in a mental pocket mirror, caught the expression of quizzical bewilderment: now why the devil did I do that? he wondered. But his elegantly featured other self seemed a total loss, offered no reply.

The door opened again, no knock; just the silent Curly giving Wyatt space to enter; but he grinned at both of them before closing the door with pistol-shot finality.

Perrins stared long and intently at the man before him. He'd spent a life time pinning labels on men, thought he knew something about character evaluation; but it was slightly disturbing to find he'd run out of labels. Realizing he stared beyond the bounds of courtesy he checked himself and indicated a seat.

'Thank you.'

'Drink?'

Wyatt looked faintly surprised, but accepted.

Perrins poured a large Scotch, handed it to Wyatt who unexpectedly stood up: 'If you don't mind, Commander – Baynard needs it more.'

Again Perrins stared, and the label – an unfamiliar one – began to show through. He answered roughly for him. 'Sit down – drink it yourself. Last thing he wants is alcohol fouling his bloodstream, you should know that.' He paused, glanced down at the frayed carpet – 'I've sent for a doctor.'

Wyatt sat, looked at the glass in his hand, then glanced at the Commander – but said nothing.

'So you're Captain Wyatt.'

Wyatt smiled faintly. 'Was Captain Wyatt – you'll need to find another label.'

Perrins started – a lucky shot or a mind-reader? 'Well, if it's any consolation, Captain, there's not much more than a hair's-breadth between success and failure, though I think Omar was distinguishing fact from fiction – so we meet on fairly common ground.'

But he directed his words at the window blank with darkness, spoke at random to cover pangs of conscience tapping on his shoulder like a desperate down-and-out looking for the price of a night's lodging. After all these years he found it beyond him to talk to a dead man. Wyatt, still clasping the glass in both hands, listened and watched the Commander closely.

'They're already turning your homeless friends out of Buckingham Palace.' He glanced at Wyatt, pouting a little as though to ask, 'what do you say to that?' 'They're already returning the pictures and furnishings. It'll all be back to rights in forty-eight hours they say – not bad going eh? The Queen's staying at the Snowdons' temporarily – there's talk of another coronation . . .'

'Why are you telling me this?'

'No one else will. You'll be told nothing – that's petty. There's only one way they know to really defeat you, Captain – but that's petty too. I want your defeat to be as bitter as I can make it – you're too big for anything less.'

He stood and walked up and down for a moment, mastering his thoughts, choosing his words . . .

'Ignominy, humiliation, as much of it as they can muster – for everyone. They're planning third class citizenship for all concerned – that'll come after they've served their sentences. They'll hound every last one of your followers – the file will never be closed. Meantime monarchy, old style Democracy, tradition, styles and titles – the whole ragbag'll be exalted to heights unimaginable. That's the bitterness for you Captain – you've strengthened the whole symbiotic system of monarchy Establishment which has a parasitic attachment to – loyal subjects . . . Parliament? it'll remain what you showed it publicly to be – a front organization for the big wheels under its bonnet . . .' Perrins rounded bitterly on his prisoner. 'Why the hell did you have to lack the only essential you needed for permanent success?'

'Ruthlessness?'

'Very well – against your code – but didn't you really know the kind of men you were up against? What was the point of caring more for her life than they do for the whole family down to cousins ten times removed?'

His exasperation moved Wyatt as much as it amused him. 'It was no part of my plan.'

'No, my God, that was plain from the start! And now – here you are.'

Wyatt remained silent in face of a self-evident fact.

Perrins considered the phone on his desk; something about it worth a moment of derision . . . The hard lines of anger streaking his features softened a little. 'Did you know you tried to resist arrest?'

Wyatt shook his head.

'It won't look good for you or your friends – reputation, reputation . . . kill it stone dead. One of my men was wounded – shot himself but not enough – your fault again. They're working out the legal machinery now – it'll be exceptional – to meet the exceptional circumstances. Only one thing'll be missing.' Perrins paused long enough to shift his contemplation of the phone to Wyatt: 'You.'

Voices could be heard outside – somewhere beyond, Big Ben sounded the three-quarters with a hint of mockery. The two men listened to the silence – unaware of the sounds . . . Wyatt nodded abruptly 'No more than I expected.' They stood almost simultaneously, the Captain put his glass on the desk. Perrins grinned and put out a hand.

'Now we're both finished.'

A moment later Wyatt was escorted from the room. Perrins stared down at the untouched drink, then suddenly he grabbed the glass and downed its contents in one. Disobeying orders and talking treason with a bugged telephone in the place. Really, it was asking for trouble. But now he could look his other self in the face again knowing exactly why the devil he'd done it. He sat back calmly and waited for a summons.

The well-bred, the well-heeled and the well-we've-made-it crowd clustering excitedly around Bookers' teleprinter made a

242

respectful passage for the old man entering the foyer. He ascended the grand staircase slowly and with great dignity. It might have been made for him.

He found Rigg, Minter and Wynlose already assembled. Compton-Douglas they informed him had hurried off to the Tower in full regimentals, clutching his baton like a man dismembered, to help present Her Majesty with the Keys. Langley snuffled with unsuppressed delight.

'Poor old Douglas – just see him, doddering forward with a velvet cushion loaded with damned great bits of iron. Philip'll lean over, hands clasped behind his back and say "Very interesting Colonel" or something equally mind-shattering.'

Rigg almost joined in the gilt-edged laughter. 'Have a care my Lord – your words could be construed as treasonable.'

Langley chuckled with the rest – it was a time for laughter and high spirits. 'Deeds not words Rigg – we took a great risk with her life.'

'At most a calculated risk,' Wynlose suggested. 'Did we have any doubts?'

'Oh yes – we had doubts,' said Langley whose memory was longer than that. He smiled to himself – sometimes a joke was too good to share.

'What happens now?' Minter asked.

'We must get the troops out of Rhodesia – that's a number one priority. I had a word with the Archbishop. He agrees Thanksgiving this Sunday is obligatory – shot in the arm for the Church. I suggested a real booster – a further coronation confirming Her Majesty's title to the Crown. He's pleased as Punch. It'll get things off to a good start. What about your lot, Aubrey?'

Minter had already seen 'his lot'. The Farm Street Brethren would be only too happy to pass on his respectful request for *Te Deum* in all churches and cathedrals to mark the happy deliverance.

'Good. Now for your department Martin – the trials must make Nuremberg look like a magistrates' hearing.'

Rigg hitched up his chin a notch or two. 'Depends on the political situation.'

'Ah well that's simple isn't it? Hamson's working on the Press and the CCO's sending out agitating directives – Wrigley'll have to go to the country.'

'Can we depend on it?' Wynlose sounded doubtful.

'We can depend on you Wynlose; he respects your judgement. We'll advise the Queen to suggest to him that he's a gentleman. What with his reverence for all things crowned plus the fact he'll be made to remember a few things he may care to overlook . . . well Martin?'

'I think we shouldn't rush a "general"; a provisional government to begin with – that way we can spread the risk.'

'Good – and in the interval?'

'We'll need the Special Powers Act plus. Need to create a sense of continuing crisis; arrest on suspicion, detention of suspects on the South African line, exit Habeas Corpus, everything possible to build up a thorough case – then a State trial with all the trimmings.'

'Can your new man handle it?'

'He's the right man for this job. A bit too theatrical perhaps – wants to use Westminster Hall for the trials. I had to restrain him on that one.'

Langley's eyes blazed with sudden enthusiasm. 'Don't be a fool! It's brilliant! Tell him he can have Westminster Hall.' The old man sat with eyes closed visualizing the drama to come, unfolding on the greatest of all London's stages . . .

'What about Wyatt?' asked Wynlose.

Langley opened his eyes abruptly and stared into the distance. 'Well . . . what about Wyatt?'

Something about the blandly reflected question set them glancing at each other.

'I wondered what arrangements . . .'

'Has he been arrested – is that what you're asking?'

'Of course he's been . . .'

'Then what else were you thinking of?'

Wynlose opened his mouth and shut it again; all of them peered through thick silence at Langley – a few words – enough to explain why he was the leader. Their branches were nothing compared with his roots proliferating in deep-down darkness . . . conceivably they feared Langley at that moment. Certainly they did not mention Wyatt again.

They delayed the Queen's departure from the Tower beyond strictly reasonable limits. Wrigley was the first to realize that a few details had been neglected in the general scramble to unseat Wyatt.

Quite simply, they need to put on a show, something eye-catching, proving to the nation, to the world, that a new page was to be written palimpsest style in one of history's left-over back numbers. Her Majesty must be attended with as much pomp as time and a cold November evening would allow. If monarchy was to be restored it had better be done properly; you can't let Royal Families be driven away as discreetly as old lags leaving the 'Scrubs' first thing in the morning.

Frantic telephone calls were made to all kinds of eminents. The Constable and his deputy were on their way. My Lord Mayor and a handful of City Aldermen were roped in – the whole of the Government and their shadowy counterparts were attached, a few judges and QCs made an appearance, and, as one TV commentator waiting for transmission succinctly put it, 'all the odds and sods Wrigley could lay on hands on'. Police, and others heavily disguised as detectives outnumbered the gathering. They were taking no chances . . .

But all that came later, more than two hours after Wyatt's arrest. She was a Queen once more – but in the public interest – she must be seen to be freed. So they made her wait.

The announcer fairly goggled at the camera, almost wriggled in his seat with the itch to tell someone . . .

'Here is the news: Wyatt has fallen. The Queen has been freed from the Tower – Britain is once again a monarchy. Wyatt's régime came to a dramatic end just two hours ago – thirty-seven days after the equally dramatic coup. For a report on what happened we go over to Gerald Selworth at Westminster.'

And there was Selworth with that peculiar stance of TV commentators suggesting the tense concentration of a man waiting his turn in a busy urinal. 'It's a desolate scene tonight here in Westminster, a police cordon still surrounds the area and in the November gloom one sees only police – plain and tuppence coloured hurrying in all directions. They're still searching through that vast and sprawling complex of buildings. Wyatt and most of his henchmen were removed more than an hour ago but it's believed some of the rebels are still in hiding. They're even searching the vaults for time-bombs – giving a new look to the old story ...

'Just behind me you can see the damage done by a mortar shell. The Army had to be called in when the rebels showed fight or casualties would have been pretty heavy I'm told. One shot and it was all over – the troops were withdrawn and armed police went in to finish the job. In half an hour Britain's self-appointed Protector was being hustled through the damaged entrance under the stony gaze of a nearby statue. One wonders what that russet-coated captain, Cromwell, thought of it all. And now back to the studio.'

'World reaction,' continued the announcer, 'was prompt. Holland, Sweden and Denmark have expressed warmest congratulations to Her Majesty. India, Pakistan, Australia, New Zealand and Canada immediately sent word of their great satisfaction, and President Johnson has cabled the Queen personally his heartfelt expression of joy and goodwill, convinced "that Her Majesty's happy deliverance will open a new era in Anglo-American friendship and understanding." In the nation at large the reaction seems to be one of stunned amazement and shock. Most people are asking the inevitable question: how could a man with Wyatt's resolve and tenacity of purpose, at the very height of power, have allowed himself to be ousted so swiftly – so easily?'

Ironic contrast: a series of pictures followed highlighting the UN coup in Rhodesia. Scowling whites and smiling Africans, lorry-loads of troops being welcomed as liberators just across the border. But it hardly seemed to count any more. History had picked up her skirts and was running hell for leather to avoid the crossfire of incompatible events. Wyatt had fallen – that was the point ...

246

Floodlights gave the scene a certain spatchcock impressiveness; a *son et lumière* production hurriedly thrown together. Journalists and press cameramen swarmed everywhere. Tension climbed as the assembly, swelled by members of the Diplomatic Corps, waited for the modest door to open . . . suddenly, ringing through the Thames-infested air came a clarionade of trumpets sounding the Queen's Fanfare in elegant unison. TV cameras panned slowly against the uncompromising severity of the White Tower – there on the battlements stood eight trumpeters peppering the night sky with notes full of good tidings.

'From where I'm standing the scene is a tapestry of rich pageantry wrapped in black velvet. A detachment of the Household Cavalry is clattering under the Bloody Tower to take up its position in the great square. Yeomen of the Guard in their scarlet dress line the short route to the car waiting to drive the Royal Family to yet another temporary lodging; but this time they go in freedom, watched by a vast concourse of dignitaries here to reaffirm their loyalty and respect. I can see the Lord Chancellor, the Lord Privy Seal, the Lord Mayor of London, the Archbishop of Canterbury – all in their robes of office – a colourful sight.

'And now . . . as the last echoes of the fanfare die away a door opens, the door of the house in which Her Majesty lay, a hostage to fortune, swings open. The Queen in a light brown travelling coat and pale blue hat comes forward – pauses for the press photographers . . . she looks very small, very pale, every inch a Queen . . . "God Save the Queen!" someone shouts – and a great cheer goes up from the assembly – she smiles – turns to her family. His Royal Highness the Duke of Edinburgh says a few unsmiling words to someone following him – I think it's – yes, it's Wrigley, the Prime Minister, who steps forward to speak to Her Majesty – she . . . she appears not to have heard . . .'

Milly Lavery sat gaping at the smoky chiaroscuro scene on her little black box and thought how nice it was to see the Queen out visiting again. She'd missed the preliminary

247

announcements and had a confused impression the Queen was opening something. She was thinking of Fred too, which didn't help. He'd gone off in a great hurry – no idea when he'd be back – something to do with the new job . . .

'Hullo John,' it was 'John' to everyone, right or wrong side of Curly. 'Now what about it, John?' he'd say, just before his fist crashed into a stubborn face. He used chamois covered boxing gloves – not to spoil appearances. 'Sorry to drag you out John – got an "urgent" on – we need you.'

He placed a large parcel on the table, larger than the first one.

'The other half, John – plus.' He smiled suddenly, watched Lavery like a scientist examining a rat for after effects. The man's gaze flickered from Curly to the chunk of El Dorado wrapped in brown paper, missed the spasm of contempt knocking Lingfield's grin askew.

'All yours when the job's done John.'

Lavery looked up wordlessly like a dog adoring its master.

'All right?' Lavery could only nod.

'Simple as falling off a log. Only thing is it means three months inside.'

'Three months!' The adoration disappeared, was replaced by the nearest Lavery could manage to honest indignation.

'Form's sake.' Curly kept explanations to a minimum. Strictly speaking the Laverys in his world deserved less.

'But why?'

'Broad daylight job. Press'll be there – Mr Anybody too, maybe – they'll all want to see the big man himself carted off to the "Scrubs" won't they – you'll be there too –' He tossed a photograph across the table. 'See the spot marked X?'

Lavery studied the half plate of a great, arched entrance and nodded.

'That's where you'll be. See the spot marked W?'

Again Lavery nodded.

'That's where he'll be – at eight o'clock on the dot he passes under the arch to a police car waiting the other side. Two of our boys'll be handcuffed to him so be careful – there'll be plenty of us around ... now you could be just another reporter, couldn't you? You break the cordon – our blokes'll put up a show of stopping you but it's only three paces – you just step right up and let him have it – bang bang bang right in the guts – can't lose, John. But we couldn't exactly let you go could we?'

'How – how do I know you'll –'

'Come off it John – you play fair with us and we'll see you're all right – this'll be waiting for you the day you come out.'

'What do I tell the magistrate?'

'Magistrates? Don't worry about that, I'll give you all the dope you need later – oh and we'll have a bit of a rehearsal – all right?'

Lavery supposed so.

The PM's face filled every screen in the country. Like a Big Benevolent Brother he gave the impression that he gazed only at *you*, but you of course are only one of millions. All he stared at in reality was the blind eye of a camera. The catch in the throat, the throb in the voice, the moistened eye rusting iron determination, all the old familiar tricks were there as he announced that 'this was a moment of pride for him and indeed for the whole nation: And let me just say this ...'

After Perrins, Wyatt was dead to the world. After Perrins no words passed between him and other human beings. Only Lingfield permitted himself a trifling lapse from strict orders. A moment before Wyatt was taken to his cell the genial-looking sergeant planted himself in the way and grinned.

'I'd flush you down the john if I knew one big enough.' Wyatt looked at him and the grin faded. 'Take him away,' was all he added.

In silence they stripped him of his few personal belongings, in silence they slammed the steel door to and turned the key. Nothing attractive to the attention except a large sheet of paper and a pencil stub lying on the table. What did they expect, an abject confession – or a suicide note? He smiled and paced the limits of his cell – a new Kingdom – four paces one way

– four the other. They'd left him his thoughts – an oversight perhaps? And the writing materials. He sat down at the table, stared at the blank paper ... ten minutes later he was fast asleep. On the sheet of paper were two words: Consummatum est.

He was ready when they came for him at 7.50 next morning.

Reporters had waited all night in the ante-room, hoping for information of some kind. The duty sergeant couldn't persuade them they were wasting their time. The clampdown on news was a hundred per cent. Their cup of bitterness spilled over when they were ordered out into the open after an all night vigil. 'In the interests of security.' They stood around disconsolate in the cold – fed to the teeth with waiting – and a light rain was beginning to fall. Why should they have noticed the little man edging his way to the front of the small crowd outside Scotland Yard? So Wyatt, they were officially informed, was being transferred to gaol. Big deal. Not only did it tell them nothing they couldn't work for themselves, but any hope of a few words from Wyatt himself was an also ran. Sixth sense perhaps kept them on the spot.

It was all over in ten seconds.

The word went round as Big Ben chimed the hour. 'He's coming! Yes – that's Wyatt.'

The figure in a crumpled uniform, hatless and without a tie, walked with an escort towards the waiting car. Another figure moved with sudden speed, broke free from restraining hands and ran to Wyatt. The man shouted something – 'Death to traitors,' they said – then fired – some say three times – the sensible ones ran for cover – others true to their professional sense of curiosity remained to watch two plain-clothes men shoot down the killer. One journalist alone commented on the expressions each man presented to death. Wyatt's calm resignation and the hint of a smile. The assassin merely looked surprised. If Lavery could have known he would later be identified as Reginald Percy Monger of no fixed address, he might very well have looked thunderstruck.

'... you are charged with conspiring together with one

Richard Wyatt to commit a treasonable act against Our Lawful and Well Beloved Elizabeth the Queen in that you did . . .'

Hartfish rose slowly to the pinnacle of his career, slowly he polished yellow tinted spectacles as his eyes ranged over the men arraigned in the dock . . .

More about Penguins

Penguinews, which appears every month, contains details of all the new books issued by Penguins as they are published. From time to time it is supplemented by *Penguins in Print*, which is a complete list of all available books published by Penguins. (There are well over three thousand of these.)

A specimen copy of *Penguinews* will be sent to you free on request, and you can become a subscriber for the price of the postage. For a year's issues (including the complete lists) please send 30p if you live in the United Kingdom, or 60p if you live elsewhere. Just write to Dept EP, Penguin Books Ltd, Harmondsworth, Middlesex, enclosing a cheque or postal order, and your name will be added to the mailing list.

Note: *Penguinews* and *Penguins in Print* are not available in the U.S.A. or Canada

Coup D'État

A Practical Handbook

Edward Luttwak

More governments are changed by coup d'état than by elections. This coolly notorious handbook is a guide to the *coup d'état*, a manual showing how a small group of men can seize the levers of power within the state and swing the bureaucratic machine into action behind them. Edward Luttwak first isolates the situations in which a *coup* is possible, and then discusses how to infiltrate key groups in the army, how to evade the intelligence network, and how to neutralize any military or political threats.

Although politically neutral, this is clearly a subversive book. Throughout it fixes attention on the real points of power within the modern state – all of which have to be recaptured within 24 hours. Luttwak illustrates his argument with fascinating examples from recent political history, and in particular illuminates many of the political problems of the Third World.

'More devastatingly cynical than anything to be found in *The Prince*' – *The Times Literary Supplement*

'Extraordinary ... a brilliantly clever, cynically methodical guide ... admirably documented' – Helen Vlachos in the *Spectator*

'Could well become an underground bestseller in nations with a history of toppling governments ... charts every step of a *coup*, from plot to power ... a little classic' – *Time*

Not for sale in the U.S.A.

The Death of Grass

John Christopher

A terrifying fantasy which invites comparison with the novels of John Wyndham.

A new virus appears in China: it kills grass. Millions die of hunger. The West is alarmed: bread rationing may be needed. But few people foresee the desperate fight for survival, the panic, and the lapse into barbarism that are to come...

also available

The World in Winter

Not for sale in the U.S.A.

The Hour of Maximum Danger

James Barlow

A conspiracy is afoot.

The aim: to discover the nature of an anti-missile perfected by a refugee scientist.

The people: a model-girl, a Communist diplomat, a factory-worker, a telephonist . . . and others.

When James Barlow's story first came out it was seen to bear a striking and almost prophetic resemblance to the Profumo and Vassall affairs. The author's close study of known Communist espionage techniques lends to his work a strong sense of reality. He has here written a book which is both entertaining and, in a chilling way, deeply instructive.

'This is not just a propaganda novel. It is a well-constructed story, and all the characters live an independent and authentic life of their own' – *Illustrated London News*

'Mr Barlow's people are essentially human, modern folk, every one of them recognizably so, even his communists . . . The writing is concrete, with innumerable touches of realism in dialogue and description' – *The Times Literary Supplement*

Not for sale in the U.S.A.

also available

This Side of the Sky

Term of Trial

The Patriots